*To*
MY SONS

# EMILIE LORING
# THE SOLITARY HORSEMAN

A NATIONAL GENERAL COMPANY

This low-priced Bantam Book
has been completely reset in a type face
designed for easy reading, and was printed
from new plates. It contains the complete
text of the original hard-cover edition.
NOT ONE WORD HAS BEEN OMITTED.

THE SOLITARY HORSEMAN
*A Bantam Book / published by arrangement with*
*Little, Brown and Company, Inc.*

*PRINTING HISTORY*
*William Penn edition published 1927*
*Grosset & Dunlap edition published June 1950*
*2nd printing ..... January 1958*

*Bantam edition published December 1968*
*2nd printing ... December 1968     4th printing ...... August 1969*
*3rd printing ...... March 1969     5th printing ... September 1969*
*6th printing ........ May 1970*
*New Bantam edition published January 1971*

*Bantam Books are published by Bantam Books, Inc., a National*
*General company. Its trade-mark, consisting of the words "Bantam*
*Books" and the portrayal of a bantam, is registered in the United*
*States Patent Office and in other countries. Marca Registrada.*
*Bantam Books, Inc., 666 Fifth Avenue, New York, N.Y. 10019.*

PRINTED IN THE UNITED STATES OF AMERICA

## Prologue

"DON'T refuse to see the boy, Claire. He is tortured by remorse and begs for a few moments with you."

The white-faced woman in deep mourning walked to the window. The sunlight revealed a trace of silver in her dark hair, accentuated the ivory pallor of her skin, pitilessly exposed the shadows under the eyes brilliant with heartache too intense for tears. It revealed also the secrets of the room in which she stood. Beautiful mahogany. Fine books. Choice rugs. But, shabby patricians all. With a sigh which seemed to tear its way up Claire Grahame faced the tall man with steel-gray hair. His eyes met hers with steady, compassionate tenderness as she demanded passionately:

"Why should I see him, Nick, now that he has been acquitted of killing my . . ." With an uncontrollable shudder she caught at the back of a chair.

Nicholas Cort waited, waited for her to go on, waited for pent-up emotion to shatter the incredible calm she had maintained since the tragic death of her son. She was still so young. Only thirty-nine. Too young to have lost both husband and boy. As though imploring his sympathetic understanding she hurried on:

"Haven't I done enough, Nick? I went to the Court House to plead for clemency if he were convicted. You told me that he was young, that always he had had too much money, that he had been drinking when his automobile struck David, that the man in the car ahead had been as much to blame morally. He doesn't need my help now. Don't think that I am sorry for that. I am not vindictive. Really I'm not. The fact that I was blessed with a son who preferred the clean ways of life doesn't make me callous to the tragedy of weak lives which are beset by temptation."

"Anthony Hamilton is not weak, Claire. If he were

he would not want to see you. He desires, if possible, to make some restitution."

"Restitution! Can he give me back my boy?" Her voice broke. She gripped the chair back tighter and went on, "Does he intend to offer me money? Didn't someone say that he was rich in his own right?"

"He is and he has a wealthy father besides. It is only just that they should make some provision for your future as David would have done."

"Not if the Court acquitted him. David! What wouldn't David have done for his mother."

The brooding tenderness in her voice set the tears thick in Cort's eyes as he explained:

"Young Hamilton has no thought of offering you money, Claire. He wants to talk with you. He insists that never again can he have a moment's happiness unless he sees you."

"Why should he have a moment's happiness?"

"You don't mean that."

He waited for a moment with his eyes on the woman's downcast lids, on her white throat with its contracting muscles before he added:

"That remark sounds too much like Hamilton's mother."

Claire Grahame's long lashes flew up. For the first time since she had lost her boy a spark of interest flamed in her dark eyes.

"His mother! Do you mean that his mother is not holding his hand tight in hers through this horrible experience?"

"On the contrary, she has raged at him because of the unpleasant notoriety into which he has plunged the family. She thinks of herself only."

"Didn't his father stand by?"

"His father told him that he was a fool to drive when he had been drinking, not a fool to drink, you notice. His brother two years older echoed that sentiment. With that family background and remorse gnawing at his heart I am afraid for his future."

"Have you grown fond of this—this boy, Nick?"

Nicholas Cort colored darkly at the reproach in her tone but he met her eyes steadily as he answered:

"Yes. More and more as I have realized the physical luxury and spiritual poverty in which he has grown to twenty-one. When I learned that next June he is to be graduated from college with honors I became interested. I looked up his record. His dissipations have been with drink and cards, never with women. That temptation appears to have left him cold. I watched him through the trial. He asked no mercy. His concern was for you. For your loss."

"My loss! Can you stand there and plead for this Anthony Hamilton and realize what it is? Ever since his father died David has had his strong arms about the children and me. Rose and little Peter do not yet know how their brother went. I hope they never will. He was such a boy, Nick, when he had to shoulder responsibility, such a boy. We hadn't much money but we four were so happy together. David and I spent hours and hours planning how we could carry on this place, White Pillars, the old Grahame homestead with its seventy acres. We decided on a fruit farm because he loved the open. The three years he put in at Agricultural College were thrilling to us all. We set out hundreds of trees and look!" she pointed eagerly to the window. "There they are for the first time faintly pink with bloom. How we planned. In ten years we would be shipping fruit to markets all over the civilized world. Fruit You Can Eat In The Dark, was to be our slogan. Such waste, Nick, such waste! If we get into this horrible war raging overseas, David would have gone and I should have been proud to have my son in the service of his country—but to lose his life like this. . . . Oh well," she dropped her hands in utter futility as the passion of emotion burned out. She walked to the window and conceded without turning:

"Write young Hamilton that he may come."

"He is waiting outside now, Claire."

"All this time? You were so sure that I would see him?"

"Yes. I know you better than you know yourself. You would never let a boy suffer if you could help it."

He opened a door across the hall. The woman at the window crushed her black-bordered handkerchief in white-knuckled hands.

"Thank you for letting me come, Mrs. Grahame."

At the low voice she turned. She set her teeth hard in her lip before she looked at the youth who had laid waste her life. He wasn't the boy she had imagined. Perhaps the last weeks had aged him. His dark hair was brushed to satin smoothness except where it rippled rebelliously above his ears. His eyes were black with emotion, his nose and mouth had the chiseled perfection of marble, he was tall and lean. His hands looked as though he had never used them. Probably he hadn't, the woman thought, as a vision of the brown hands she had loved, with their hardened palms, flashed into her mind. She seated herself by the old table and motioned to the wing-chair opposite:

"Won't you sit down?"

"Thank you, no. I only want to tell you . . ."

She put her hand to her throat.

"Please, please don't! I—I couldn't bear it. Now that I have seen you I know what you feel. I am not bitter any longer. Really I am not. Tell me about yourself. Your plans. All my life I have loved boys."

She bit her lips to steady them.

"Plans! I have no plans. I want to do what I can for you and then—then I don't care much what happens."

"Oh, but you must care. You must. Don't you see? Accidentally you have robbed the world of a young, beautiful life. You have no longer the right to waste yours. You must take its place. My son meant to put so much into the world and now—now—oh, my God!"

With the agonized cry Claire Grahame flung her arms on the table and dropped her head upon them. Cort sprang forward but Hamilton was before him. He dropped to his knees and encircled the black-clad figure with his arms as he implored:

"Let me take your son's place. Of course, not in your heart, but if you can bear seeing me around let me work for you, help you—love you."

The last words were a mere whisper. Nicholas Cort held his breath as though by the slightest movement he might tip the scales in which a future hung in the balance. It seemed hours, though the old clock in the corner had ticked but seconds, when the woman raised her head. Hamilton withdrew his arms and stood as though awaiting judgment.

"Look at me!"

His eyes, which she could see now were gray, met hers steadily.

"Do you mean that you are willing to work for me? Willing to give up your way of living for my way?"

The color rushed into his white face.

"Give me the chance. Only give me the chance."

She gazed back at him for a moment before she stared down at the hands clenched in her lap.

"Suppose—just suppose that I accept your proposal? What would your parents say?"

Hamilton took an impetuous step forward. Unobserved Nicholas Cort left the room. The boy's voice was rough with bitterness.

"They don't care what I do. They are furious with me now. They have my brother Mark."

"You don't realize what you would be giving up, Anthony. My life runs in an entirely different groove from yours. Three years ago I invested all I had, except enough to carry us until the crops could help, in peach and apple orchards. If you were to take David's place you would have to work as he worked, as he planned to work for ten years. Do you mean that you would give that time to me? Share our fortunes? Live as we live?— without using your own money, without help from your people? Temperately?"

"Temperately! After living through the hell of these last weeks do you think I'll ever drink again? Give me the chance to help you, Mrs. Grahame. I have no right to ask you to lift this intolerable load from my heart but if you will . . ."

"Give me a few hours in which to decide. I want to help you but I wonder if—if I am big enough. I will talk with Mr. Cort and—Rose darling . . ."

She tried to smile at the little girl who entered the room. The child's head was covered with short black curls of satin softness. In her simple pink linen frock she looked younger than her twelve years. In one arm she clasped a doll. Its head was shattered. One rosy cheek, one sapphire eye alone remained intact. Between wet lashes her eyes were brilliant with expectation. She tiptoed forward. Her lovely lips trembled as she slipped her hand into Hamilton's and asked shyly:

"Are you my new big brother?"

She clung tightly to the fingers which gripped hers as she explained eagerly:

"Mummy, Uncle Nick told me that I had a new big brother. Have I, Mummy? I've missed Davie so."

The dimpled chin quivered. The dark eyes filled with tears.

Claire Grahame bent over her. Her voice was sympathetically tender as she asked:

"Rose darling, what happened to Annabel Lee?"

The little girl looked at the doll clasped in her arms. Tears made deep dark pools of her eyes as she answered her mother:

"Nap Long strung Annabel to a tree and—and shot her head off and then—he offered me striped candy." The scorn in her voice choked in a convulsive swallow before she added: "I wouldn't let him see me cry, I *wouldn't.*"

"Nap Long again! The village bad boy. He delights in hectoring the younger children," Claire Grahame answered the question in Anthony Hamilton's eyes.

He dropped to one knee and caught the child in his arms as he comforted:

"Dear, Tony will get you another doll."

Rose leaned contentedly close and shook her head:

"I don't want another child in place of my darling Annabel Lee. I—I'm grown-up now." With a heartbroken little cry she pressed her face against young Hamilton's shoulder.

For an instant Claire Grahame stood motionless looking at the boy and girl before she crumpled to a chair and hid her face in her arms outflung on the table. Her slender body shook with sobs. The child regarded her for a moment in startled uncertainty. Two big tears coursed down her cheeks. She looked through drenched eyes at the youth who still held her close:

"Mummy mustn't cry like that. If you really are my new brother put your arms about her. That is what Davie did when Daddy left us. Don't cry, Mummy. Don't cry. Davie would be so sorry."

She knelt at her mother's feet and snuggled her head against her arm. Hamilton laid a tender hand upon one shaking shoulder. At the touch a cry of infinite love and longing welled from the woman's heart:

"David! My son! My splendid son!"

# Chapter I

A GEM of a laugh. A thrilled whisper:

"Ready boys!"

The girl, perched on the newel-post of the stairway which swept gracefully up to the hall above, put an harmonica to her lips. A shaft of September sunlight from a window on the landing illumined her, set a bit of nickel on the instrument ablaze, lingeringly tipped with gold the pink and white cosmos in the Georgian bowl of silver on the half-moon table. Her laughter-brimmed eyes were on the three dogs on the stairs. Rusto, the Belgian, loomed in majestic dignity above the shaggy, black wire-haired Pinschers. His ears were cocked, his eyes were on the girl. The smaller of the two dogs tilted his head and rolled his eyes heavenward as though preparing to scale Carusonian heights of tone. The beady eyes of his twin fixed on a door across the hall suggested dark and dour reflection as he flexed sensitive nose muscles.

At the first note of reveille all three threw back their heads, spread their jaws and flung their voices on the air. On her tricky perch the girl swayed with laughter. She stopped playing to chant in a sweet, husky contralto:

"We must get him out!
We must get him out!
We must get him out of that of-fice!"

She repeated the call on the harmonica. The dogs accompanied to their individual satisfaction. As their wails increased in volume and tunelessness the door across the hall was flung open. A man in riding clothes appeared on the threshold. With much the spectacular effect of the sun breaking through a cloud his exasperated frown cleared away in a flashing smile as he regarded the quartette on the stairway. The girl's old-rose skirted knees were crossed in an effort to maintain her equilibrium, her lovely face was dimpled with laughter, white teeth gleamed between

1

boyish lips, her dark eyes were brilliant with triumph. The soft hat on a slightly deeper shade than her frock was crushed down at a rakish angle on her black hair. As she resumed her efforts on the instrument the dogs increased the volume of their output. They gave the impression of attempting the feat of keeping one eye on their conductor and one on the man at the door. Anthony Hamilton held up his hand:

"Lafayette we are here!"

The girl jumped to the floor. As though released from a spell the dogs dashed across the hall. The Belgian reared on his hind feet and thumped a paw on the man's chest. With the other he bowled over the clamoring terriers.

"Shame, Rusto! Give the little fellows a chance," Hamilton reproved as he stooped to pat the small dogs. The large one tried to thrust his cold nose under his master's soft collar. Anthony laughed:

"You did the trick, Rose. Here I am. What do you want?"

"Want! Have you forgotten that you promised to have tea with me at the river this afternoon?"

"Today!"

He ruefully regarded the sheaf of papers in his hand. He pulled a memoranda book from his pocket. Rose Grahame leaned her head against his arm as she followed his eyes. Exultantly she tapped the page with a pink-tipped finger:

"There it is! Under this very date! 'Tea with Rose.' Let's see you wriggle out of that and get away with it, Mr. Anthony Hamilton! Come on, Tony, I want a nice long afternoon with my best pal. I have the tea-things in a basket. I cajoled Juno into making cream scones. They're bursting with strawberry jam. It gets dark early now and we must be back in time to dress for dinner at your mother's. I haven't met your brother Mark yet. I intend to make myself irresistible."

"Don't try too hard, Rose."

"Silly! Do you think I meant it? I have more important things on my mind. I have a world-shaking proposition to make to you. I returned from Europe three days ago. Do you realize that this is the first chance for a heart-to-heart we've had since I left college? You and Mother hustled me abroad immediately after graduation. While I was gone you cut out Peter in the lady's fickle affections and got engaged to Daphne Tennant. Poisonous of you, I call it, not to give me an inkling of the state of your young affections before-hand."

A slight color burned beneath the bronze of Hamilton's skin. His eyes were on the papers in his hand as he directed:

"Wait for me in the living-room. I'll be with you before you can say, 'Hands up!' Are the dogs invited to the tea-party?"

"Of course. Good boys! Didn't they help rout you out of that old office? Hurry or we won't get to the river before the sun drops behind the trees."

As Rose Grahame crossed the hall the dogs looked after her then at one another with the shifting, impersonal gaze canines employ when they wish to appear indifferent. One after the other they thumped to the floor in front of the office door. They rested their noses on outstretched paws. From the threshold of the living room the girl regarded them. They wig-wagged tails in languid acknowledgment of her attention.

"Why make it so blatantly evident that it is Tony whom you adore? That you play with me only when you can't get him or Peter?" she reproached in answer to their apologetic eyes. She crossed to the window. Her thoughts reverted to the past summer. It had been a wonderful experience but, why had her mother and Tony been so determined that she should go? How had they financed the trip? For the last five years the orchards had provided a comfortable income besides paying off loans but, with Peter and herself at college, there couldn't have been much margin for travel. She had rebelled against leaving the family and the beauty of White Pillars to travel in a Europe—no matter how interesting—crowded with printed-silked and tweed-suited Americans. Nevertheless, she had made the most of every moment. Perhaps now she would be permitted to enjoy life here.

Her glance rested on a hazy blue line of hills, followed the silver river, patterned in emerald islands, which spooned between banks sometimes rough and gray with granite, sometimes fringed with willows, sometimes

marshed with rushes, until it purled leisurely by the fields
of White Pillars. Glittering little creeks fluttered back
through mellow meadows into the green distance like gay
follow-me-lad streamers floating from a charmer's shoulders. Her thoughtful eyes lingered on a white colony of
beehives, returned to the near-by orchards. As far as she
could see in all directions were rows and rows of trees
laden with fruit of crimson and gold. She parodied aloud:

"Apples to right of her
Apples to left of her
Apples in front of her reddened and ripened."

Tony had made royally good, the girl thought as she
reveled in the mystic charm of the iridescent gloom into
which the sunshine melted. Memory flashed back to the
day more than ten years before when for the first time
she had seen him. She had not half understood her mother's
grief but she had sensed the solemnity of Anthony Hamilton's promise. He was to be son and brother to them for
ten years. Forsaking all others to cleave only unto them.

How absurd that that bit of the marriage service should
slip into her mind in connection with Tony. He had kept
his promise. A year after he had come to White Pillars
he had been sent to a Southern camp and there he had
stayed through the war training raw recruits, such raw
recruits! How he had rebelled! How he had tried to get
across. She and her mother had hoped for his sake that he
would be sent overseas. For their own—that was a different matter. He had returned with two silver bars on
his shoulder to lay aside his uniform and resume work in
the orchards.

Rose forsook retrospection to watch an airplane hovering above Headless Hill. Was it a mail-carrier a little off
its route? Was the pilot considering the advisability of
landing on the plateau which gave the decapitated effect
to the near-hill? He was coming down! The girl watched
breathlessly. The great birds with a human mind in control
never ceased to thrill her. He was up! He was off!
Curious that he should have landed there even for a few
moments. Perhaps he was a friend of Nap Long who kept
a plane in a hangar on the hill. Napoleon Bonaparte Long!
Mention his name to Tony and one got figuratively the
reaction as from waving a red rag at a bull. Long had

spent the two years of the war in the midst of fighting and had achieved distinction as an aviator. Disliking him, as he had before, it was a little more than Tony could bear.

She mustn't think of Nap, she detested him. Much better to think of what Tony had accomplished. He had installed Eddie Timmins, who had been his orderly at camp as foreman. When the hard times came he had adopted a policy of employing only natives of the county or responsible naturalized citizens in the orchards. The men were given a chance at agricultural college in the winter.

At heart had Tony been restless under the restraint of his promise, Rose wondered. Apparently his family had unlimited wealth. Never had she talked with her mother about his past. Whenever the thought had arisen of what his life had been before he came to them she had smothered it. Whenever friend or neighbor had veered toward the subject she had sidetracked them. Curious. Was she jealous of the time before he had belonged so entirely to White Pillars? The ten years of his contract were accomplished. Had been since last spring.

He was free to go. Why should he continue to work, why continue to fight an attacking army of pests, why labor in the laboratory working out formulas, why longer shoulder the hundred and one problems and disappointments incidental to the business of orcharding?

The plot had thickened this summer. Tony's mother, realizing, doubtless, that his contract as manager of the Grahame orchards had expired, had leased La Mancha, the magnificent estate which adjoined White Pillars. Nap Long had bought it on his return from nowhere a year before—how had he made the money? Last spring he had met Mrs. Hamilton in France. She had wanted to hire a house for the season in his village. He had offered La Mancha as being the only suitable estate for her, so he had explained glibly.

Tony had been white with anger when he heard it. Mrs. Hamilton had kept the place overflowing with guests, had demanded her younger son's presence at all festivities. What had been her object in coming to their quiet village?

To bring pressure to bear to separate Tony from his adopted family?

Rose blinked long lashes to clear sudden angry tears from her eyes. If his mother didn't get him Daphne Tennant would. Daphne and Tony! It seemed incredible. Peter had been fairly eating out of her hand when his sister sailed in June. Daphne was harmless enough but she was two years older than Peter and entirely under the domination of her mother. The invalidish Mrs. Tennant and the pretty daughter had come to town a year before. They appeared cultured and not too eager to make friends. Perhaps because of the latter attitude they were taken up by the Country Club set. It didn't seem quite fair that Tony with his solid-gold family background and charm, who never before had singled out a girl for his attentions, should poach on Peter's preserves. Why had he done it? Rose wrinkled her patrician nose disdainfully as she visualized his fiancée's colorless daintiness:

"Hmp! Clinging-vine stuff! That's what he fell for," she commented under her breath as she crossed to the fireplace. She vented her indignation on the smoldering logs. They blazed into protest under the vigorous attack of the poker. Something in her heart always went off like a flashlight flare when she thought of that engagement.

She frowned at the tall Willard clock topped by three brass balls. On its face a full-rigged ship was about to dip below the horizon. It was ticking the minutes away with exemplary fidelity. If only Tony would hurry. If they didn't get away soon someone would buttonhole him about something. It was the busiest season of the year. The peaches were being picked. As soon as those had been shipped the fall apples would be ready to market. Her brother David's vision had materialized. "Fruit You Can Eat In The Dark," was being sold all over the world.

Perched on the arm of the davenport at right angles with the fireplace Rose looked about her. She loved the restfulness of the plain Japanese cloth walls with their dull gold hangings, the absence of clutter of detail. A coppery bowl of russet helenium was on the piano, a happy-go-lucky arrangement of marigolds glinted in a shadowy corner. She had known the room and its heirlooms as far back as she could remember. She had learned to write at the Sheraton secretary which treasured behind its tambour doors great-great Grandmother Grahame's pink lustre tea set. She had learned to play cards on the Hepplewhite table. In front of the Georgian mirror she had balanced on the edge of that Chippendale chair in a vain effort to admire the huge pink bow in her black hair before she fared forth on the breath-snatching adventure of her first party.

At right and left of the fireplace rose tier upon tier of books. On one side was her grandfather's library. Sets of Dickens, Thackeray, Macaulay, Irving, Parkman. She smiled as her eyes rested on the Cadell edition of Scott. How she had reveled in the stories in those small volumes. Every valiant knight had been Tony. Every lovely lady in distress had been her mother.

Her glance fell on the Chinese Coromandel screen of vivid red lacquer which stood at the entrance of the garden room. She prickled with imagination. Always it had that effect upon her. Always it seemed to whisper mysteriously: "Dare you to look behind me! Dare you!"

And always she had forced herself to look before she dashed away as though a legion of imps were at her heels. Of course she had outgrown that foolishness now, but—that bit of Oriental color still exuded an aura of sinister mystery. She looked quickly beyond it to the garden room gay with chintz. From it drifted the scent of moist warm earth, the fragrance of blossoms. Between two sunny plant-filled windows was the wall fountain Tony had given her mother. A bronze nymph held to her bronze ear a shell from which crystal drops fell rhythmically into a miniature pool below. The drip-drip of water kept time to the tick-tock of the massive pendulum of the old clock in the corner.

"Ready, Rose!"

"Not really, Tony? Before I could say 'Hands up!' you said. I have had time to review my whole life," the girl mocked as she deserted her perch on the arm of the davenport.

Thoughtfully she regarded Anthony Hamilton smiling at her from the doorway. He was so good to look at. Strong. Lean. Tall. His gray eyes were clear and dependable, just

now with cool laughter in their depths. His smooth, dark
hair kicked up perkily above his ears. His teeth were
even and white, his mouth under the slight mustache was
determined but so—so sweet. That was the word for
Tony's mouth, the girl decided. And his smile? She
couldn't describe it. It just caught at her heart. Couldn't
he rage though! His riding clothes were shabby from constant wear in the saddle but she loved their suggestion
of past distinction.

"Young woman, for one in a rush you are taking your
time. Almost—you give the impression that you are considering the advisability of keeping your date with me."

"I was considering how nice you are," she answered
gravely. A flash of emotion routed the laugh from the
man's eyes. The telephone on the desk rang. Rose answered it.

"Yes." She made a little face at the instrument.

"He is here. Wait a minute." She pressed her hand over
the mouthpiece as she flung over her shoulder:

"It's your ball and chain, Tony. Darn! Now I suppose
our party is off."

Hamilton took the instrument from her hand.

"Daphne? . . . Ride with you? Can't. Have an engagement with Rose" . . . His brow contracted in annoyance.
Impatience chilled his voice as he persisted, "No. I can-
not . . . Sorry . . . I am not to call for you tonight? . . .
Very well. Good-bye!"

He hung up the receiver.

"Come on, Rose."

"If Daphne wants you, Tony . . ."

"Don't you want to go?"

"Don't snap my head off. Of course I do, silly, but I
appreciate the fact that your steady company has first
claim." With a gleeful chuckle she slipped her arm through
his. "Let's go! The basket is on the veranda. If we don't
hurry . . ."

The telephone rang. It rang again imperiously. The
man and girl looked at one another before, with the
guilty air of near-conspirators, they tiptoed out of the
house with the dogs leaping and barking at their heels.

## Chapter II

AT THE foot of the broad steps Rose waited while Hamilton unhitched a horse whose coat shone like black satin, whose soft nose nuzzled his pockets. Rusto dexterously caught the bridle rein in his mouth as his master commanded:

"Take Pierrot home!"

The captive whinnied a reproach, pirouetted daintily before he submitted to the steady tug on the rein. The dog, lordly with responsibility, led him in the direction of the stable. As Rose and Hamilton started on, the faint ring of the telephone pricked at her conscience. They should have waited to answer that call. She looked back. How lovely the old house was in this light. Sunshine filtered through two immense oaks and patterned the exquisite proportions of the classic columns and cornices with fluttering shadows, stenciled the long, broad steps with patches of gold. The trees cast into darkness the picturesque little balcony above the old entrance door. Many a time had she swung from its intricate iron railing into the big tree and slid to the ground to escape pursuing Peter and his pals. Charm. Dignity. Simplicity. The Colonial perfectness of the mansion impressed the girl as never before. From the kitchen ell drifted a woman's voice singing with negro richness and pathos:

> " 'I'm on mah way to heaven
> An' I don' wan' stop;
> I don' wan' be
> No stumbelin' block
> An' I come all de way to tell yuh
> Ain' da's good news?' "

Rose's throat contracted. She slid her hand into Hamilton's. As his closed firmly about it she confessed:

9

"All my life I have heard Juno sing and even now her voice twists my heart into a tight knot. Was there ever a homier home than ours, Tony? Jeer if you like, but I saw nothing as charming as White Pillars in all my travels."

"I never jeer at you, dear." The tenderness of the last word shot through Rose's consciousness like a ray of warm sunlight.

"Confess that you think me a hide-bound conservative. If you didn't would you pry me away from my native heath at every opportunity?"

"Your mother and I won't allow you to narrow down to life here until you have seen something else. Ignorance of the world outside one's circle isn't the best foundation for enduring happiness within it."

"Wasn't college *enough?* Pulling me up by the roots every little while won't make me happy. Look at that orchard where our men have started the fall plowing! See the shades of brown in the freshly turned furrows! Here comes Rusto tearing back for fear he'll miss the scone-party. Oh, how I love the country!"

In sympathetic silence the man and girl crossed the garden back of the house, stopped a moment to consult the sundial, opened a rustic gate. A broad path ambled downgrade to the river. The dogs crowded by them to stage mad forays among the trees, dashing back at intervals to sniff at the basket Hamilton carried.

The banks of the stream were vivid with cardinal flowers. A few maples had shaken out their brilliant autumn finery preparatory to dropping it into cold storage. Oaks showed a suspicion of tan. Pines, spruces and cedars gloomed deeply green in contrast. Far upstream, spanning the sparkling current, like a misty tight-rope flung from shore to verdant shore, hung a bridge. At the right of the path a cedar bathhouse snuggled close against the bank as though fearful that its broad veranda, which extended out over the river, might drag it from its safe and sane seclusion. A swan sailed majestically in midstream. His consort watched him from the sanctuary of a small island.

Rose dropped to her knees on a carpet of brown needles. Over her head green boughs canopied to shut out the blue brilliance of the sky. Woodland music

crooned through the top of the pine, resinous fragrance
stole from its branches. A squirrel tenant chattered. A
bluejay marauder squawked an insolent defiance. Swallows
skimmed. The river flowed by, sudsy in spots, glitteringly
swift in others, sometimes still and sullen with a sinister
suggestion of undercurrent. The girl drew a deep breath:

"Isn't this glorious?"

"It is. Shall we have tea here or in the boathouse?"

"Here. No roof over my head this wonderful afternoon.
Tony, my heart like all Gaul, is divided into three parts.
Mother and White Pillars one, you and Peter. When I
would get desperately homesick last summer I would close
my eyes and picture you and me having tea here. Then,
quite distinctly I could hear you say, as you always have
said when there was something I hated to do:

" 'Get it behind you, dear. It has to be done. Get it
behind you.' "

Hamilton lighted the wick of an alcohol lamp under
the kettle he had set on the shore of a sandy shallow.

"Ungrateful child, to think of that opportunity as
something to get behind you. *Madre* and I sat up nights
planning it."

"*Madre*. I love your name for mother, Tony. How did
you manage to finance the trip? How could you, with
Peter and me getting through at college? Of course he's
the original infant prodigy to do his work in three years,
but you should have spent the money set apart for his
fourth year on him, not on me."

"He could have gone across had he wished. He was
eager to get to work in the orchards. He has done won-
ders this summer. In two weeks I'm putting him in the
shipping end of the business. He'll clerk there this winter
—I hope—happily."

Rose regarded him thoughtfully. His tone was troubled.
Did he suspect that Peter had wanted to get to work
that he might have at least a prospect to offer Daphne
Tennant? Did Tony realize, as she did, how the boy had
changed this summer? Was he always to shoulder the
burdens of others? She watched a gaudy maple leaf sail
buoyantly down stream like an adventurous crimson and
gold galley before she confided dreamily:

"Tony, always you remind me of my first hero, the

solitary horseman in *The Talisman*. I know that story by heart. Remember how when you first came to White Pillars I used to curl up in your lap while you read it to me? How when I was housed with measles and chicken-pox you read and re-read it? It began like this:

" 'When the burning sun of Syria had not yet attained its highest point on the horizon,' etc., etc. 'The surcoat of the solitary horseman bore in several places the arms of the owner much defaced. These seemed to be a couchant leopard with the motto:

" 'I sleep; wake me not!'

"This is where you come in, Tony. Remember with what ferocity the Saracen charged on the Knight of the Couchant Leopard? 'When within twice the length of his lance the heathen whirled his steed and rode twice round the horseman, who, without quitting his ground presented his front constantly to the enemy thus frustrating the Saracen's attempts to attack him on an unguarded point.' That's you. You never turn your back on difficulties. You face things."

Memory shadowed Hamilton's eyes as he demanded:

"Isn't every man who gets anywhere a solitary horseman? Doesn't he wheel—to quote old Scott—'with inimitable dexterity' to face temptation, doubt and indecision as they attack? If he lets those enemies get a chance at his back he's licked."

"But every man isn't facing a lot of problems which belong to other people as you are. To proceed with my cross-examination. From whence, O Horseman, came the money for my trip? I know that the orchards have prospered, but, enough to finance the Bilt-Feller luxury in which I traveled? Enough to provide the appropriation you insisted was to be spent for clothes? Oh, I used it. Wait until you see my winter sports costume *et als!* 'Mademoiselle is charming! Superb! Ravishing!' " She rolled her eyes and clasped her hands with French abandon.

"Who said that?"

"Rusto growls like that when one of the little dogs approaches his bone. Why shouldn't I be considered charming? Tony, you're due for a terrific bump which will

wake you up to the fact that I am twenty-two years old
—plus."

Hamilton watched a golden squall of bees blow through
a clump of purple asters; watched the motes of yellow
pollen which shook from bodies and wings float down
stream on a soft breeze. His lips flashed into a smile:
" 'I sleep; wake me not!' " he warned theatrically. The
laughter left his voice as he mused aloud:

"Twenty-two—plus. Are you really, dear? I never
think of you as grown-up. Always to me you are the child
who slipped her hand into mine and whispered:

" 'Are you my new big brother?' "

The girl put her hand to her throat as though it hurt.
Her lips were unsteady as she persisted:

"Whatever you think, Tony, I am almost twenty-three.
Old enough to know something of our business affairs.
How did you finance my summer?"

"Oh, we dipped into some accumulations."

"*You* and *Mother!* You two who have brought me up
to regard touching my anaemic savings account as the first
downward step on the road to ruin. I can't believe it.
Perhaps you wanted me out of the way? Poisonous idea.
You needn't have troubled. You could have fallen for
Daphne with me here. I wouldn't have stopped you even
if I do think she's a flat tire."

"Rose! Did you major in slang at college?"

The girl flushed brilliantly.

"Don't be icy, Tony. How can I help picking it up
from Peter? It's so darn—so expressive. I'm sorry I called
Daphne a—I shouldn't have spoken so of the girl to
whom you're engaged. But, you did wait until I was out
of the way, didn't you?"

"You are unjust to Daphne. The pity of it is that she
knows that you consider her a nonentity. That kettle will
boil over."

Rose glanced at him surreptitiously as she prepared tea.
She recognized certain storm signals. She had learned to
tread softly before that steel-like set of his jaw. She and
Peter had labelled that expression, "When Tony drops
his visor." It was her own fault if never again he took
her into his confidence. How could he when she had
called his fiancée a flat tire? A laugh tugged at her lips.

Just the same she was. Tony would find it out when the
first fine frenzy was over. As a peace-offering she prof-
fered a plate of scones, flaky, delicately browned, in-
dented by little wells of ruddy strawberry jam.

"Aren't those luscious? Is your tea *quite* as you like it?
I want you to be blissfully comfortable before I ask you
something."

"Shoot."

"I want to work. I want to be your secretary."

"What?"

"Don't shout. Don't twist that mustache off, Tony, I
like it. Stop glaring and listen. At college I studied stenog-
raphy and accounting, besides municipal government and
administration; state and local government; constitutional
law and a few other more ornamental courses. I am
equipped to help in the clerical end of our business. It is
ours, isn't it? When you go . . ."

"Go! What do you mean?"

"Aren't you between Scylla and Charybdis? Your mother and Daphne? Either one will do her best to pry you
away from your adopted family."

"Cut out that word, adopted. You Grahames are my
family. Go on with your crazy proposition."

"Don't lose your temper because I feel the prick of
independence wings. We haven't much money behind us.
One blighting season in the orchards, one strike of the
pickers would make an awful hole in a year's profits. To
date you and mother have ordered my life for me. Because
I adore you both I haven't had the heart to stage a declaration of independence. I'm a meaty problem for a psy-
choanalyst. When I'm with you I'm absurdly young. Always I have the impulse to slip my hand into yours. Is
it because in your heart you refuse to let me grow up?
You'll have to admit that a girl who was president of her
class in college can't be kept legitimately in the Teddy-
bear stage."

"As long as possible I want to keep you from coming
up against the rough edges of life, dear."

"Tony, you're archaic. It is time I took a few bumps.
Isn't it better to start walking alone while there are still
plenty of years ahead in which to fall down? It is so easy
to scramble up when one is young. Look at that river!

It's off on an adventure of its own. See it sparkle and darkle and foam and bubble. Little it cares if it gets caught in the reeds and rushes or eddies into a Sargasso Sea—my mistake, the scientists say there isn't one. It knows that it is young enough, strong enough, gay enough to wriggle free from all entangling alliances. It's taking its chance at living before it is submerged in the ocean."

Hamilton's eyes warmed with affectionate amusement as he teased:

"I'll bet a hat you've taken to writing free verse."

"Laugh if you'll only listen. I intend to do something! That's that! I ought to be trained in the business while you are with us. I know nothing of the affairs of your people but I suspect that they will give you all the money you want if you will leave us. Of course Daphne Tennant knows that. Will she settle down in an apple orchard? Not a chance. If you think she will you have another guess coming to you, simple child."

Hamilton pressed the tobacco into his pipe with a force which rendered it unfit for smoking whatever its virtue for packing.

"I will meet that problem when it presents itself, Rose. Just now I have one more urgent. I had not intended to tell you but as you wish to be taken into my business confidence, here it is. Our peaches are being stolen."

The statement was as effective as a brand new broom wielded by a brand new housemaid on a brand new job. It swept all thought of self from the girl's mind.

"Not the Elbertas, Tony? Just as you have begun to harvest! Are you sure?"

"Yes. We monogrammed some for exhibition purposes. They are gone."

"Of what use could they be to anyone but ourselves? If a thief wanted them to eat why risk discovery by snitching marked ones? Who would buy them?"

"He could represent himself as our salesman. There are fruit dealers who would not ask questions."

"Whom do you suspect? That new man, Sam Hardy? I haven't seen him yet. Except for him we have the same crew of pickers we have had for the last two years, haven't we?"

"We are short half a dozen. I suspect that Nap Long

hired them for his building enterprise. You can't blame the men. They have families and money talks. I won't suspect Hardy. He was jailed, he assured me, unjustly. I like his face. I trust him."

"How did he happen to come here?"

"He had heard that I was interested in men who had served time."

"You are, Tony. I have often wondered why."

"Dear, don't you know?"

"I know that you are old-fashioned enough to believe that to some extent you are your brother's keeper. Do you suppose that Nap Long is behind the peach thefts? He was so furious when you declined to hire those foreigners he recommended and to buy his boxes."

"Long? No. He's a realtor of the build-you-a-house-while-you-wait, type. He wouldn't dare. Haven't you heard?"

"What?"

"That he's out for the office of selectman? One of the board died last summer. The two left can't agree. A special town meeting has been called for the second week in November to elect a man to fill the vacancy."

"Tony, why don't you try for it?"

"I can't now—some day I will. I'll confess that at times I hear the political Lorelei twanging her harp. I'll have to stuff my ears with cotton for the present. The man elected should devote a lot of time to town matters as the present board's been asleep at the switch. I've bought three abandoned farms to use as apple plantations. My plan is to lease them to trustworthy men in our employ. Incidentally, I have blocked Napoleon Bonaparte Long in his scheme to dot this valley with two-story frame houses. He's boasted that he'll boom the town, bring factories here because of the river power."

"He never can be elected, Tony. Think of his old peddler grandfather. Think of his shop-keeper father, weak-eyed, always buried in books, when he wasn't drowned in liquid. Think of his horde of dirty brothers and sisters. Napoleon was the oldest. There is no doubt but that he inherited his grandfather's flair for big business. His first venture was to trade a broken knife for a shabby bill-folder. In its depths he found a crumpled dollar bill. Somewhere, somehow he heard of his illustrious namesake. That settled his career. Like Napoleon the First, 'Long's star' has become his obsession. Notice how he stands with one hand thrust in his coat the other behind his back? Exactly the pose of the Emperor of Paul de la Roche. He is even training his hair to fall in a Napoleonic lock on his forehead. Apparently he has been uncannily successful, how else could he have bought La Mancha? He even equipped it with servants in character before he rented it to your mother. A sense of artistic values is the last trait with which I would have credited him. Curious the way his family vanished into thin air just before he came back here to settle."

"He is ambitious socially. That family would keep him down. He is one of the Oliver Optic-Trowbridge heroes come to life—from newsboy to multi-millionaire type. I repeat my platitude. Money talks. Nap is already hobnobbing with one of the governors of the Country Club. Before you know it you will be taking tea with him there!"

"I! Never!"

"He appears to have money to burn but I can't rid myself of the feeling that there's a colored gentleman in the woodpile."

"Is he the only candidate for selectman?"

"No one seems to have time to run against him."

"I detest him. I can't forget the burrs he stuck in my hair nor the day he strung my Annabel Lee to a tree and shot her head off, then offered me striped candy. That doll is in a box in my room now. I remember thinking all the time I hugged her close in my arms, 'I won't let him see me cry. I won't.' I asked mother for some black ribbons. You tied the box for me, never have I opened it since. Remember, Tony?"

"Remember! I do, as though it were yesterday. I remember also, that the next time he teased you I gave him the thrashing of his life."

"He hasn't cared for you a lot since, Tony. Ugh! How I hated him. He was such a hector. What a racket the dogs are making! Nothing smaller than a treed bear would justify that pandemonium. Here they come! They're trailing something! Perhaps the mysterious peach thief."

Rose sprang to her feet as the approaching clamor of yelps and barks drowned the chatter and purl of the river. Rusto and the Pinschers dashed into sight on the bank a hundred feet down stream. They halted. They snuffled around in baffled uncertainty. After a bewildered instant they retraced their steps until they sniffed and growled themselves out of sight. Rose dropped back on her heels.

"What could it have been, Tony? A world-shaking pursuit for them to have ignored the fact that we were having tea. They're scone-gluttons."

"A hedgehog would have set them off. It might have been a woodchuck. I saw one nibbling the lettuce yesterday and told Sam Hardy to shoot it if he got the chance."

"Where were we when so rudely interrupted? I know—peaches. Shocked as I am at the news I shall return to my business proposition. Will you engage me as your secretary?"

"Why tie yourself down at present? You worked hard at college. Play for a year. Devote yourself to your family. 'O woman! . . .'"

"If you say that woman's place is in the home I'll throw something at you. Preferably something that squashes."

"I was about to quote from your favorite Sir Walter. 'O woman! in thine hours of ease,' etc. I'm dumb."

The girl laughed with him as she admitted:

"I'm not denying that woman's place is in the home—when she's needed. Some day I'm going to marry and have five or six children—they will keep me busy. But, I ask you, what is there for me to do at White Pillars? Juno and Jupiter have been with mother since she married. The household machinery never even creaks. Mother has her welfare work in the village. She doesn't need me. Peter doesn't need me. You do not need me—now."

Hamilton took careful aim and fired at the angry chatter of a squirrel he could not see.

"Where did you get that silly notion? I . . ."

The descent of an extraordinarily large, an extraordinarily perfect peach in place of the cone which had gone up snapped off the sentence. Speechless from surprise the man and girl stared into the green above them. Its density was broken by gleams of sunshine like glinting fragments of tinsel on a Christmas tree.

Rose brushed her hand lightly across her eyes as though to sweep away a cobweb of imagination. She whispered incredulously:

"A peach from a pine!"

She held her breath as Hamilton swung up into the tree. She heard the ripple of water among rushes, the hum of wings in the purple asters as filching bees lighted and loaded and zig-zagged hiveward, the excited yelps of dogs in the distance, the swish of branches.

Her heart pounded with excitement. Was the orchard thief overhead? How could he have escaped the dogs? By swinging from branch to interlacing branch, of course. Curious that she had not heard him. Why had the dogs turned back? Tony was coming down. As Hamilton reached the ground and brushed one pitchy hand against the other he announced:

"Not a sign of anybody. I couldn't get near the top of the tree nor see into the dense foliage. There go the dogs again! They've treed something. Leave the tea-things. We'll come back for them. Come on! Don't make a sound."

Rose followed at his heels as he made his cautious way along the bank of the stream. At an opening in the trees ahead he halted and caught her by the shoulder. She followed the direction of his eyes. A tall man in a canoe was pushing off from shore. The portion of his face visible below the down brim of his soft hat was white and streaked with sweat and dirt. The dogs stood in the water up to their middles watching him. Their mouths hung open. Their red tongues dripped. Their tails wagged friendly encouragement. Rose felt the fingers on her shoulder tighten, heard Anthony's quick breath. They watched the canoe till it disappeared around the bend, till its white wake was but a frothy memory. Hamilton released the girl's shoulder. He pulled the peach from his pocket and frowned down upon it. Rose slipped her hand under his arm and whispered:

"Who was the man, Tony?"

His voice matched his troubled eyes as he answered:

"Sam Hardy."

# Chapter III

CLAIRE GRAHAME in a heliotrope frock which made a lovely bit of color in the cool hall, paused on a stair as a stubby black tail whisked out of sight barely escaping further decimation by the closing front door. The same shaft of sunlight, slightly aged, which had illumined her daughter, transmuted the soft waves of her hair to the bluish silver of the Georgian bowl, accentuated the clear coloring of her skin. She listened till the fusilade of barks diminished in the distance. Evidently Rose had succeeded in luring Anthony from his work, she thought. The telephone in the living room had been ringing for the last three minutes. Why had not the young people waited to answer it? Evidently having secured Anthony, Rose would risk no interference with her plans. Smiling she ran down the stairs and answered the call.

"Mrs. Grahame speaking. . . . Mrs. Hamilton? . . . Anthony is not here . . . I don't know where. May I take a message? . . . Yes. I understand. You want him to come early. Alone. I will tell him. Good-bye."

She wrote the message on a pad in the office and returned to the living room. Mrs. Hamilton was decidedly arbitrary, she thought, as seated in a corner of the davenport, hands clasped about her knees, she watched the burning soot on the back of the chimney shift in design like the pattern of a kaleidoscope. Why had Anthony's mother come to this quiet village? To make her younger son realize the splendor and ease of the life he had given up? La Mancha was the last word in luxury with its horde of Spanish servants. It was quite evident that she disapproved of Anthony's engagement to Daphne Tennant. In that they two were in accord. Nothing which had happened during the years he had lived at White Pillars had surprised her as had that. The girl was colorless, "pulpy" Rose called her. She had had Peter securely hooked for a while but she had cast him into the waters of discard—as promptly as Peter himself flung back a small trout—when the manager of the Grahame orchards swam into her social pool. She herself had been concerned when her young son had been attracted to the girl who must be twenty-five though she looked and dressed eighteen. She had confided her anxiety to Anthony. He had counseled her not to worry and then—he himself had fallen victim to Daphne's charm.

Ten years since Anthony had come to White Pillars. She remembered the day she had seen him for the first time, remembered her anguish of spirit as though it had been yesterday. At first she had had to fight an undercurrent of bitterness but his tenderness and help had been like a soothing hand upon her aching heart. Never could she forget her first born but in the years since she had lost him the man who had so valiantly slipped into his place had been an unfailing comfort. Sometimes she wondered if she could have loved her own David more. Anthony's word and example had been law to her children. His tenderness had kept her spirit youthful. She felt younger today at forty-nine than she had ten years ago. Life was vital, packed with interest. He had kept his promise. He had shared their fortunes, had lived as she and Rose and Peter had had to live in the lean years. Lean! There had been some which losses had picked to a skeleton; years when she had wondered if the place and all they had put into it would have to go. When last spring she had reminded Anthony that his period of service was accomplished he had demanded:

"Don't you want me to stay with you, *Madre?*"

"Want you! My dear boy . . ." her voice had turned traitor.

"Then don't think of my leaving you. The new orchards are beginning to bear. Timmins is capable of taking my place. We will try Peter outside this summer before we put him into the shipping house. If he makes good, as he will, next year I'll begin to make an ambition of mine come true. It will be nothing which will separate me from you and Rose."

She had had difficulty in steadying her voice sufficiently to answer:

"It is time you realized an ambition. You have put yourself absolutely aside. While your friends have set up bachelor quarters you have remained here with us."

His smile had warmed her heart to the roots.

"You forget that I am the head of the family. Heads of families don't live in bachelor quarters."

"You have been an unfailing joy and comfort to me, Anthony. Sometimes I feel guilty in taking so much. You really belong to your own people."

She remembered the grip of his hands, his turbulent eyes, as he had corrected:

"I belong to you by right of salvage. Had you not been so divinely forgiving that day . . . If you feel that I have fulfilled my pledge I shall take but one advantage of it. I shall use my own income. Since Grandfather Hamilton's death two years ago it has been doubled. We'll divide my salary between Timmins and Peter—when he earns it. There are so many things I want to do for you and Rose. I want her to have clothes, she has been so sporting about having little. She must go abroad after she gets her degree."

"But, Anthony . . ."

"Give me my way in this, *Madre*. Your love and devotion have enriched my life. Have made me what I am. Let me repay. My boyhood was bleak and barren. Rose need not know how the trip is financed. If she does she will not question accepting it from me more than from her other brother. She is such a conservative that if we don't watch out she'll be married and settled in this village before she has seen anything of the world. I want her to go while she is still too young to think of marriage."

"You won't realize that she is grown up, Anthony."

"She isn't to me. Grown up with that boyish mouth? Oh, no. Promise me that Rose may go, *Madre*."

"I will consent to anything you think right," she had capitulated.

And so, in spite of Rose's plea that she be allowed a long, lovely summer at home she had gone abroad with friends. What had Tony meant by realizing an ambition? He had said, "Nothing that will separate me from you and Rose." He had confided that before he had become engaged to Daphne. Perhaps . . .

"Am I late for tea?" queried a voice behind her.

She roused from her revery with a start. How long had she been staring into the fire thinking back, she wondered as she turned to greet the man standing in the doorway.

"Nick! Deserter! We haven't seen you for days." As Nicholas Cort pressed his lips to her hand she observed:

"I hope that you appreciate my restraint, that you noticed that I didn't ask, 'Where *have* you been?' I have discovered that that question or its twin, 'Where are you going?' irritates Peter beyond words. Nothing but interest prompts the query but I have been assured that it enrages even the most innocent-intentioned male."

"As a reward for such heroic control I'll volunteer the information that I have been to Texas on business."

"Thank heaven you're back. I need you. I'm panicky."

The blue of Nicholas Cort's already intense blue eyes deepened. The years had been kind to him too, she thought. His hair was white but his skin was fresh and young. Except for fine crinkles about his deep-set eyes when he laughed his face was unlined. He carried his tall body with military erectness. Years ago he had set up bachelor hall in the home of his forebears in the village. He and her husband had been boys together, college classmates. In these last years he had been a devoted friend. Friend! The soft color heightened in her cheeks. Hastily she lowered her eyes from his as he repeated:

"Panicky! You? What has happened?"

"Ring for tea. Then I'll tell you."

Cort pulled the old-fashioned bell-rope. With the air of one perfectly at home he fussed around on the top of a smoker's paradise. The tall clock boomed:

One! Two! Three! Four!

It resumed the day's business. The wall fountain caught step.

Drip-drip! Tick-tock! Drip-drip! Tick-tock!

The monotonous duet was interrupted by the entrance of a tall, straight, colored man with grizzled hair. He pushed a laden tea-wagon in front of the davenport, then lingered to unnecessarily rearrange its equipment.

"Jupiter, bring fresh tea when Miss Rose and Mr. Anthony come in."

The flash of eyes and teeth in the servant's black face was like the unexpected ripple of foam on a sea suddenly stirred by a slight breeze. The man's chuckle was silver-toned:

"Dey won't want no tea, M's Claire. Dey wen' down froo de garden cahy'n a basket. I say to Juno, 'Yo' gone mak scones fer dem chillen again, 'ooman? After all yuh biggedy talk 'bout dat Mistuh Caloric?"

"If they had the tea-basket they won't want anything here, Jupiter."

"I don' know, Missy Rose, she eat a powerful lot, she sure does." As he left the room Claire Grahame explained:

"On one of my daughter's vacations she tried to imbue Juno with a respect for calories. For a while we were in danger of starvation. Sugar?"

"You ask having poured tea for me for ten years—plus?"

"Then you do take it?" she tormented.

"Stop looking at me like that or take the consequences."

He laughed as quick warm color spread to her hair. He seated himself in the wing chair opposite.

"I can see that I have you properly quelled. What's on your mind?"

"How long have we been friends?"

"Friends?"

"Nick—please. I need your help."

"Since the day I was best man at your wedding. Why?"

"I'm collecting evidence. After all these years you must have a working knowledge of my character. Had you ever a shred of suspicion that I thought of Anthony Hamilton's fortune when I consented to his coming here ten years ago?"

"Good Lord, no. Has it been intimated?"

"It has. By Anthony's mother."

"Doesn't she know that when he came here you refused to take the money settlement which was offered you?"

"Evidently not. It was hard to have him come—but, I couldn't let him drift back into his old life. She intimated that we Grahames were dependent upon his income, that he had financed both children through college. It is so untrue. Rose doesn't even know that Anthony has a fortune in his own right. She thinks that his mother is here to bribe him to leave White Pillars. Never has he used his money for us, for himself, never, that is, until last summer. I did consent to his financing Rose's trip abroad."

"You allowed him to do it when I have begged and begged . . ."

"Don't roar. It was quite a different proposition."

Cort's face was darkly red as he demanded:

"Is that all you have on your mind?"

"No, Nick. I'm frightened."

"Frightened! You? Where's that one-day-at-a-time philosophy which has carried you buoyantly through years which would have reduced the nerves of the average woman to ribbons? What's the trouble?"

"The children. First, I know that Anthony will wreck his future if he marries Daphne Tennant."

Cort leisurely stirred his tea, looked up under level gray brows as he suggested with a trace of amusement in his voice:

"Tony is over thirty years old."

"Old enough to realize what he is doing, you are reminding me. I know it. But always I have thought of Tony as smashing, crashing into love. This affair isn't even lukewarm. My heart fairly stops when I think of that marriage. Second—there is Peter."

"Peter! What's he been up to?"

"He behaves so queerly. I thought at first that he resented Tony's cutting-in on Daphne—but—I don't know. If it weren't light-hearted Peter I should think that he was worrying."

"Peter is all right. He worships Tony. If Daphne is at the bottom of it, all the boy needs to straighten him out is to meet another attractive girl. Twenty-four hours after he will be assuring himself that Daphne Tennant would have played the dickens with his life. That's youth."

"She'll play the dickens with Anthony's. What do you think of her, Nick?"

"I can't judge. She seems to have a curious distrust of

me. Her personality withdraws like a snail within its shell when I speak to her."

"Afraid of your third-degree eyes perhaps. She must have a guilty conscience."

"Not necessarily. She may be hiding some trouble that she is afraid I will suspect. Don't worry. That I should live to say that to you! Both of your boys are men older than their years. Peter went through college popular, respected, straight, in an age when the youngsters who didn't get into the war were making that conflict an excuse for all sorts of deviltry. When I probed him he came back coolly:

" 'Can't see the use of messing up my future getting plastered, running into debt or after cheap girls. Tony doesn't and he's the best fun, the best all round sport I know. He's A in everything. He claims there's such a lot in life that's fine to keep him sprinting that he hasn't time for the other things.' So, you see, 'Tony doesn't' is his talisman. Claire, you have put the best of yourself into those children. All you can do now is to stand on the side-lines and trust them." He smiled into her troubled eyes. "Still panicky?"

"I'll get it all off my mind. I'll confess the most foolish apprehension of all. Rose."

"Rose!"

Her short laugh was more of a sob.

"Who is panicky now? It is nothing real, Nick. Just my hectic imagination. Suppose—just suppose, that she should fall in love with Mark Hamilton? In some ways he is so like Anthony but, where Tony's skin is clear and brown, his is thick and beefy. Where Tony is lean he is heavy. His eyes in their puffy setting lack the clear straightforwardness of his brother's . . ."

Cort interrupted with an irrespressible laugh.

"Otherwise he's just like Anthony."

"Don't jeer at me, Nick. Doubtless the two brothers started with the same mental and physical equipment but looking at Mark is like looking at a blurred duplicate of Anthony."

"Why not credit Rose with your power of discernment?"

"She is young and he is fascinating. Gay. Caressing.

Cosmopolitan. And his technique with women—masterly."

Cort's eyes were tender as he reassured:

"Claire, you are beginning to show the strain of the years when you amazed us all by your courage. Don't worry about Rose. Don't worry about anything. Marry me and give me the right to help you help them all."

"Please don't ask me again, Cort. The children need me."

"They may leave you."

"Peter will have to be a fixture on account of the orchards."

"Suppose he goes away?"

"Away!"

"Now I have frightened you. Come here." He caught her hands and drew her to her feet beside him. "You know that you will marry me. You can't escape. 'If eventually, why not now?' "

"Please, Nick . . ." He released her and lighted a cigarette. She attempted to inquire lightly, "Are you dining at La Mancha tonight?"

"Yes, luckily. Mrs. Hamilton is a delightful hostess."

"Nick! You don't admire her! You can't. Her face is as soulless as—as the face of that Chinese woman on the Coromandel screen."

Nicholas Cort thoughtfully regarded the expanse of red lacquer. His eyes narrowed in an appraising squint as he protested:

"I don't agree with you. There is a lot in Mrs. Hamilton's face when she speaks to me. If you dislike a woman you can see no good in her. If you don't watch out you will get provincial. Living in this narrow environment . . ." his shrug broadcast waves of suggestion.

Claire Grahame experienced the same sensation as when, months before, an earthquake had set the room to swaying. Nick had criticized her! She felt two red spots flare in her cheeks. She must now have as much color as the woman he so admired, she thought sarcastically. She was grateful for the entrance of her daughter and Anthony. She glanced at the clock:

"Aren't you back early?"

"Yes, Mother. We . . ." The girl looked at Hamilton.

Did he shake his head or did she imagine it, Claire wondered. Rose slipped a hand under Cort's arm and cajoled:

"I hoped that you would be here, Uncle Nick. You always take my side, don't you? You'll make Tony see reason, won't you? He won't listen to me."

"Play fair, Rose. Tell him what you want to do," prompted Anthony Hamilton.

"I want to be his secretary. Wa-it a minute," she commanded as Cort opened his lips. "I shan't be taking the bread from the mouth of the present incumbent as I have heard Tony say scores of times that if he could get someone as good here he would transfer her to our New York Office."

"What humility! Do you think you are as good?" teased Nicholas Cort.

"Why don't you take the New York position? You and I might live there together. We are both threatened with an attack of narrow outlook, it seems."

The moment she had spoken Claire Grahame was ashamed of the sting in her tone. Nicholas Cort turned to poke the fire. She was conscious that Anthony regarded his broad back before he looked at her. Rose shook her head:

"You and I! Leave our men here without anyone to spoil them? I can see you doing it. I won't go away. I have just come home and at home I stay. If Tony won't engage me I'll find someone who wants a secretary. I'll find something to do, something that will keep me here."

Nicholas Cort turned from the fire. There was mischief in his eyes as he suggested:

"If you feel the urge to get busy why don't you run for selectwoman against Napoleon Bonaparte Long?"

"Don't make fun of me, Uncle Nick. Why don't you oppose Nap?"

"I've served. The town needs someone full of new ideas and pep. If only one of the young men would give his time he would set the pace for others. Having once seen the wheels of administration revolve from the inside never again would he be indifferent. He . . ."

A shriek from the direction of the kitchen resounded through the house. Instantly it was followed by a woman's voice shouting:

"Lawdy, Jup'ter, don' let dat debil . . ."

Cort and Hamilton started for the door. A long, lank figure in a torrid bathrobe shot down the bannister rail and landed on bare feet in the middle of the hall with the agility of an acrobat.

"Wow! Who let out that war-whoop?" demanded Peter Grahame.

His mother regarded him with adoring eyes. The panic which had gripped her on his account vanished in a surge of pride. What a dear he was! Clean. Wholesome. So good-looking. How unconsciously he imitated Anthony. There was the same flashing smile. The same imperious lift to his sleek head. The same touch of reserve. He had had an example worth following, thank God. How unjust to imagine that he was in the grip of a guilty conscience. His startled black eyes might have been his sister's, they were so like. Back of him, through a partly open door, she glimpsed two grizzled heads, the whites of eyes rolling in two black faces. Something shot by Peter? It couldn't be! It was . . .

A monkey landed on top of the tea-wagon. A poilu cap, held in place by a strap under the creature's chin, was tipped rakishly. A cockade of red, white and blue bristles adorned the front. A skinny claw scooped up the cream from a silver bowl, spattered it off in a shower of white beads. The three men dashed for the intruder. He jumped to the floor. With a rubber-ball bounce he landed on the Sheraton desk. An instant after he was peering down from the top of the tall clock in the corner.

The ancient timepiece swayed and regained its equilibrium. Safe from interference the monkey sampled the delicacy on his paw. His bald brow wrinkled. Sybaritically over the experiment. His pale cheeks were flecked with cream.

His melancholy eyes, dashed with cunning, darted from face to face staring up at him with dazed incredulity. He chattered, pulled off his cap, nervously ripped out the white lining which drifted to the floor. As he replaced his head covering at a rakish angle a brass ball on top of the clock caught his roving eye. He worked it free. In scowling inspection he turned it over and over. He at-

tempted to set his pointed, yellowed teeth in it. In an
ecstasy of mirth Peter flung himself to the couch:

"Look at him! Look at the cream on his whiskers!
Larry Semon stuff, what?" He flung up his arms to protect his head as something round and hard and shiny
whizzed past his ear. His mother struggled out of a nightmare of amazement:

"Anthony! Nick! Peter! Don't let him ruin Grandfather's
clock!"

She ducked as a second ball pitched with the precision
and despatch of a big-league outfielder struck her shoulder. The monkey, who looked as though his face had
been lathered for a shave, chattered and mouthed horribly as he seized the third ball. With a diabolical leer
at his audience he flung it to the tea-wagon where it
landed with a splash and crackle of china. Rose, weak
from laughter, snatched up a cake and cajoled:

"Come and get it!"

Head on one side the tempted one appraised the bribe,
swung by the tail from the top of the clock, skimmed
through space and landed in the girl's arms. As Hamilton
and Cort reached for the monkey she held the shivering
creature close:

"They don't like you, Mr. Monk. Mean old things!
Never you mind, somebody does, evidently. You're as
sweet and clean as a pet kitten. Let Rose wipe your
face?" With her handkerchief she dried the wizened brown
cheeks. The creature submitted to her ministrations with
ludicrous resignation. She pulled the poilu cap into place
and removed a bit of cream from the tri-color cockade.

"There! That's better. Why did you frighten him," she
protested indignantly as the monkey wriggled free and
landed in the hall. Instantly from the ell issued a series
of shrieks followed by a mellow voice singing with camp-
meeting fervor:

> " 'When I die, Lawd, I wanna die right,
>     Dat suits me.
> When I die, Lawd, . . .' "

A furiously slammed door cut off the song. Claire Grahame drew a long, relieved breath.

"Jupiter will take care of him now. How do you account for that visitation, boys? Is there a circus in town?"

"More likely a hurdy-gurdy man," Hamilton responded. He laid the brass ball which he had been regarding thoughtfully on the table. "Peter, you ought to be able to stalk the mystery. Come to the office for a moment after you are dressed, will you? I want to consult you about shifting the pickers tomorrow."

"All right, Tony. I—I want to talk with you . . ."

Claire Grahame noted the boy's embarrassed glance at Nicholas Cort. He was white under his summer tan. What did it mean? She had been right. Peter had something on his conscience. Nick knew. Why, oh why, hadn't he told her this afternoon? As she turned toward Cort he encouraged:

"Better get it off your mind now, Peter. They are all here. This is as good a chance as any. Time is flying."

Hamilton, who was leaving the room, stopped in surprise. Rose glanced up inquiringly from the broken china she had been collecting on the tea-wagon. Cort laid a detaining hand on Claire Grahame's arm as she took a quick step toward her son. Peter looked steadily at his mother. He tried twice before he succeeded in announcing gruffly:

"I don't want to carry on the orchards. I want to study law."

"Peter!"

Her shocked exclamation brought the color surging back to her son's face. In a flash she realized what the declaration would mean to Anthony. If Peter didn't stay at White Pillars the achievement of his ambition might have to be postponed. He had done so much for the boy. She watched him with troubled eyes. After the first surprised moment he seized Peter by the shoulders and administered an affectionate shake. His voice was gruff as he addressed him in his own vernacular:

"You big stiff! Is that all you've had on your mind? Thank God!"

# *Chapter IV*

AN HOUR later, seated at his desk in the office at
White Pillars, Anthony Hamilton affectionately regarded
Peter Grahame backed up against the mantel. One of the
boy's hands was thrust hard into the pocket of his dinner
coat, the other gripped the ear of Rusto. The dog sat on
his haunches, head tilted with the air of an important
third in conference. The older man threw back his shoulders as though ridding them of a burden. The relief! To
know that the boy's aloofness had not been due to that little matter of Daphne Tennant.

His eyes traveled round the walls of the room which
were hung with framed illustrations of fruit, blue-ribbon
certificates, pictured pests in all stages of development.
They rested for a moment on a huge outline map of the
United States which showed the distribution of apple
trees of bearing age. He had labored early and late, he
had studied nights, to help New England make an im-
pressive showing on that map, to make the texture and
flavor of its apples appreciated. And now, Peter would
not carry on. The boy was entitled to select his career.
It should not be forcibly fed to him. Hamilton's voice
was rich with sympathetic understanding as he encouraged:

"You have the right to choose your profession, Peter.
But, when you knew what you wanted why didn't you
come straight to me?"

"I hadn't the nerve, Tony. I hated to be a quitter. Boy!
Don't I know how you've worked in the orchards year
after year? And now, just as you have me trained to shoulder some of the burden I quit. Raw, I call it."

"You have talked it over with Judge Cort?"

There was a tinge of hurt reproach in the question.

"I had to get it off my chest to someone, Tony. I
couldn't tell Mother. She's so dotty over you she'd see only

your side of it. Rose was away. One reason I told Uncle Nick was that he might guy me out of the idea. I thought he'd tell me I had about as much brain for law as—as Rusto." The dog responded to the tweak on his ear with an indignant yelp.

"And he didn't?"

"Nope. He says that I have the legal mind. That if I'll work I'll make my mark. Applesauce perhaps, but I'll take a chance."

"Good for you, Peter. The country needs sound, un-bribable lawyers quite as much as it needs sound laws."

"Uncle Nick said that the profession lost a great judge when you took to apple growing, Tony."

"Did he? His belief in me from the first time I met him has been one of the big things in my life. I had the same idea once myself, Peter. Not that I would make a great judge but that I would like to practice law. It is late for that now. When I have the time I'll step into the political ring. You have a flying start for your profession. You have had a mother with ideas and ideals the influence of which you are bound to carry into your work. I started wrong. Then—then White Pillars needed me and I came here. I never have been sorry but I'll move heaven and earth if necessary to give you a chance at the career you want. Have you made plans?"

"I'm entered at the law school where Uncle Nick took his degree."

"Then you don't need me."

Rusto sprang to his feet, ears cocked, as the boy took an impetuous step forward:

"I always need you, Tony. I hadn't the courage to tell you, that's all. It seemed like slipping from under."

"You'll work better at work you want to do. Timmins will get your chance."

"Tony, put Rose in the shipping room. She's crazy to get into business. It's in the air. The girls all want a try at it. Lucky for their husbands if they get it out of their systems before marriage. If you don't take her on she'll get a job somewhere. One you won't like perhaps," warned Peter darkly.

"What do you mean by that?"

"Nap Long told Tim that he was trying to get a college

girl for a private secretary. Thought it would raise the tone of his office. Wondered if Miss Grahame would like the job."

Hamilton put his hand to his neck.

"If that laundry continues to shrink my collars I'll blow up the works!"

Peter chuckled.

"It isn't the laundry which makes your collars tight, Tony. It's fury when you think of Rose and Napoleon Bonaparte Long. Wow, how you hate him! I don't wonder. I'll bet he's had a spattered career. He'll try anything once. The bigger the risk the more kick he gets out of it. 'Long's star!' If he's elected selectman he'll turn this valley into a factory town. I should worry. You've taken a load from my mind. I feel as skippy as a young doe bird." He clogged around the room to the accompaniment of his own whistle. Hamilton laughed in sympathy.

"You've taken a load from my mind. I thought you had kept aloof from me because of . . ."

"Because of Daphne Tennant? I was sore at first. It didn't last. Mother and Rose took that too seriously. They ring the wedding bells if I look at a girl. I had this other thing on my mind. But, about Daphne—I have been wanting to give you a tip for some time. I've had so much more experience with girls than you have," patronized Peter.

With difficulty Hamilton derailed a shout of laughter. He coughed violently.

"Excuse me. Dust in my throat. You were saying?"

"Don't trust Daphne. She's clinging and appealing but I'll bet a hat she's living a double life. There's a worm in that good-looking chestnut, all right."

"Her life must be rather drab."

"What's the matter with her getting out from under? In these days need anyone with half a brain be dependent? Why doesn't she go to work? She's a little gold-digger, that's why. She'd rather roll her limpid eyes at a rich guy and moan about being a beggar-maid. . . ."

"Perhaps I should remind you, Peter, that . . ."

"I haven't forgotten that you're engaged to her—worse luck. Just take a tip from me, Tony. Watch your step."

"Thanks for the warning. Have you time to drive your

mother and Rose to La Mancha? Mrs. Hamilton telephoned for me to come early."

"Sorry, but I'm dining out too. I'm late now. Let Rose
drive. You coddle her too much, Tony."

"Do I? I'll have Eddie Timmins take them over."

"I must be off." Peter turned at the threshold to demand
with boyish embarrassment:

"Sure you don't think me a quitter?"

"Sure. We'll talk finances in the morning."

Hamilton watched him dash through the hall and take
the stairs two at a time to the accompaniment of a joyous
whistle. Thoughtfully he emptied his pipe into the fire.
Rusto, flung at full length on the rug with his back to the
blaze, flopped his tail lazily, raised his head languidly,
blinked tawny eyes at his master and relapsed into a doze.

As Anthony Hamilton refilled his pipe his thoughts
were with the boy. Peter's determination to study law had
changed everything. It meant that his own ambition to
enter state politics must be set aside for the present. He
would have to remain in the orcharding business until he
had trained another man. Timmins couldn't do everything.

Thank the Lord that a girl had not come between him
and Peter. Claire Grahame need not have worried over
that slight heart squall. Her son had a nice sense of values.
Had he analyzed Daphne correctly? No. She was more
frightened than scheming. When the mourning-swathed
woman and her pretty daughter, from that indefinite re-
gion, the South, had taken a house in the village one year
before he had suspected mystery. The pallid-faced mother
rarely appeared in public. Perhaps because they held
themselves aloof the two were taken up by the Country
Club set.

He had liked Daphne Tennant at once. Peter had fallen
a victim to the O-for-a-strong-arm appeal of the violet
eyes behind a bewildering tangle of lashes. Claire Grahame had been troubled by his infatuation. She had
been one of the few who had felt an instinctive distrust
of mother and daughter. Peter had no money, she had
argued to Anthony, all the girl wanted of him was to
secure a firmer social foothold while she stalked bigger
game.

He had laughed at her fears but to save her anxiety
had drawn the girl's fire from Peter with disastrous results.
As he had said good-night to her one evening in her
living room suddenly she had turned her face against his
sleeve with a strangled sob. In an effort to comfort her as
he would have comforted Rose he had put his arm about
her shoulders. Enter Mrs. Tennant with a timeliness which
suggested dirty work at the keyhole. Her face had been
ghastly. Her eyes had glittered. She had gushingly assumed
an offer of marriage and an acceptance. Such old stuff! In
a flash she had blazoned the news of the engagement to
friends in the room adjoining.

"At least, I've saved Peter," he had grimly assured himself before he protested:

"Daphne, you know as well as I that this is not an
engagement. I have not asked you to marry me. I never
shall."

She had winced. He had felt like a brute. With furtive,
tear-drenched eyes on the doorway through which her
mother had staged a dramatic exit she had whispered:

"I know, Tony. But, let it stand. For a few weeks. It will
help me immeasurably. It can't hurt you. You are not in
love with anyone are you? Please."

He had weakly consented and Daphne had added bitterly:

"Promise that you won't tell Rose Grahame the truth.
She tries hard but she can't wholly conceal the fact that
she thinks I'm ninety-nine and nine-tenths per cent moron.
Promise not to tell her. Please, Tony."

He had rebelled but in the end she had won. If he intended to help her he had better help in her way. Besides
the farce would be ended before Rose sailed for home.
He had had such a fight to make good in the orchards,
the Grahames had so filled his life and heart that, except
as friends, girls had played no part in his life. He had
rather envied Peter the youthful ease with which he
plunged into love. Since that night he had not so much as
touched Daphne's hand. He had acted as escort when
occasion demanded but she had become repellent to him.
Rose had come home and the farce dragged on.

He had laid the situation before Nicholas Cort. What
was Mrs. Tennant's game, they wondered. How much

was the girl a party to it? Was she determined to entrench her daughter socially or was it money—a breach of promise suit? Cort had counseled standing pat. He had taken a little trip to the southern town from which the women claimed to hail. He had returned today. What had he discovered? He must get the matter cleared up. With Peter gone he would be infernally busy and if he trained Rose in the business . . .

Why not? The orchards were one third hers. She was clear-headed. She had a nice sense of values. She had accomplished a prodigious amount in her studies. Interest in business might prevent her falling in love with a man who was unsuitable. Deep in his heart he feared Mark. Propinquity was insidious in its attack. He had been glad to get Rose out of the neighborhood this summer. His brother was fine in many ways but not good enough for little Rose.

The dog at his feet sprang to attention, ears erect. The rumble in his throat sounded like the premonitory warnings of distant thunder-heads. Anthony Hamilton listened. A whistle? A long, low whistle?

He followed Rusto in his precipitate dash through hall and living room. The dog flattened his nose against the crack of the garden room door. He sniffed, whined, growled. Hamilton's eyes raked the place from the golden shower of acacias to the bronze nymph ceaselessly listening to the drip of water. Nothing seemed to have been disturbed. He returned to the living room. A pair of shaded lamps shed their soft light on table and davenport. He listened. There was no sound outside. None inside save the snuffle of the dog, the drip of the fountain, the tick of the Willard Clock, the expiring snap of burnt-out logs. From the ell came the music of a spiritual crooned to the plaintive accompaniment of an harmonica.

Who had whistled? Warning or signal? Anthony snapped on the overhead lights. He picked up a gay little handkerchief from the floor. Rose's, of course. She had a way of leaving a trail of her belongings. He smiled as he remembered how solicitiously she had dried the monkey's cheeks. A few red and white and blue bristles from the cockade on the creature's cap still clung to the filmy bit of linen. He thrust it into his pocket and whistled to the dog:

"All right, boy! Are you and I developing nerves in our old age to get wrought up over a whistle? Tim is coming for you." He glanced at the tall clock. A bit of white on the floor in front of it attracted his attention. Curious! What could it be. He picked up a carefully folded scrap of paper. With the dog rumbling and grumbling at his heels he unfolded it beneath the light of one of the lamps. Scrawled in red ink was the word

## DANGER!

Beneath it was a crude drawing of a fruit laden tree with a lopped top.

"Not content with stealing the fruit someone is threatening the trees, Rusto," he confided to the dog.

Back in his office he scrutinized the paper. It had a hint of age and more than a hint of grime. Someone was warning him. Who? How had the scrap come in the living room? Had it been thrown in at the door? Had that been the sound which had first roused Rusto? He visualized the windows and doors in relation to the clock. Instantly on the screen of his mind flashed a close-up of a wrinkled brown face, of beady eyes staring down at him. The monkey! The paper had been in the lining ripped from his cap! Who had sent him?

"Come in," he called in answer to a knock at the veranda door. As a short, stubby man entered the room he added:

"Lock it, Tim."

The clean pink skin of Eddie Timmins' round face wrinkled into tiny, concentric lines like mountain ranges on a map. He rested one arm on the mantel above the fireplace as he absent-mindedly shook the paw Rusto politely offered. Anthony Hamilton seated himself at the desk. The dog flopped to the rug beside his chair. The foreman's voice was worried as he announced:

"More peaches gone today, Cap'n. The chap who's getting them certainly has a hunch for the best."

"It may not be a chap, Tim."

"Do you mean perhaps it's a crow or a hedgehog? You're on the wrong trail, Cap'n. Now I ask you, how

would a bird—he'd only bite them anyway—or an animal
know enough to take marked ones?"

"Only because they are the best. But you are right,
Tim. It must be a human. Whoever is doing it is doubtless
getting in form to steal our prize apples. Those are not
marked. Perhaps someone is itching to clean up a few
prizes at the fruit show next month. There are dozens
of them offered this year. How is Sam Hardy coming on.
The more I see of that man the more I trust him."

Timmins stared into the blaze. His eyes, under the
brows which protruded in two lumps above them, were
troubled, his shoulders, even his ears which in the long
ago had been transformed by nasty, glancing blows into
the variety known as cauliflower, registered affection as he
protested:

"You trust everybody, Cap'n. Sam Hardy does his work
fine—seems to have an instinct for the right thing in
the orcharding game—but the pickers don't like him.
Asked if he might bunk by himself at the old Allen
house you bought last summer. Now, R. E. Morse is all
right in moderation but being a gob of gloom don't do
anyone any good, least of all the bunch you're working
with."

"Give him time."

Timmins chuckled.

"That's what he's complaining about, he got it, didn't
he? I'll say one thing for him, he seems to love animals.
Saw him hugging a kitten the other day. The horses and
dogs are crazy about him and you can take it from me,
they know a hard egg when they see one."

"He may have found animals more companionable than
people. We'll trust him, Tim. We'll give him every chance
till he gets a foothold. Put him on the job Peter has had.
Give him a gang of pickers to superintend."

"Mr. Peter! For the love of Mike, where's he going?
I thought you were keeping him outside till the picking
season was over. There's a go-getter for you. When you
told me you were putting him to work in the orchards
this summer I got cold feet. I thought he'd be soft from
college living notwithstanding he's a ball player. But he
hung on through heat and storm like a champ of champs.
The men like him. No lugs, friendly with 'em all."

"He will enter law school."

"Back to school! Ain't he got enough of that? Some folks never know when they're well off! Giving up a fat sure income from the trees to be a lawyer! I can't believe it."

"His going will give you a better opportunity."

"I wasn't thinking of myself, Cap'n. I was thinking of you. It seems as though you ought to have first chance at breaking away."

"My turn will come. Meanwhile we have a job on our hands to catch the peach thief."

"Now you're talking." Timmins crossed to the desk and confided in what apparently he intended for a whisper:

"Two more foreigners came to the office today asking for a job."

"How did they get into town?"

"Search me. That makes four so far this month."

"Perhaps they're the same ones."

"No. The first two left by train the morning I got off those crates of peaches."

Hamilton produced the paper he had found on the floor of the living room.

"What do you make of that?"

Timmins' ruddy face went blank with amazement as he studied the drawing.

"Looks as though there was a plot on foot to cut down the fruit trees, doesn't it, Tim?"

The foreman's face turned chalky. His eyes burned like flames. Twice he moistened his stiff lips before he whispered:

"For the love of Mike, Cap'n. That drawing isn't a fruit tree! Can't you see? Those round things aren't apples. They're flowers! That—that darned thing's meant for a rose-bush."

# Chapter V

"TIM! You mean?"

The two men glared at one another. After a throbbing instant Timmins protested roughly:

"It isn't possible that any one would dare, would want to harm Miss Rose but this paper looks like someone's warning us. Of course there's lots of feeling in certain quarters because you won't hire every hobo that comes along but—where'd you get it?" he demanded abruptly.

"On the floor in the living room."

"On the floor—Cap'n, you've had a nightmare."

"No. That is where I found it."

"How did it get there?"

Anthony Hamilton hesitated. Better not tell Timmins yet about the monkey. The news might travel and the creature be spirited away from the neighborhood before he had discovered to whom he belonged. He evaded:

"Rusto and I were here. Suddenly he tore into the living room. I followed. I looked around. Nothing there to make the dog so uneasy. I knew that it was time for you to take him to the garage. Looked at the clock, and saw this on the floor in front of it."

Eddie Timmins' eyes were skeptical, his voice dry as he remarked:

"Um-m, guess it must have been radioed there. But how it landed doesn't make so much difference. It was there. For the love of Mike, Cap'n, don't let Miss Rose go riding round alone. This may be just some dumb egg playing a prank—there's been a lot in the papers lately about these fake red-ink warnings—but, we can't take a chance. You'd better set Mr. Peter to sleuthing."

"No, he's a firebrand. A spark of suspicion and he'd undo all you and I have accomplished trying to smoke out the peach thief. I'll consult Judge Cort. I'll give Miss Rose the job she wants in the shipping room. We'll keep her so busy till we get to the bottom of this mystery that she won't have a chance to ride. Rusto will help. Watch Rose, old man."

The dog sat erect the better to present his paw. His master gravely accepted it. The color stole back to his face.

"We'll be on guard, Tim, but we mustn't frighten either Mrs. Grahame or her daughter. Drive them over to La Mancha tonight, will you? Mrs. Hamilton wants me to come early. Have the sedan at the door in half an hour. I'll bring them home."

"Sure, Cap'n. I can't get that red-ink drawing out of my mind. Nap Long and his followers are sore at you because you won't buy boxes and hire the men he sends you and if that had been a warning to watch our trees, I shouldn't have been surprised, I've been looking for trouble there. But Miss Rose, why, Long spoke about getting her to work for him. He wouldn't harm her."

"No. I don't like the man, but I wouldn't suspect him of that."

"Perhaps some fresh kid's been reading about those plots to kidnap the movie stars and is trying to be funny."

Encouragement without conviction.

"We'll hope that is the explanation. Meanwhile we'll watch. Go on, Rusto," he commanded as Timmins opened the veranda door. He added casually:

"Just a moment, Tim. Do you know of any one in town who owns a monkey?"

"A monk? I've never seen one in this burg. Not thinking of annexing another pet, are you? Better not. Rusto'd chew him to shoestrings out of jealousy and the small dogs would cheerfully tangle up the dripping remains."

"Then I won't get one. Good-night!"

Timmins responded with an affectionate grin and a snappy salute. He pushed the reluctant dog before him and departed. As the door closed Hamilton rapped his pipe clear and dropped it to the desk. Tim had tried to be encouraging but it was evident that he was worried. Blights, pests, petty thieving paled to insignificance beside the menace implied in that warning. But, perhaps Tim was right. Perhaps it was someone's fatuous conception of fun.

Fun? No. Nap Long? No. No matter what his sentiments were in regard to her adopted brother he wouldn't harm Rose. He was ambitious socially, politically. He was making money out of the town. Would he risk that?

Anthony frowned down at the fire. Since the years had released him from his promise not to use his own money he had bought three large estates to keep them from falling into Long's clutches. Why clutter the beautiful valley with small frame houses and factories when the demand for New England farms from Westerners who had waked up to their possibilities had just begun? It was his intention to plant the land he had bought with orchards and lease them to trustworthy men in his employ.

He had planned to offer one to Sam Hardy but—suspicion which had been coiled sluggishly in the corner of his mind since afternoon raised its horned head and hissed. He envisaged the man paddling off in the canoe. He had been laboring under intense excitement. Why? It would have been a human impossibility for him to so quickly have made his escape from the tree which had shed such extraordinary fruit—for a pine tree. He couldn't believe that the man to whom he had given a chance to make good was the peach thief. Ever since his own trial for carelessness which had resulted in the death of David Grahame his heart had been tender toward first offenders. Had it not been for the boy's mother, in his remorse and humiliation he might have wasted his life.

Curious that out of the whole country Hardy should have applied at White Pillars for a job. Had he heard of the manager's sympathy with released prisoners or—had someone hostile to the Grahame interests been behind the request. He would not believe evil of Hardy. Nicholas Cort liked him and the Judge had been too long a trained observer of the human comedy to be hoodwinked.

The old clock in the living room booming the hour recalled him to the present. If he were to reach La Mancha before the arrival of his mother's guests he must go at once. As he slipped into his topcoat in the hall the spirit of peace which brooded over the old house folded its wings about his heart. His tense muscles relaxed. He was absurd to be anxious but—he regarded the stairs uncertainly for a moment before he ascended them two at a time. He would make sure that Rose waited for Timmins. He tapped at her door.

"Rose!"

"Yes, Tony?"

"Open the door."

"Can't. I'm dressing. Wait until you see me tonight. I'll put your eyes out with my gorgeousness."

"I'll get my smoked goggles. One of the French frocks?"

"You'll see."

"Timmins will be here with the sedan to drive you and *Madre* to La Mancha."

"Tony! Aren't you going?"

"Of course. Mrs. Hamilton wants me to come early."

"For one awful moment I feared that the time I had spent to impress you with my grown-upness had been wasted. We don't need Eddie Timmins. I can drive."

"Mind your big brother. Go with Tim."

"All right, Tony."

As he settled behind the wheel of his roadster the storm-centre of thought shifted to his own family. What motive had been behind his mother's descent upon this quiet village? For what stake was she playing? He had known nothing of her plans until a letter from Mark had announced that she had leased La Mancha for the season. She had met Long in Paris and when he learned what she wanted he had obligingly turned over his own place to her and moved into the Lodge, on the estate. That information had come from Mark who knew nothing of Long except from casual acquaintance.

Anthony's eyes narrowed as he thought over the few times in the last ten years when he had seen his mother. She had been fiercely angry because of the promise he had made to Claire Grahame. Since his father's death her headquarters had been in France. Mark had drifted between the two continents, idle, bored, except for the two years he had served with distinction in the war. Good old scout. He hadn't had half a chance. Emotion twitched at his lips as he thought of his brother's evident pleasure in being with him.

His grave face flashed into a smile as he regarded the house he was approaching. The wave of fashion for things Spanish had stranded it on the side of a New England hill. It was of the type native residents refer to as someone's "Folly". A copper-king—back in pre-war days when copper-shares paid fabulous incomes—had unlocked his mint, and architect and builder had plunged in with both hands. The result was a Palm Beach palace in a Puritan setting. And Napoleon Bonaparte Long owned it! The grandson of the illiterate peddler; the son of the down-at-heels small shop keeper; the boy who had delivered goods at the back doors of the very houses to which his wealth now provided a key to the front doors! America the Magician!

Santa Anna, the butler, in the scarlet sash and regalia of a Spanish servant, met him as he entered. A darkhaired, dark-browed maid hovered in the distance. Man and girl were quite in character with their surroundings. The huge hacienda hall was embellished with little balconies which flaunted gay embroideries flung over their railings. There were unexpected winding staircases, curious casements, lace-like grills of forged iron-work. The effect could have been achieved only by an interior decorator gone color-mad, Anthony Hamilton decided, as he crossed the thick rug to greet his mother. He caught the twinkle of jewels on her white fingers, with their rosy nails, as she laid aside the book she had been reading. Diamonds and emeralds glittered on her bare arm as she motioned him toward a mammoth carved chair drawn near the couch on which she was seated. With difficulty he repressed a laugh. Good theatre! Thus might Egypt's Queen have commanded an humble courtier to advance.

What did she want, he wondered, as after the first word of greeting her eyes wavered from his. By the ties of law and blood she was his mother, by the ties of love and devotion and sympathetic understanding Claire Grahame held him. She had challenged him, inspired him to do his best by her unselfishness, her steadfastness, her contagious sweetness and buoyancy in the years when all the powers of orchard evils had conspired to blot out her small property.

The woman facing him in the glittering frock with emeralds about her throat, at her ears and on her fingers was a stranger. What did he know of her? Her life was as a sealed book to him. Her face, the jacket of it, gave no inkling of what was within. Were there pages of tenderness, or were they all of ambitions, passions, schemes?

Her copper-colored hair, doubtless henna-cured, was
drawn back in the prevailing fashion, her features were
marbleized, her eyes were as green as her jewels, she
was fashionably slinky. A wave of remorse and shame
burned through him. He was thinking all this of his
mother, his . . .

"You have not answered my question, Anthony."

Self-reproach receded before the chill voice like a heat
wave before the shrill vanguard of a Nor'easter.

"I repeat, what are you going to do about it?"

"I beg pardon for inattention. About what?"

"Giving up these people. Devoting a little time to your
own."

The inflection of "these people" set off a bomb of fury
in his consciousness. His voice showed the strain of con-
trolling anger as he repeated:

"Give them up! Why should I? Their interests are mine.
You have been content to live almost without seeing me,
without writing to me for ten years. Why this sudden ma-
ternal urge?"

"Don't be disagreeable, Anthony, that sounds just like
your father and grandfather. I never write letters. The
court had exonerated you. Why should I try to see you
after you made that quixotic promise to serve the Grahame woman?"

"Mother!"

"Sit down, I didn't mean that to sound disparaging. Your
father said to let you go. You were your own master. Your
grandfather had seen to that when you were twenty-one.
And two years ago he left you more money and—the
family pearls."

Motive at last! The pearls. Always she had coveted
them. They were a priceless, perfectly matched string. He
tried to hold her eyes with his amused ones as he reminded:

"Surely, you can't want those with all you have of your
own."

"I have nothing equal to them. There are few necklaces
in the world as fine."

"Is that why you are trying to put the clock back? I
don't flatter myself that it is affection. Is it the pearls?"

Her jeweled fingers picked at the arm of the couch,

Her blackened lids were lowered, concern was delicately impinged on suggestion as she cautioned:

"Things happen suddenly. You—you might be seriously ill. I am merely suggesting that—I hope that you have made a will so that should anything happen to you your money will revert to the family from which it came."

"You are giving yourself needless anxiety. It would be to your advantage were I to shuffle off this mortal coil without leaving a will. If I die unmarried and—intestate—everything I have will go to you."

"Really Anthony?"

Her tone was exultant. As she met her son's keen eyes she had the grace to color. He sensed the scurry of her mental retreat.

"I didn't mean that as it sounded. I thought only of the pearls . . ."

"Forget the pearls. You need those no more than you need me in your life. If ever you do—I am your son, I will help in any way I can. I shall remain at White Pillars. You have Mark."

Flora Hamilton's shiver was involuntary and genuine.

"I—I am afraid of Mark."

"Afraid of Mark! Mother, how unjust. He is the kindest-hearted, the tenderest man in the world."

"When—he is himself. I am no prohibitionist—I hate the breed—but Mark's steady drinking is getting on my nerves. He is disintegrating. Behind his face I seem to see a skull grinning at me. I—I am ashamed to be seen with him. I want you."

Fury robbed Hamilton of his voice. What had the woman before him done to help Mark out of the slough of temptation? Back in college days she had accepted the fact of her sons' dissipations with a laugh and a shrug and a flippant:

"Boys will be boys! They all do it."

He had had to find out for himself by soul-searing experience that the vast majority of men who made good didn't "do it." Also he had found out for himself how enormously a real mother counted in the scheme of things. He had had one for the last ten years. He had been faring forth shoulder to shoulder with his brother on the hilarious broad way when Claire Grahame had come into his life. He could hear her shaken voice demand:

"Do you mean that you will give ten years of your life to me? That you will live as I live? Without your money? Without help from your people? Temperately?" Youth and wealth. She had realized the menace in the combination.

If only Mark could have had a woman like that in his life. Could have been salvaged as he had been. It was not that he had leaned on Claire Grahame—he had been a solitary horseman in those days—had had to whirl with inimitable dexterity to face temptation and doubt as they attacked—he had fought his battles with set teeth and lips tight closed, but, always he had felt about him her ideals, her belief that men were the finest force in the world, her faith and trust in him which must not be betrayed. His own mother had thought only of herself. She had been mad for pleasure, excitement, admiration, jewels. From the nursery her sons had been sent away to school. His most vivid memory of her was of a nervous, irritable woman smoking endless cigarettes.

And now she demanded a place in his life. They were as far apart as the North Sea and the South Sea. Continents of antagonisms separated them. Yet—he felt a sudden tenderness for her, for the mother she might have been. She was terrifiedly grasping at him, at even a straw of affection to retard her onward rush to a loveless old age, to the port toward which she had been gaily and selfishly paddling her shell of life. She had been a beautiful woman. She retained much of her attractiveness, but her carmined lips were slightly drawn, there were lines of self-indulgence about her eyes. They were as cold and green as her emeralds as she leaned forward and reminded:

"I never give up working for what I want, Anthony. I want you. I shall stay in this village until I get you. I want you to sit at the head of the table tonight."

"In Mark's place? No. If you attempt to give it to me I will never enter any home of yours again."

White, shaken, he defied her. She opened her lips, snapped them together as Daphne Tennant, followed by her elder son, entered the hall. She rose and greeted the girl without warmth, then resumed her reading.

As his fiancée, *pro tem*, crossed the rug toward him

Anthony regarded her with critical eyes. Her fair hair had been waved to closely follow the outline of her small head. Her skin was an exquisite result of powder and rouge at applied perfection. Her features were lovely. Her eyes were violet. Her ultra short blue frock was deeply bordered with gold lace. There was a spoiled-child pout to her lips as she protested and explained in the same breath:

"Mark took pity on the poor beggar-maid who has no mount and took me riding this afternoon."

Anthony smiled at his brother though it hurt intolerably to see that hint of vacuity in his eyes. Mark laid a not too steady hand on his shoulder as he apologized:

"I didn't mean to butt in on your preserves, Tony, but you can't expect a charming girl to play the nun while you neglect her for business."

"It wasn't business. He had a date with sister Rose."

The edge in the words sent the color to Anthony's face. Daphne was going a bit too far even if she did want the engagement to seem genuine. He ignored the implication and greeted his brother.

"I missed you today, old scout. I like to have you prowling about telling me how to manage things."

"I was on my way to your office when I met the ever-ready Long. He insisted upon personally conducting me over the houses he is building. While exhibiting his Homes Beautiful he monologued steadily. Theme, your indifference to the excellent cheap labor and boxes he is altruistically yearning to supply. I smelled powder from a late combat. Yes?"

"I have steadily refused to employ labor which he finds too raw for his own use. If we buy our boxes from him he will build more factories." He turned to throw his cigarette into the fire. The sepulchral voice of the Spanish butler announced:

"Señora Grahame. Señorita Grahame."

Anthony's eyes were on the blaze, his thoughts were busy with Mark's interview with Nap Long. What a persistent devil—he turned at his brother's touch on his arm, at his low exclamation:

"So that is 'sister Rose'! I don't wonder you kept your date, Tony."

The quality of the voice clanged an alarm through his consciousness. He turned. Claire Grahame in a violet frock which shimmered with silver sequins was speaking to his mother. Who was with her? Not Rose? Was that lovely girl the child he had seen grow up? Was the French frock responsible for her air of sophistication, the frock which left her ivory tinted neck and arms bare? Its color reminded him of the Lyons roses in the garden, it was the same perfect blend of warm salmon pink with an undertone of yellow. Her boyishness had vanished. She was a woman, young, radiant, shyly conscious of her charm. Her eyes flashed with mischief as they met his.

At the contact something within his mind wrenched away, it was as if a curtain had been thrust aside forcibly. Then the child he had known seemed to regard him wistfully before she vanished. In her place stood— Realization snatched at his breath. He smiled grimly. And he had thought he was too old to feel.

As Nicholas Cort and Napoleon Bonaparte Long joined the group about Flora Hamilton, Rose slipped away. Anthony could feel his brother's fingers tighten on his arm as she joined them. She nodded to the girl beside him.

"Greetings, Daph." Her voice was tantalizingly gay as she challenged:

"What's wrong, Tony? You look as though you had lost something. Your memory, perhaps? Could I by any chance have wrecked it? I look grown up at last, yes?"

In the process of tormenting she had quite forgotten his brother. She was delightedly absorbed in the transformation achieved by the French frock. His jaw set. She must not suspect—yet, the fact that he had just discovered, that she was the one woman in the world for him. His voice gave no indication of the turmoil in his mind as he conceded:

"I have lost something but not my memory. Mark is reminding me of my manners. I want you to know and like my brother, Rose."

The girl extended her hand.

"Of course I shall like him. If he is yours isn't he my brother also?"

"Thank you, Miss Grahame."

"What nonsense to call me Miss Grahame. Tony, tell him to call me . . ."

"Rose?" Mark dared.

"Of course. Call me anything you like except Pomona. Because I live in the midst of orchards every man whom I meet sooner or later declaims sentimentally:

> " 'Pomona loves the orchard,
>     And Liber loves the vine.' "

Mark Hamilton threw back his head with a laugh which was own twin to his brother's.

"I didn't know that the modern boy read Macaulay," he teased.

"Boy! Don't you believe that I am grown up, either? I said, men. They don't. They doubtless pore over *Bartlett's Quotations* till they find a line which includes the word orchard. Why else should they all quote the same sentiment?"

The butler, who looked like a musical comedy character at large, murmured something at the threshold.

"Anthony!"

Hamilton straightened at the low reminder in his mother's voice. Almost he could feel her eyes strike sparks as they met his across the intervening space. After his protest would she dare humiliate his brother? He saw her set her teeth in her lips before she substituted:

"Mark!"

Her elder son, who had been laughing with the two girls, hastened forward to offer his arm to Claire Grahame. As Rose followed with Long, Daphne Tennant observed to Anthony:

"Your brother seems profoundly impressed with his new —sister."

He answered evenly though a curious premonition of loss and pain shook him.

"I hope that they will be friends. You are as careless as Rose about dropping your belongings, Daphne." He stooped to retrieve the enamel cigarette case of blue and gold which had slipped to the floor. As his fingers closed about it his mind did a merry-go-round and steadied. Caught in the gold mesh of the girl's skirt were wisps of red, white and blue bristles.

## Chapter VI

HE SLIPPED the bit of tri-color into his waistcoat pocket. What did its presence in the gold lace of Daphne Tennant's frock signify? What could it mean but that the monkey who had stormed the living room at White Pillars, who, he suspected, had left the red-ink warning, had been recently with the girl beside him.

He was still pondering the question as he regarded the faces above the refectory table in the magnificent dining room. They were tinged with pink from the glow cast by the strip of red brocade under the light from the candles in massive silver sticks. The room was softly illumined by wax tapers which made the coloring of the Florentine frescoes on walls and ceiling especially exquisite.

Two men, aided by the dark-browed maid he had seen in the hall, were serving. The picturesque costumes gave him the sense of being a part of a stage production. Rose sat at Mark's left. Rose! His heart pounded. How could he have been so unconscious of what she meant to him? She and his brother were engaged in an animated argument as to whether a much acclaimed novelist were a creator or a recorder. Mark's usually bored eyes were alight with interest. The wine in his glass remained untouched. Thumb screws of apprehension tightened brutally about Anthony's heart. At last had his brother found the girl to whom he would be constant? He couldn't have her. Not Rose. She was his, had been for years only he had been too blind to see. Would she, could she change from sisterly affection to the love he wanted? For ten years she had regarded him as a brother. Could he teach her to regard him as a lover? If she were once repelled never could he undo the mistake.

Another challenge. The highway of his life serpentined from one problem to another. Suppose that around the next bend a radiant reality awaited him? He knew now why no one of the many charming girls he had met had had power to stir his pulses. He had been immune because of Rose. He tried to summon a vision of the child who had caught his hand in hers back in the long-ago. Useless. She had really waved good-bye to him in the hall before dinner. He had not imagined it.

His thoughts snapped back to the girl beside him. Daphne! For the moment he had forgotten that mix-up. He would take her home tonight and eliminate the absurd complication. Nicholas Cort could take Rose and her mother. . . .

"Don't disturb Tony. He's crystal-gazing."

Rose Grahame's laughing protest flagged his train of thought. The eyes of his mind returned to his fingers clenched about the stem of the ornate goblet at which he had been staring.

"I beg pardon! Did anyone speak to me?"

"This one did several times," mocked Rose gaily. "I appealed to you for confirmation. I told your brother of the visitor who dropped in—to be literally correct—bounced in at White Pillars this afternoon. He insists that I am the victim of a nightmare. A monkey did appear at tea-time, didn't he, Tony?"

"He did."

The water in the glass he still clenched overflowed. He looked up at the maid who had filled it.

"Pardon, *Señor!* Pardon!" she murmured. With a furtive glance at the butler she removed the goblet.

His attention, diverted for an instant, flashed back to the girl beside him. Daphne Tennant's face showed no tinge of self-consciousness. Yet, she must know something of the monkey. What other explanation could there be of the bristles caught in the gold lace of her frock?

"Perhaps he dropped from the airplane I saw hovering over Headless Hill this afternoon," Rose speculated.

Long, at the left of his hostess, bared white teeth in a smile. His black hair was lacquered—Anthony suppressed a laugh. Rose was right. He was training it in a Napoleonic droop—his rather small black eyes were points of light. His finger nails glittered like pink glass. His clothing in cut and material was the last word in fashion. His voice was indulgently amused as he suggested;

"That would be something of a drop, Rose."

The familiarity of that "Rose" sent the blood to Anthony's temples. As Long had known her through her school years there was no reason why he should suddenly adopt a formal manner with her, but . . .

"The plane landed. Perhaps merely to leave the monkey. It stayed down but a short time."

"Where were you?"

Was there a slight edge to the question? Anthony kept his eyes on Long's face while Rose explained. The man was interested in the descent of that plane. Why?

"In the living room at White Pillars."

"That monkey was too well groomed to be a castaway," observed Claire Grahame. "Perhaps he is the pet of one of the village children, perhaps—my knowledge of geography leaves much to be desired, isn't Texas somewhere near the monkey-belt? Perhaps Judge Cort brought him from there concealed about his person. Nicholas, are you guilty?"

"Texas!"

"Texas!"

Daphne Tennant's startled repetition of the word followed Long's. Anthony Hamilton detected a blaze of suspicion in the eyes of the man across the table as he looked quickly at the girl. Her face, which had remained coolly undisturbed at mention of the monkey, had broken into consternation like the still surface of a pool suddenly ruffled by an unseen force below, at mention of a state. Long also had been startled but he glibly explained the cause of his exclamation:

"I was amazed that you had been in the state in which I have large interests. Had I known that you were going I could have given you worth-while letters of introduction, Judge Cort."

"Thank you. The next time I go, perhaps. Your real estate investments must keep you busy. They seem to be widely separated."

Long swelled visibly. He thrust one hand into his waistcoat.

"They are. I've just cleared up thirty thousand in an

Oklahoma deal." He stroked his smooth-shaven chin with the back of his hand. "If it were not for this selectman's job I should go out there. But, one's native town should come first, Judge, first."

For an instant Anthony's eyes met Rose's. Hers brimmed with mirth. Nicholas Cort replied to Long:

"A fine sentiment. How goes the fight?"

"Fight? There is no fight. The townspeople want me, they realize what I can do for them." His tone was arrogantly complacent.

Lovely color flushed Rose's cheeks as she retorted:

"Don't be too sure, Mr. Napoleon Bonaparte Long. There is still time before special Town Meeting for some one to prepare to cross swords with you. You may have to fight."

The spirit of the boy hector danced impishly in Long's eyes as he patronized:

"Years ago I learned a lesson. I never fight a business opponent. I buy him out. The method ought to work in politics."

In the hall after dinner he leaned over the back of the large couch where Rose was seated. Anthony, who had brought her coffee, lingered beside her. Long's eyes and teeth were agleam as he proposed:

"Rose, when I am selectman I shall need another secretary. I hear that you are looking for work. Come to me. I'll pay well. The hours will be short. What say?"

Anthony lightly touched the girl's shoulder.

"You're too late. She has accepted a position as shipping clerk in our office."

With characteristic theatricalness Long threatened;

"Hamilton, sometime you're going to block me once too often. You're such a snob about family that you're trying to crush me under foot as you would a gypsy worm in your orchard. I'll get even . . ."

"Long, you're forgetting, don't make me forget that we are guests here."

Anthony felt Rose's frightened grip on his arm as she propitiated:

"What nonsense to accuse Tony of blocking you because I have decided to work in our own business. Isn't it the logical thing for me to do?"

"Perhaps, but remember, I'll make a place for you any time. You may be glad of it. One never can tell what may happen. I'll go talk with Miss Tennant, with your permission, Hamilton. I'm curious to know why she is interested in Texas." He bowed with exaggerated deference before he departed. Rose breathed a sigh of relief.

"For an instant, Tony, I feared bloodshed. Your eyes were flames in a white mask. He was unbearable. I didn't care for his, 'One never can tell what may happen.' It gave me the shivers. Did you notice the tone in which he spoke of Daphne? He's discovered some way in which he can hector her. Tony, you duck! Am I really engaged for the shipping office? Of course I would rather work for you, but if you hadn't been Johnny-on-the-spot, much as I detest him I believe that I should have considered Nap Long's offer. Think of working for an honest to goodness selectman! Who knows but what I might have acquired a flair for politics. Haven't pages become United States senators? Perhaps I showed a lack of public spirit in refusing the position," she teased. She stroked her smooth chin reflectively, her voice and intonation were Long's as she mimicked:

" 'One's native town should come first, Judge, first.' "

She laughed up at the man behind her as she placated:

"I know that you hate the idea of my working, Tony, but you'll like it, see if you don't. I'll be stony with business. Watch me." As Mark Hamilton joined them she announced with laughing empressement:

"I'm a business woman. I have just signed on the dotted line as shipping clerk for the Grahame orchards."

"Shipping clerk! Rose-Pomona, have you been looking for work? I need a secretary. Chuck Tony and come to me."

"Stimulus and response! That was the first topic I had in my business psychology course. I'll file your offer with Nap's to hold over my boss when I demand a raise in salary."

A few hours later to Anthony Hamilton's intense annoyance Daphne coolly declined his escort home. He was afire with impatience to end the farce between them. His brother was hovering over Rose. Daphne looked in their direction before she suggested:

"Mark brought me . . ."

"Please go with me, Miss Tennant," interrupted Long. His eyes met and held the girl's, as he added: "There are still so many questions I want to ask about your friends in Texas."

Anthony's brows met in an annoyed frown as he protested:

"Daphne, I . . ."

She made a laughing little face at him though he could see that her cheeks had whitened under her rouge.

"I shall go with Mr. Long, Tony. You are not my dictator—yet."

Rose slipped her hand within his arm. She regarded his fiancée disdainfully as she proposed with old-fashioned charm:

"I'll keep you company, Tony. Uncle Nick will take mother."

When a few moments later she snuggled down in the roadster beside him she counseled severely:

"You shouldn't let Daphne turn you down like that. Isn't she engaged to you? One man at a time should be enough for any girl."

With superhuman control he refrained from throwing his arm about her and crushing her close. Never had he felt the desire before and many and many a time had she been beside him. He smiled grimly. Deaf! Dumb! Blind! Awake now, his arms ached to hold her close. He would have his reckoning with Daphne tomorrow. Had she sensed what was in his mind? Was she fencing for time? She wouldn't get it. Tomorrow he would be free! Free to begin a cautious assault on the fortress beside him. And it was a fortress, a fortress barricaded and intrenched from donjon to tower behind sisterly affection. He laughed under his breath. What a flowery comparison. It sounded like one of Sir Walter Scott's heroes. As the car turned from drive to highway Rose suggested eagerly:

"Let's go home via Headless Hill. The upper bridge is but a short way from here. We'll cross the river there, follow the Hill road, return by the lower bridge and home."

"Would *Madre* be anxious?"

"Anxious! When I am with you? What have you on

your mind, Tony, to ask that? Forgive me. I forgot.
Daphne's a cat. That doesn't help matters either, does it?
Let's forget her. Isn't this a glorious night?"

He didn't answer. Under pretense of tucking the rug
about her silver-shod feet he drew her closer. The middle-
aged moon was slanting westward. Silvery radiation. A
river of enchantment. The bridge as frail and unreal as
a mother-of-pearl mirage. The world of reality remote
and legendary. Rose sighed with utter content:

"Isn't this perfect?" then with a sudden return to mun-
dane details, "This bridge isn't too safe, Tony. Those
rails appear to have the stability of a paper cutout."

"It should be of concrete. The town fathers will wait
until some one crashes through, then they'll replace."

The road they followed cinctured the waist of the low
hill. The stillness was rippled by the splash and leap of a
brook among trees. The air was crisp, frosty, heavy with
the night scent of sweet fern and spruce. Anthony drove
slowly. Rose straightened into sudden animation.

"Tony, I can't get the atmosphere we have left out of
my mind. Exotic. Drenched in luxury. The Arabian
Nights produced in modern setting. Never have I seen
anything so gorgeous as your mother's background, her
oval and square diamonds. Where, oh, where, are the
round stones of yesteryear? And you turned your back
on that life to live with us! Incomprehensible. Of course,
we've never been grubby but we have been poor. When
we've made a little money it has had to be chucked into
the hungry maw of utility; there has been little to spend
for sheer beauty. If it hadn't been that we couldn't drive
Juno and Jupiter away we should have had to do everything ourselves. And when I contrast those two funny,
bossy darkies with that retinue of servants—Santa Anna
—alias Ali Baba and his Forty Thieves—it's inexplica-
ble. Why, why did you stay with us?"

"Had you the choice, which of the two atmospheres
would you choose."

"Heroically strangling the memory of that delectable
dinner I'll say White Pillars, of course. But, it is my
home."

"It is my home," he denatured the curtness of his
voice with a laugh:

"I'll bet the culinary genius of La Mancha can't match Juno when it comes to rice waffles or scones."

The car hurdled a rock in the road.

*"Nombre de Dios,"* growled a voice from a tangle of underbrush.

Anthony jammed the accelerator. The car sprang forward. The man who had blinked dazzled eyes in the glare of the motor lamps shrank back with a mumbled oath of surprise. Not until he had turned the roadster into the village highway did Hamilton's heart resume routine work. At the hail a vision of the red-ink warning had flashed through his mind to the accompaniment of Tim's hoarse correction:

"For the love of Mike, Cap'n, that drawing isn't a fruit tree! Can't you see? Those round things aren't apples. They're flowers. That—that darned thing's meant for a rose-bush."

As the car slowed down Rose twisted in her seat to look over her shoulder:

"What occasioned that speed-burst, Tony? You are a superb driver but don't do it again. All of my maline scarf and the breath left in me after the bump are back in the road a way. That man must think he touched off a rocket. Poor chap, perhaps he was lost. You didn't give him a chance to speak. Have you forgotten the story of the Good Samaritan?"

"As I remember it that charitable and benign gentleman didn't have a girl with him. Ready to go home?"

"Ready if not resigned. Don't you love the scent of the orchards at night? I could tell that we were getting near White Pillars if I were blindfolded. Mark spoke of the fragrant air and beauty of the river. Had I not been prepared to like him for your sake I should have liked him because he was enthusiastic about our village. In fact I liked him so much that I wish . . ."

"What, dear?"

"That—that he didn't drink—things."

"Like him in spite of that, Rose. Make allowance for the life he has lived. Plenty of money and no especial interest in life. The Devil's own twins, if you ask me."

"Why doesn't he get an interest. Why fuddle his mind

because he's bored? You don't, and goodness knows you've had to fight discouragement often enough."

"I don't because—because quite early in life my heart was skinned alive because I did."

"Did you lose a girl you loved because you—did, Tony?"

"A girl? *No*. Have charity for Mark. Except for that fault he is solid gold."

"I like him. He is rather like you, only Mr. Worldly-Wise. Did he mean really that he would engage me as his secretary?" Through the gloom he could see the laughing triumph in the eyes which sought his. "With two employers clamoring for my valuable services you'll have to watch your step. I forgot to ask—it may make a difference—what salary do you pay your shipping clerk?" The smile left her eyes and voice as she added:

"To think of having money I have earned."

"Have you wanted money so much, dear?"

"Everyone wants it. It's poisonous to conceive a glorious plan and then have it fade out for lack of funds, to see an air castle crumble because one can't finance the building. Shall I have a desk in your office at the storage plant?"

He welcomed the question. The pungent aroma of September, the moonlight, the girl's slender self so near were undermining his self-control. For the remainder of the way he talked shop without a break. As the car stopped before the door Rose laid her hand on his:

"Tony, don't think because I have chattered incessantly that I do not realize what you are feeling about—about Daphne. I'm sorry. It is unbearable to have you hurt."

He caught her fingers in his.

"It is all right, dear, don't worry."

Claire Grahame and Peter were in the living room as they entered. As her mother glanced at the clock Rose explained:

"We came home the long way."

Anthony lighted his pipe.

"No more late hours after tonight, *Madre*. Rose has accepted a position in our shipping office. She must settle down into a hard-working business woman."

The girl's frock petaled about her like the leaves of a

Lyons rose as she nestled into a corner of the couch. She made an adorable little grimace as she protested:

"Don't talk as though I were a slave bound to the orchard wheel."

"Go to it, Tony," approved Peter. "She's spoiled. She needs discipline. Boy! If you put her through the training I got—Rosy, while you're still free, white and twenty-one let's raid the ice-box."

As the brother and sister disappeared in the direction of the kitchen Hamilton rested his arm along the mantel and frowned down into the fire.

"Anything wrong, Anthony?"

He shook his head in answer to Claire Grahame's tender question. Should he tell her of his soul-shaking discovery? He must. It was only fair. Perhaps because of what happened to David she would not trust him with her lovely girl. The thought whitened his lips. Better get it over. Better adopt his own advice to Rose. Get it behind him. His voice was low and not too steady as he confided:

"*Madre,* I made a discovery tonight. When I looked up and saw Rose in the hall at La Mancha I knew that I loved her."

"Loved Rose! But Daphne?"

"That is not a *bona fide* engagement. For some reason—to double-cross her mother, I suspect—Daphne begged me to consent to it. Wrong. All wrong. I shouldn't have tried to help her that way. A lie always proves a weak, a betraying link. Now that I realize my love for Rose the situation is unbearable."

"Why not tell her the truth?"

"I promised Daphne that I wouldn't. She feels that Rose regards her with indifference tinged with contempt, that she couldn't and wouldn't sympathetically understand the reason of this fake engagement."

"I regret to admit that I doubt if Rose would sympathetically understand any girl to whom you became engaged, Anthony. She would indignantly refute the charge, but she's jealous."

"If I can make her care would you think our marriage unsuitable?"

"Unsuitable!"

"I mean—because of David."

Tears were thick in Claire Grahame's eyes as she answered:

"My dear, every year you have lived since that tragic day has been an atonement. I shall be happy and proud, I shall feel safe, oh, so safe, about my daughter's future if she loves and marries you."

"Thank you, *Madre*. It will be difficult to make her realize the change in my love for her."

"So difficult that you must proceed cautiously. Boys and men have counted only as friends with Rose. She has been happily absorbed with college and sports. You and Peter have filled her heart. You and Peter. The quality of her love for you both is the same."

"I realize that. But tomorrow—tomorrow I'll begin to change the quality. The farce between Daphne and me will end tomorrow."

"Dear—are you sure that you can end it?"

"Sure? What could stop me?"

His voice was vibrant with assurance. He sensed Claire Grahame's involuntary shiver. He caught her gently by the shoulders and exultantly repeated:

"What could stop me?"

"I don't know, Anthony. For a moment I had a curious sense of foreboding. Don't mind me. Nicholas says that I am developing nerves. Remember always that my love and confidence are yours."

He pressed his lips to her silver hair.

"Thank you, *Madre*."

"Close-up! The return of the prodigal," dramatized Peter at the door. Rose regarded her mother and Anthony with wary eyes as she demanded:

"Are you two conspiring about me? I warn you that I shall knuckle no longer, so don't waste your gray matter. I announce in Peter's inelegant but expressive vernacular, 'From now on I'm on my own.' Fearless but feminine. Good-night, everybody."

She kissed her mother, patted Peter's arm and with a touch of defiance nodded to Hamilton:

"Good-night, tyrant."

His mouth and eyes flashed into laughter. He followed her to the foot of the stairs.

"*Madre* and I accepted your ultimatum, Miss Grahame. Here are your bag and gloves." As he laid them in her extended hands he confessed unsteadily:

"I got that terrific bump to-night, dear."

"Bump! What do you mean, Tony?"

"Didn't you predict that sometime I would be shocked into a realization of the fact that you have grown up? It has happened. My little girl has gone."

## Chapter VII

ROSE recognized the man who was directing the unloading of a truck full of boxes of apples in the storage cellar. She smiled and nodded as he touched his cap.

"Good-morning, Hardy. Have you seen Mr. Hamilton? Mr. Long wants him to call him at once on the telephone and I can't locate him."

"Not since early morning, Miss Grahame. He rode through the lower orchard. He is usually back at the office at this hour. Have you tried the packing room?"

"I rang the foreman but no one answered. I will go there now."

She stopped for a moment to breathe deeply of the clear air before she entered the building in which were located packing and shipping rooms and offices. It set back from the main road on a gentle slope to the river. In the packing room a half dozen girls were busy at tables wrapping apples in white tissues printed with the Grahame trade-mark, "Fruit-You-Can-Eat-in-the-Dark." Two men were painstakingly putting McIntosh Reds through a sizer. They handled the fruit as though it were spun glass.

Unsuccessful in her quest Rose returned to the office. What an infinite amount of labor and care Tony had put into developing the business, she thought as she glanced about the room. Behind glass doors shelves were stacked with agricultural reports. Sample crates and boxes were piled in one corner; a bunch of planting boards four or five feet long with notches at the ends and in the middle leaned against a wall. What detail there was to orcharding. Nothing seemed too trivial for his attention. Doubtless that was the reason the Grahame fruit had made good. After all, there was nothing truer than that you get out of life and interests just about what you put into them. There was no gilt-edge dividends, no melons cut in fruit raising unless one worked like a demon to earn them.

The girl rested an elbow on the sill at the open window and looked out over acres of trees. Just beyond the building stretched a nursery. How thrifty the young stock was. October! She had been at work two weeks. She loved it. She watched a truck loaded with ladders—light ladders, pointed ladders, extension ladders—swaying toward the tool house. Saturday. Tony would permit no tool to be left at large over Sunday, particularly the ladders which might suggest apple-picking-made-easy to a passing marauder.

What a day! Warm as June. A single purple finch, doubtless left behind when his relatives and friends flocked southward, hopped about on a tree branch. His delicate and rosy coloring was marked by tiny brown stripes. The river mirrored the glory of fields and hills. Little islands dotted through a quicksilver stream had turned to russet and gold.

Rose swiveled to her desk at sound of a hand on the doorknob. As a matter of example she mustn't be discovered by an employee dreaming at the window. She glimpsed herself in the mirror she had tucked into one corner of her desk. "You do look business-like in your brownish rose jersey frock with snowy linen collar and cuffs," she assured her reflection.

"Boss away?"

The sepulchral whisper hissed through the crack afforded by the slightly open door. Rose laughed as she swung around to face the inquirer.

"Tony is in the orchard. Come in."

Mark Hamilton entered with an exaggerated air of relief. He dropped a magazine to the capacious blotter before he perched on one corner of his brother's desk. He clasped his hands about one of his knees. Thus comfortably balanced he confided:

"The last time I appeared in this office, Rose-Pomona, I feared violence. Your boss was dictating to you. If a look could have slain I should have flopped out like a headless rooster."

"Tony doesn't approve of callers in business hours. This is no place for the gilded-leisure class."

"Don't you like the gilded-leisure class?"

"Don't wheedle. I like workers."

"A thorny rose this morning. I strive to please. I'll apply for a picker's job. Can't you see me in overalls climbing a tree and ripping the fruit into baskets? I'd show more speed than some of the Johnnies I've seen working here."

"Climb! Rip! That shows what you know of the business of orcharding. I'd like to see Tony's face when you climbed into your first tree. Ladders, my ignorant youth, ladders everywhere. Rip off the apples! They are handled as carefully as eggs, gently, oh, so gently removed that the stem shall remain with the fruit, not with the tree. Evidently you don't know that markets refuse apples that have twenty-five per cent of the stems missing."

Rose warmed to her subject.

"Every broken spur means that several apples are deducted from the next three or four years' crops. Think what that would amount. . . ."

"Help! I'm buried under an avalanche of information! You've missed your vocation. You ought to get in touch with the Bureau of Agriculture and go on the lecture platform, or into politics. You're a born soap-box orator."

The girl colored.

"Perhaps if it were your living you'd know something about it. I'm very busy," she suggested crisply.

"I'll wait till you are through. My roadster is at the door. I'll run you home for luncheon. Isn't this a half-holiday?"

"Yes. But Tony may want me to stay. He may have some letters to get off."

"You are not sure? I'll take a chance. I'll wait."

"I am sure of one thing. If you don't go I shan't get away till midnight." She back-spaced to correct a mistake in the invoice she was typing.

"I'm dumb."

He dropped into the desk chair and opened the magazine. For a while only the tap-tap of the machine and the crackle of turned pages stirred the stillness. Suddenly he straightened in his chair:

"Listen!

" 'Bootlegging of aliens across our land frontiers continues to be a well-paying industry. Some authorities declare that from three hundred to a thousand aliens a day are smuggled into this country across the Canadian and Mexican frontiers. The border patrols are said to be doing good work; but their numbers are far too small to guard as they should the 3800 miles of boundary under their jurisdiction.'

"That's straight from the shoulder. I happen to know that it's true."

Rose's dark eyebrows drew together ever so little. Her voice registered amazement as she observed:

"I am glad to know from your indignant tone that you draw the line at some branches of the bootlegging industry." As he colored she went on, "It seems incredible when one thinks how much harder a dishonest person works for a living than an honest one. And on a chance, too. Probably these smugglers don't get more than ten dollars a head—if they get that—for the live freight they deliver this side of the line."

"Ten dollars! When I was in Mexico two years ago— I went down to look at some mines in which our estate has an interest—the immigration authorities were after a ringleader who had boasted that he had cleared up twenty thousand dollars that year on aliens."

"Twenty thousand! Did they catch him?"

"I heard they did but only after an awful fight. He was slippery as an eel. They tried all sorts of bait to lure him to the American side. I don't know how they caught him finally."

"Is there nothing that can be done about a man like that?"

"A nice long term in Leavenworth, if—they catch him the side of the border. Nothing if he plays safe on the Mexican side. I understand that we have no extradition laws which cover that special crime." He flung the magazine to the desk and crossed to the window:

"What a day!"

"Isn't it wonderful. October, and the window wide open. The hills are flaming with color. They suggest the explosion of a fireworks factory. See that gash of sumac close to the water? The air is like wine."

"Lot you know about wine." Mark Hamilton grinned engagingly. He intoned theatrically:

> " 'Lips that touch likker
> Shall never touch mine.' "

Rose whirled from her fond inspection of the world outside.

"I wish you knew as little. Do you know how I feel about you, Mark? I like you before noon. After that— I wish—I wish that you wouldn't speak to me."

"You don't mean that." He was patently amused.

The girl's eyes shone like black brilliants under tears but she stood her ground:

"I do. Can't you see that you are ruining your health, your future? I hate you when your hand is unsteady, when your skin is red and thick and looks as though it ought to be scraped, when your eyes are dull and glazed, when your breath—ugh, it's so—so disgusting."

Mark Hamilton was white with fury.

"I'll remind you, Rose-Pomona, that this country is bulging with people who are trying to regulate other people's lives."

"I am not trying to regulate your life except as it touches mine. Surely I have a right to choose the kind of companionship I like. You ought to be as fine as Tony and—and what are you? I'm frightened to death—and I'm no short-sport—to motor with you at the wheel. I refuse to be mushed into a messy mass of skin and bones because you can't say 'No' to yourself."

"I thank you for this vote of confidence." He drew a gold cigarette case from his pocket.

"Put that back, Mark. Smoking is not permitted in this building. We've neither time nor money to fight a fire. If Tony were to come in and find you with a lighted cigarette he'd rampage good and plenty."

"He'd have to go some to beat you at it."

"I'm sorry. I was hateful. But it makes me see red when I realize how you are throwing away your life."

"Then you do care?"

"Of course I care." She held him from a nearer approach with one slim hand. "Aren't you Tony's brother?"

"Is that the only reason?"

She dimpled with provocative laughter.

"You can be rather nice. I was rude, Mark, but I know that you worry Tony."

"He never sermonettes. He never even looks reproach."

"I know that, but it hurts him just the same. He adores you. Too bad, when he has so many other things to think of."

Mark's attention was seemingly absorbed by something outside the window as he asked:

"You mean Daphne?"

"I suspect that she is one of his problems. He hasn't seemed the same since that night we dined with your mother. He has set up a barricade of reserve. 'Dropped his visor,' Peter and I call it. Remember how she refused to go with him and accepted Nap Long's escort? I am sure he hasn't seen her since."

"She hasn't seen anyone. Mrs. Tennant is ill."

"How do you know? Are you responsible for Daphne's change of manner toward Tony?"

"Your tone is distinctly hopeful. I'm sorry to disappoint you, but that sort of thing isn't done between brothers."

"Forgive me, but you seem to admire her and—and she isn't the one for Tony and—and you are fascinating but . . ."

"Am I? To you?"

He bent over her eagerly. She laughed.

"Permit me to finish my sentence. But, imagine throwing Tony over for anyone."

"He isn't the only man in the world."

"No? Meaning?" Her laughing eyes flouted him. She joined him at the window. "Here comes another. Nap Long in his resplendent roadster. Mark, do you like him?"

"No. I ran into him at an Officers Club in Paris. When I found that he came from this town, naturally I inquired for Tony. Mother had been obsessed by the idea of spending a summer here. I asked him about a house and—here we are."

"You did like him at first."

"That was before he commenced slamming Tony. I may think that my brother is quixotic but I won't allow anyone else to say it to me. Long harps on that string or on the fact that the Grahame outfit won't order his boxes or hire the men he recommends. I can't stand anyone who is eternally airing a grievance. Besides—what's he doing at the Tennants'?"

"Does he go there?"

"I have seen him coming away several times. Perhaps he has matrimonial designs on the mother."

"Perhaps he is in love with Daphne. Joy! He has a heap more money than Tony and. . . ."

"How do you know how much money Tony has?"

"I know what his salary is, do I not? Of course his family has money. But that isn't the same thing for a wife, is it? Napoleon Bonaparte Long's is his own. That pompous, bombastic man is simply walking away with the selectman candidacy. If only there were someone to beat him! If you were a voter here, Mark, I'd take a chance on you rather than on him."

"Thanks for the delicately implied compliment. Why don't you beat him?"

"I!"

"Yes. You have studied town government, haven't you? Get the Woman's Club to back you."

"That couldn't be done. Clubs affiliated with the General Federation are pledged not to mix into local politics as a club. Can't you imagine what would happen to their other work if they did? It would scatter like a ripe peach thrown into an electric fan."

"Then get the town mothers back of you. You have pep, common sense, and being a bred-in-the-bone New Englander, you'll fit into the national thrift program like a chestnut in a burr."

"Am I so prickly? I'm thrifty in practice because I've had to be. I'm horribly extravagant in imagination."

"The practice will hold you if imagination breaks loose. Isn't there a lot of housekeeping about the administration of a town's affairs? There ought to be a woman on the board. At least you'd do as well as some of the rubes about here."

"Thanks. Can you imagine a solid citizen voting for 'little Rose Grahame' whom he has seen grow up? Rose! What a name for a political candidate."

"It's a charming name. Whenever I hear it or say it I step suddenly into a zone of fragrance, sweetness, beauty, color."

"Mark! How dear of you! I shall love my name after that. If only Tony would try for the office. But he won't. He has such a lot on his mind. At least I might help by getting on with my work. I wish you'd go."

"Why should I? I'm sitting pretty. You'd have to see it silhouetted against the window to appreciate the lovely lines of your head." As the girl regarded him with indignant eyes he laughed: "Don't beat me! I'll go—as far as the steps." He backed into someone in the doorway and turned:

"Oh, it's you, Long."

Napoleon Bonaparte Long brushed by him unceremoniously.

"Good-morning, Rose. As I couldn't get hold of Anthony Hamilton on the telphone I came here. Where is he?"

"Still in the orchards."

Rose Grahame struggled to conceal her aversion as she answered. Long appeared a trifle more glossy than usual. His eyes seemed a little nearer together, his black hair more lacquered, his teeth more tombstonely white, his fingernails more glittery. One hand was thrust into the breast of his light top-coat, the other held a gray hat behind his back. The Emperor! She shut her teeth hard on her lips to steady them. She met Mark Hamilton's eyes. He was evidently amused at her absorption in the caller's apparel. A smile twitched at his full lips as he inquired:

"Is there an embargo against smoking outside this building? No? Then I'll sun myself on the steps till Tony comes. Remember, I'm there if you want me. Better think over my proposition. I'll help."

He set the door wide and departed. Long appropriated the chair by the desk. Rose felt his eyes on her as she resumed work. For a few moments there was no sound save the click, click of the typewriter.

"Like your job?"

She nodded and increased speed.

"Stop work for a minute. I want to talk to you." As she dropped her hands into her lap he demanded:

"Why do you treat me as though I were the dirt under your feet? Haven't I just as much money as you have?"

"Don't be silly, Nap. You know perfectly well that you have more, heaps and heaps more."

"I didn't say that to brag. But, neither you nor your mother have asked me to come to White Pillars. Mrs. Hamilton entertains me. I am welcome at the Tennants, in a dozen other homes of the best families in the town. I own the biggest place in the county. I'm going to be selectman. Just what's the matter with me that you hold me at arms' length? I . . ."

At the sound of a footstep on the stairs she sidestepped suavely:

"I came here, bought that old factory above the bridge and set it going from a public-spirited desire to wake this place up. What's the big idea in refusing to buy my boxes? They are cheap and good and near at hand. You are as much an owner in these orchards as Anthony Hamilton is. Persuade him to order them."

Rose gasped at his quick change of subject. Was that Tony coming? He would be furious if he knew of Long's protest against his social ostracism by her mother and herself. Perhaps they had ignored him but always they had disliked him. Because he had returned to the village with money made no difference in their estimate of him. The footsteps passed the door and died away down the corridor. Better to keep him on the subject of his business rather than have him revert to his social grievance, she thought.

"We never question our manager's decisions. Why did you start a factory here? You are spoiling the town. Tony told you before you equipped it that he would not buy boxes of you. With the shortage of labor everywhere aren't your building operations enough?"

"I can get plenty of labor."

"Plenty of the kind that can't speak English."

"Poor devils, don't they need work as much as the natives Hamilton is so keen for? I'm glad to give them a chance."

He gestured grandiloquently. His hand swept the magazine Mark had left to the floor. The sight of the sprawled pages set a flare in the girl's memory. Words came back to her:

"From three hundred to a thousand aliens a day are smuggled across the Canadian and Mexican borders."

Suppose Santa Anna were Mexican and not Spanish? Suppose—an absurd supposition of course—but suppose he had been smuggled into the country? She rested her chin in her hand and regarded the man across the office.

"Give them a chance! Merely to help them? You! That sounds too disinterested to be in character, Nap."

"Cut out the high-hat stuff. I like it in Rose Grahame. I won't stand it from Hamilton's stenographer. I understand that your boss will harvest from acres of orchards. I intend to supply the boxes for that fruit. If I don't—I'll reduce your force of pickers till you beg for mercy."

"The men we have employed for years won't listen to you."

"The new men will and in time the old ones will listen to my money. I need more intelligent workers on the tract I'm developing. Of course if you can afford to let your fruit stay on the trees until it drops . . ."

"We can, Long," assured Anthony Hamilton from the doorway.

His expression and voice set Rose's heart pounding with excitement. The man in the chair tilted his head at a cocky angle. Hamilton's face grew darkly red as he commanded:

"Come away from my desk. Rose, take this list to the shipping room."

The girl took the sheaf of papers and hesitated. Had Tony invented the errand to get rid of her? She wouldn't leave the two together. She remembered Long's threat to "get even." He rose leisurely.

"Don't send her away, Hamilton. I'm no wild man as she—she will know some time." An undertone in his voice stopped Rose's breath. How dare he smile at her as though there were an understanding between them? Fortunately Tony was engrossed with papers on his desk.

A maddening weapon, the chill of inattention. Long took fire.

"I dropped in to deliver my ultimatum. You're short of pickers for your prize crops, aren't you? I keep tabs on your business. You'll be shorter if you don't give me an order today for boxes."

He made a careful selection from the army of cigars in his waistcoat pocket. With a pencil Anthony Hamilton thoughtfully designed arabesques on the blotter on his desk. His tone placated as he inquired:

"Why should I?"

"In the first place it will save you money, second . . ."

"Mighty thoughtful of you, Long, to take my affairs to heart. However, I repeat I shall not use your boxes. This is my busy morning . . ."

At the suggestion in his voice Long's eyes blazed. He adjusted his coat-collar, struck a silver-sheet attitude in the doorway and threatened:

"Wait until I'm selectman, Hamilton. I'll grant myself a permit to build a box-factory on my La Mancha property snug against the White Pillars' line. Good-morning."

As he banged the office door behind him Hamilton already was busy with the papers on his desk. Rose resumed work with her thoughts on the men across the room. It seemed as though she had endured silence for an eternity before she asked:

"Can Nap grant himself a permit to build that factory, Tony?"

"He seems to think he can—he'd have to get one other on the board to confirm it. Has Mark been in the office this morning?"

"For a few moments."

"What did he want?"

"If you snap at me like that I won't answer you."

As her indignant eyes met his the merest wraith of a strange emotion flitted along her pulses, caught at her breath and was gone. Humiliation, of course. She had been at work but two weeks and already she was intruding personalities in business. She had been so sure that she could hold herself coolly aloof from that.

"Mark came to take me home to luncheon," she volunteered in a low voice.

"Sorry. I can't let you off early. I want to dictate letters. Ready?"

The girl's heart smarted as she picked up book and pencil. If this was what working for Tony meant she hated it. The telephone rang. She answered and transferred the call to his desk.

"The shipping room."

She watched his face as he talked.

"Hamilton speaking . . . How many? . . . Tell the three to come for their pay, Monday . . . We can't lock them in, can we . . . Good-bye."

Rose waited as he turned over the papers on his desk. Had he forgotten the letters? What had happened? Had Long staged a walk-out already? Would Tony tell her? That tricky Napoleon Bonaparte was right in one thing, the business was partly hers. Her eyes followed him as he crossed to the window from which he could look out over acres of orchards. On some of the trees the leaves had begun to curl. The Baldwins were taking on their winter color of crimson. The perfect fruit represented years of work. Not so long ago New England merchants had regarded that apple with suspicion, they wouldn't buy it. Now it was firmly established. Would Tony sacrifice a goodly part of a year's income for a principle? She stole up to him and slipped her hand within his arm.

"Tony, has Long begun to carry out his threat to hire away the pickers?"

"It looks so. He's a fast worker."

"What will you do?"

"Were I the only one concerned I would fight him if I lost every apple in the orchards, but, your mother, you and Peter are the ones to decide. I don't believe in this box factory of Long's. He's employing a lot of foreigners. He says that he is sorry for the poor, underfed devils.

"I don't believe in him. He has self-interest tucked up his sleeves, I'll bet a hat. If we don't harvest those apples on time it means thousands of dollars loss. Peter is coming home tonight. We'll hold a family pow-wow. Meanwhile . . ."

Rose tightened her clasp on his arm.

"Meanwhile—this is Saturday. Forget your problems. Let's spend the whole heavenly afternoon on the river. I know where there are chestnuts, the only ones left since the blight. Please, Tony."

"How about your date with Mark?"

"I haven't a date with Mark. He said he should sit on the steps outside until I came, but, do you think that I would go with him if I could get you?"

The smile she loved flashed in his eyes and widened his lips as he teased:

"T.B.W. so soon?"

"I am not a tired business woman but I just can't bear to see you worried. Haven't I been at work every minute since I started? There have been times when I suspected that you and Eddie Timmins were inventing work to keep me busy. I have even been personally conducted between home and office. Look! Here comes that plane again!"

The unmistakable thrum of an air-engine drifted in at the open window. The speck in the distance materialized into a great winged creature. It circled as though in indecision before it descended to the top of Headless Hill.

"Why say 'that plane'?" Anthony asked as it disappeared.

"I have seen it twice before. Both times on Saturday. It is earlier today. I saw it first the day the monkey crashed into the living room at White Pillars. I thought that he might have dropped from it but now—wait a minute!"

She ran across the room and picked up the magazine. Hastily she turned the leaves until she found the page she sought. She indicated a paragraph:

"Read that, Tony."

She rested her head against his arm. She could hear the pounding of his heart. In spite of his apparent coolness Long must have angered him to fury to make it beat like that. She followed his eyes till he came to the end of the article. He smiled down at her.

"Well, what of it, dear?"

"Tony, I've had a perfectly mad idea that that might be what Nap Long was doing?"

"What?"

"Smuggling aliens. An air-route. The men who come so mysteriously. The airplane. His insistence upon your taking them. Remember the man on the Headless Hill road? *'Nombre de Dios'!"*

Anthony looked from the page in his hand to the window. The airplane was rising above the hill.

"Say nothing of your suspicion of this to anyone," he commanded in a low voice as a hand turned the knob. He returned to his desk. Sam Hardy opened the door. He advanced into the room and halted. His eyes went from the man to the girl at the window. His face was curiously white. His eyes almost expressionless.

"What is it, Hardy?"

"May I speak with you a moment, sir?"

"Certainly. Hood the typewriter, Rose. We are through work. Go to White Pillars with Mark. After lunch we'll hunt those chestnuts."

"Tony, you duck!" she whispered. Aloud she agreed demurely;

"Yes, Mr. Hamilton."

She nodded to Sam Hardy. Anthony held the door open for her. Had any one in the world such a heavenly smile, she thought as she ran down the stairs. Hat over his eyes, pipe in mouth, in a sunny corner slumped Mark Hamilton. He struggled to his feet and reminded:

"I told you I'd wait. Where's Tony?"

"Listening to Sam Hardy's troubles, I suspect." As the low-slung car started smoothly, she added thoughtfully, "I wonder though if he came to give notice. I have seen that man but twice before but each time he produced an uncanny feeling."

"Sort of footfall of Destiny stuff?"

"Exactly. The creepy rolling up of mystery."

"What did Long want?"

"He came to deliver his ultimatum. We are to buy his boxes or he will lure away our pickers. And as soon as he is elected selectman he will build a box factory snug against the White Pillars' boundary."

"Was that all?" demanded Mark Hamilton caustically.

"Wasn't that enough? Imagine a box factory next—oh, I can't say it. Tony won't knuckle to him and he'll do it."

"Only—if he's elected."

"Who is there to beat him?"

"I've told you."

"I! Mark, how can you be so absurd?"

"Nothing absurd about it. Look what the women in England do. I wouldn't want to see you president . . ."

"Wouldn't you? Now I had seriously considered . . ."

"Don't be catty. As I was saying, when so rudely interrupted, I think that a woman in town government would be worth trying."

The seed threw out a tiny root.

"Tony wouldn't hear of it."

"He'd hear a lot about it if you decided to do it. Never mind him. He's early-American anyway, when it comes to girls. Trust brother Mark. Talk with some of the town mothers."

"They'd think I was too young."

"Suit yourself. If you want that factory built against your line . . ."

They maintained silence till they reached White Pillars. As Rose stepped from the car she suggested:

"Come in for luncheon, Mark. Tell Jupiter to set a place for you. I'll be down in a jiffy."

She ran upstairs and into her room. She flung her coat on the candle-wick spread of the slender four-poster with its curtains, valance and tester of sheer ruffled net. Primrose yellow walls. Slip covers of gay chintz. Old mahogany. On the mantel over the fireplace a gilt and crystal clock with a blazing rhinestone pendulum. A Cavalier among Puritans.

Rose thoughtfully regarded the chimney cupboard before she pulled a chair in front of it and mounted. She opened the door and from the top shelf produced a box tied round and round with black ribbon. Seated on the floor she opened it. She removed layers of soft paper before she looked down upon a doll dressed in the fashion of ten years back. The head was shattered. One rosy cheek and one sapphire eye alone remained intact. The tears were thick on the girl's long lashes as the memory of her childish heart-break swept over her. She cuddled the mutilated treasure against her neck as she murmured:

"Annabel Lee! Annabel Lee! I saw the boy who shot you lurking behind the eyes of Nap Long today. We won't let him be a selectman, will we, my dear? We'll fight him!"

## Chapter VIII

ANTHONY HAMILTON laid the opened magazine on the desk as he sat down. He looked up at Sam Hardy. Not the common workman type. A college man, he decided. How had he drifted into his present position?

"What can I do for you?" he encouraged.

"I came to give notice, Mr. Hamilton."

"Why didn't you do as the other men did? Give it through my foreman?" He was conscious of a sickening sense of disappointment. He had been so sure that he could count on Hardy to stand by.

"Because I am not leaving for the same reason. Long has not bribed me. I—I have work to do and I must get about it."

"Sit down. Tell me about this 'work'."

"You wouldn't understand."

"Try me."

"I have been in prison."

"I know that. I might have been."

"You!"

"A man lost his life through my carelessness. Because I had sympathy and trust and help I have been able in a slight degree to make amends. Now you know why I have been interested in you. Why I should be glad to help you."

"Thank you, sir, I—I—I am not guilty of the crime for which I was jailed. The authorities released me because of new information. I . . ."

"Take your time. Tell me the facts. If you feel that you can't, I'll help just the same."

The rumble of a truck, the soft thud of wood on wood, the scent of apples drifted through the open window. The skin strained white over the knuckles of the man's brown hands as he answered:

"Hardy is not my name. I took it when I came out of

the army. After the war I went wild. I hadn't made good—I don't mean overseas, I did well enough there—I drifted across the border." He hesitated and fumbled with his hat. Quite casually Hamilton closed the magazine spread open on his desk.

"Take your time, Hardy."

The man straightened.

"Why should I slump here as though I were guilty? I did some bootlegging. Not much more than is being laughed at and encouraged here every day. Then one morning when I rode across the border into Texas I was surrounded by a posse. The sheriff accused me of having smuggled aliens into the States. Said I had boasted that I had cleaned up twenty thousand dollars in one year. Twenty thousand! I hadn't seen so much money as that in all my grown-up life. But the party for whom I was mistaken had laid his plans perfectly. The government produced witness after witness to swear that I was the leader of a smuggling gang."

"Had you no friend to appear for you?"

The man's white face darkened to purplish red as he evaded:

"What was the use of dragging anyone else into the mess? The real culprit had me signed, sealed and delivered."

"Have you made no effort to discover him?"

"I'm on his trail now. I've had a tip he's working the other border."

"I'm sorry to have you leave us. I liked and trusted you before. I like and trust you now. I had planned to offer you one of the new plantations to be run on halves until you had acquired enough money to buy it."

The man rose abruptly.

"Thank you. Sorry that I can't stay. But . . ."

"See Timmins before you go and get your pay."

"I saw him before I came to you."

"Good luck to you. If ever you need legal advice, Hardy, go to Judge Cort."

"Thank you. Good-bye."

As the sound of the man's footsteps died away down the corridor Anthony Hamilton drew the magazine toward him. He read the article Rose had indicated from beginning to end. He dropped it to his desk and walked to the window. Headless Hill glowed like a burning bush in autumn foliage. He could hear the soft rush of the river, the challenging squawk of a pheasant. Just outside a fly-catcher was harassing a warbler. Life. Something or someone always in pursuit of something or someone. Rose's whispered words echoed in his memory:

"Could it by any chance be the station of an air-route?"

An incredible suggestion—and yet—it might account for the surprising influx of aliens, who, if the suspicion were fact, were criminals at the start for entering the United States by a direct violation of the country's laws. Could a man who had crashed through them ever have respect for them? Could he be anything but a menace?

If it were true, who was responsible? Napoleon Bonaparte Long? No. He mustn't allow his detestation of the man to make him unjust. Long was utterly selfish. He had too much to lose. The Spanish butler at La Mancha? He didn't look intelligent enough. Hamilton's eyes rested on the gaily patterned Hill. Rose had reminded him of the man who had started from the brush when they were driving home from his mother's. On that same evening the maid had overfilled his glass when the mysterious monkey had been under discussion; on that same evening he had found the red-ink warning. Were the events linked together?

Was Sam Hardy wise to what was going on—supposing Rose's suspicion were correct? Did fear that again he might he drawn into the net account for his eagerness to leave the town? What had he been doing on the afternoon he and Rose had seen him paddling down river? He had been white with excitement. Had the story he had just told been true? He himself had wanted to believe the best of him.

Timmins flung open the office door and slammed it behind him. His green eyes bulged.

"Look at that, Cap'n!"

Hamilton glanced down at the richly red, perfectly formed Baldwin apple in the man's extended hand.

"Where did you get it, Tim?"

"You'd never guess if you tried years. You know that windowless room at the old Allen house, the one we figured they stored their invalids in in old times to keep them safe from fresh air?"

"Yes."

"I was over to the place this morning to test the soil so we could decide what variety of apple would thrive best. I went into the house for something and I smelled apples. 'Boy,' says I to myself, 'you've got apples on the brain. There can't be any this side of the river.' Just the same I followed my nose. Up those creaky stairs. Into that little room. Shot my flashlight round. Surprised! For the love of Mike! In front of me, spread on an old sack like they were a prize display, were a dozen of these beauties."

Anthony turned the apple over and over before he looked at his foreman. Eddie Timmins answered the question in his eyes. "You know who's bunking in that old house, Cap'n. Play that on your piano!"

"Hardy has just given notice."

"I know. He came to me. He'll go back. Would he risk snitching those apples and then leave them? We'll have to watch the old house, Cap'n."

"We'll watch him, Tim. Sit down while we plan."

Anthony Hamilton mentally reviewed Hardy's story and Timmins' discovery. Monday morning soon after daybreak he paced the floor of the old Allen house. He paused at the window. The indistinct color of trees and shrubs sent his thoughts back to his Saturday afternoon with Rose. They had canoed on the river. They had hunted chestnuts. She had been gay, debonair, unchanged except as his love for her had changed her in his own mind. Once as she had stepped from the boat she had slipped. He had caught her close. For an instant he could feel the pounding of her heart. With an impatient laugh she had freed herself. Her mother had warned him to proceed cautiously. How could he when the sound of her voice set his pulses rioting? Suppose while he waited Mark should win her? Twice Saturday evening at the Club he had come upon them in eager confab. He had heard his brother whisper:

"Remember. I'm behind you."

Behind in what, Anthony wondered uneasily. Two weeks ago he had boasted to Mrs. Grahame that he would stop the farce of his engagement to Daphne. He had written. He had telephoned. He had called. Daphne had sent a note in reply:

"Mother very ill. Please let things remain as they are at present. Can't tell what the consequences would be if I told her that our engagement was broken. Matter of life and death. Please!"

Should he tell Rose the truth about the engagement? No, he had promised Daphne. Through the very force and passion of his love the girl he loved must love him. But suppose Mark . . .

He dragged his thoughts from unbearable possibilities to the present and resumed his restless pacing. Who had stolen the prize apples? Timmins had spent all day yesterday in the house on the chance of surprising the thief. He had relieved him in the evening. All night he had been on guard. Neither a suspicious sight nor sound had rewarded his vigilance. Even Hardy had not appeared to collect his belongings. The cot neatly spread with blankets in the room at the left of the hall had not been disturbed. A cheap one-tube radio set was on a packing box.

The estate had been purchased from joint heirs, a niece and uncle. Thriftily the woman had kept her share of the buildings in repair. The man had refused to spend a cent on his. In consequence one half of the roof was neatly shingled. The sky was the limit of visibility through the other half. The house groaned and sighed like a rheumaticky old person attempting to turn. The cloying smell of decaying wood permeated the place. The early morning light added atmospheric verity to an illusion of flitting wraiths of long-dead loves and hates and hum-drum duties. Vividly as imagination might conjure romances about the long-passed occupants of the old house the apples in the room above were real. Those were a solid, indisputable fact. A dozen of the orchard's most perfect specimens were laid out in a row on an old sack.

Anthony leaned against the window-casement and looked through the dusty, cobwebbed pane. Since he had come on watch the groans and sighs of the old frame had been the only sounds to ripple the stillness. The house faced the road. Behind it the land sloped gently to the river, a river of dreams in the rosy light. It smoked in spots as though the water-nymphs below had set their morning cauldrons on the fire. Between the mists were red patches like isinglass where the water reflected the flushed and radiant dawn. The ragged outline of hills loomed like phantom castles through an opalescent haze.

The old Allen place was an ideal orchard location. A natural windbreak of spruce, pine and hard maple protected it from northwest blows. It was time to set the trees. If successful—as why shouldn't it be—this venture ought to convince the neighboring landowners of the economic desirability of dedicating the valley to orchards. Already they had had an object lesson in the growth of the Grahame business.

Hands hard in his pockets he gazed thoughtfully toward the crimson-streaked east. Yesterday he had discussed with the Grahames Nap Long's threat to call off the apple-pickers. Peter had been keen to fight to a finish, he had proposed giving up his work at law school until after harvesting. That would be unnecessary. Picking time was comparatively short. Grading and packing required the most labor. If worst came to worst the apples could be transferred from the trees to cold-storage. It had been the custom to pack the choicest in the orchards. The situation reminded him of the lean years when he and Eddie Timmins had worked through many nights because the smallness of the crop had made the hiring of pickers an extravagance. Many a time had he been tempted to tide over difficulties by using his own money but his promise to Claire Grahame had held him. He had agreed to be as her own son. Her son would have had no principal into which to dip. He had set his teeth and worked and held on with bulldog tenacity. Combating droughts, windfalls, and interminable stretches of wet weather had but steeled his determination to make good. They had won without his money. After the difficulties already surmounted, it would take someone bigger than Long to . . .

What was that? He wheeled from the window. Was the old house merely turning in its sleep with a super-sigh or had he heard a step? The sound had been like the drop of a light body on the floor overhead. The

windows upstairs were neither open nor broken. Timmins
had made a careful inspection. There was no opening
above save the hole in the roof. Would anyone in his
right mind risk climbing over those shingles?

Crash! Snap! Crack! Rip! Splintering wood! The house
shivered awake in every beam. Hamilton tugged at the
latch of the woodshed door before he remembered that
he had had it nailed fast. With a yank which threatened its
rusted hinges he jerked open the front door. He plunged
through a jungle of neglected shrubs and rounded the
corner of the house. Directly in his path was a pile of
boards and shingles. Debris from a collapsed lean-to. He
stopped! He stared! He brushed an impatient hand across
his eyes. He wasn't dreaming. The person perched on top
of that wreckage was the last person in the world he
had expected to see. Daphne Tennant!

"Good-morning, Tony!"

For a st nned moment Anthony was unable to decide
whether it was the crimson publicity-van-guard of the sun
or guilty consternation which colored the girl's face as she
smiled up at him. As one in a nightmare attempts to confirm as real each object in sight so he checked up every detail of her costume. A gaily plaided sportscoat revealed
the skirt of a straight frock of dark blue. She was as fault-
lessly complexioned as though but a moment before she
had turned from a highly satisfactory self-inspection before
a mirror. Her blue felt hat had been jolted over one
eye. Its angle contributed a ribald touch out of character
with her demure expression. With an effort she withdrew
her gaze from the grilling eyes above her. She became
absorbed in the button of her shoe.

As though released from a spell Anthony picked up
the shotgun which topped the debris beside her. He
turned it over and over in his hands as though doubting
his eyes. He broke it and removed the cartridges.

"What are you doing here at this unholy hour?" he demanded.

"After pheasants. I gave my ankle a horrid twist." She
rubbed the injured member as she flung the crumb of
explanation over her shoulder.

"Pheasants?"

Had he butted in on a rendezvous?

"I was stalking a blatantly defiant cock who flew almost into my face. He disappeared into one of those shrubs behind you. I crept up on him. I must have struck a concealed upright of this miserable lean-to for in an instant I was catapulted into the midst of this wreck. Fortunately I came out on top. Lucky you didn't appear a moment sooner. I might have mistaken you for that pheasant."

Obviously she was talking against time. Was it embarrassment because she had evaded him these last weeks or, was she giving someone a chance to escape? Had he not sensed the twang of a false note through her explanation her touch of bravado would have confirmed his suspicion that he had stumbled on a trail of mystery. Where did it lead? Never mind that now. He had his chance. She shouldn't escape until she had released him from the net of that absurd engagement. As he helped free her from the light wood piled about ʰer she demanded in her turn:

"What are you doing here at this unholy hour?"

"I came to look over the place. The men are to plow here today. I felt a Monday morning urge to be ahead of them. During the short days we have to work fast in the orchards. How did you come?"

"In my canoe."

Hamilton considered. He must get back to White Pillars. He would not leave her. With spectacular effect the morn fused into a glorious October day. He looked at his watch.

"That wise bird won't appear again so why wait?" Was it imagination or had her eyes narrowed in suspicion? "Come back to breakfast with me. You must be famished. You never tasted anything more luscious than Juno's rice waffles floating in real maple syrup. We shall be just in time. We sons of the soil breakfast early."

"How did you get here?"

"My roadster is in the barn. I'll have one of the men paddle your canoe back. Better come."

"Are you sure that I won't shock Mrs. Grahame by such an early visitation?"

"Shock *Madre?* You couldn't. Come on."

"I will. Give me my gun."

"I'll carry it."

He was conscious that she followed the disposal of it

with observant eyes. Did she breathe a little sigh of relief as the car started? As they sped over the road the silence between them widened and deepened like the thick drab water between a departing ship and the shore. He flung a conversational pontoon across the space:

"I hope that your mother is better?"

The girl's throat contracted nervously.

"Not much. This is the first time I have left her for days and days. I was sorry not to see you when you called, Tony. I knew what you wanted, but, as I wrote you, please, please, let the situation remain undisturbed for the present."

She had left her mother for the first time in days to go shooting pheasants at dawn. Did she think that he was a fool? That he would credit such an explanation? The certainty that he was being used as a smoke-screen hardened his voice as he refused:

"No, Daphne. We should have corrected your mother's misunderstanding at once. I will help you in any other way I can. But this farce must . . ."

The patter of hoofs! He looked over his shoulder. Rose with Rusto running ahead of her mount! Alone! Red letters spelling DANGER flickered before his eyes. Was she also after game? The girl on the horse waved her gloved hand and called:

"I'd recognize the sound of your car if I heard it in Mars, Tony! Don't you wish you knew what I'm out after?"

She rode alongside the roadster and looked down. Her brilliant color faded. Her smile became set as she incredulously regarded his companion.

"Daphne is coming to breakfast with us. I lured her with rice waffles and floods of maple syrup," Anthony explained before she could utter the question her lips were framing. She made no answer. She pulled in her mount, who with eyes rolling and slender feet pirouetting staged an imitation of fear. The girl ran her gloved hand down his satin neck as she admonished:

"Don't be silly, Pierrot. You are no more afraid of that car than I am. Go on, Tony. We'll follow."

What had she imagined to drive the color from her face, he thought as he drove on. He maintained a rigid silence that he might listen to the pad-pad of the horse behind them. Under the porte-cochere at White Pillars he waited for Rose. Before he could help her she had slipped to the ground and had flung the bridle rein to Rusto. As the dog led the horse down the drive she disappeared into the house with a low word to her mother whom she passed on the threshold.

If Claire Grahame was amazed at the identity of Tony's companion she gave no sign. She stood at the top of the steps lovely and youthful in her simple heliotrope morning frock. Her hair had the sheen of silver. She extended a cordial hand:

"Good morning Daphne. I am delighted to see you. I love breakfast guests. They start the day in a holiday mood. Aren't the orchards beautiful in this light? Anthony, Eddie Timmins has been trying to get you on the 'phone for the last ten minutes. Come in and take off your hat, Daphne?"

Hamilton's eyes were shadowed with conjecture as he closed the door of his office. He laid the gun on his desk. Daphne's explanation of her presence at the old Allen place was bunk, pure bunk, he decided. He would keep his eyes open. Meanwhile he would find out what Timmins wanted.

The prompt response to his call on the telephone suggested an impatient foreman sitting with his ear at the receiver.

"You called me, Tim? . . . Two more leaving? Who are they? . . . Put the men in the sizing room on the trees. . . . Nothing, that is, nothing we looked for. . . . Coming as soon as I have breakfasted. Wait a minute! Where is that shotgun I gave you last fall? . . . Yes, the one with the notch in the barrel. . . . To Sam Hardy? . . . Yes, that's all right. . . . Yes, I remember that I told him to get after the woodchuck that was eating the lettuce. . . . No, no, I don't want it. Get the gang at work on the Allen place as soon as possible. Good-bye."

He thoughtfully replaced the receiver, thoughtfully examined the gun on his desk. It had been on top of the wreckage Daphne Tennant had brought crashing about her. It must have been outside the lean-to when it fell. There could be no mistaking it. He had given it to Tim.

Tim had loaned it to Hardy. There was the notch Tim had cut when he brought down his first bird. Had Hardy left it in the lean-to, the shotgun would have been under the debris, not on top.

As he changed to riding clothes his thoughts kept busy with the tangle. No sooner would he extricate one end of the mystery than it would be lost in a hard knot. Hardy's story of his unjust imprisonment had enlisted his sympathy, but—all signs pointed to him as the peach and apple thief. Hadn't he been living at the old Allen place? Why should he want the fruit? Presumably he had left the village on Saturday. Had he lost his courage about carrying off the apples? Why had Daphne been there? How came the gun in her possession? Hardy might have left it outside—Nonsense! Daphne had said,

"Give me my gun!"

As he entered the hall he heard voices in the breakfast room. He was late. Rose Grahame ran down the stairs. She took the last two steps at a jump. She caught the lapels of his coat and administered an indignant shake. Her voice was husky, two deep pink spots burned in her cheeks as she demanded:

"Tony, what do you mean by bringing Daphne here to breakfast? Were you at home at all last night? I wanted to tell you something, something that Peter and I suspect about Nap Long, and I waited and listened for you to come until toward morning I fell asleep curled up in the big chair by my window. When I started out for my ride the door of your room was wide open. Then I knew that you hadn't come in at all." She stopped to draw a ragged breath. "You—you haven't gone and eloped with Daphne, have you, Tony?"

She hid her eyes against his coat. Anthony clenched his hands behind him. If she didn't move her head quickly he'd wreck every chance he had of winning her. His voice shook, not entirely with laughter, as he echoed:

"Eloped! My darling—girl, look at me." He lifted her chin as he accused:

"Rose, I have before suspected you of having a scenario-complex. Now I'm sure of it. Confess! You are writing for the movies. Nothing else will account for that hectic suspicion. I ask you, if I wanted to—if Daphne wanted to marry me—why should we elope?"

The color stole back into the girl's face.

"You gave me an awful shock, Tony. Of course you'll marry some day, but—if you weren't eloping, where did you come across her?"—She nodded in the direction of the breakfast room from which came Daphne's rather high-pitched voice.

"At the old Allen place. She was out for birds."

"For birds! With a camera?"

"With a gun."

"A gun! She can't shoot. Mark told me that he took her once and he almost lost his mind at her stupidity. Tony, you and Eddie Timmins are getting too mysterious for words. If you don't want to tell the truth at least you needn't fib. Come on. I'm starving."

## Chapter IX

THE Town Hall was filled when Claire Grahame entered. The leading feminist in the community—she didn't call herself a feminist, but what's in a name—had telephoned her a few days before:

"A subject of vital interest to every woman voter is to be discussed. We need you."

Judging by the expressions of the women about her they were as much in the dark as was she as to what the summons meant. They stiffened to attention as the Chairman of the meeting stepped forward on the platform. She was smartly attired and perfectly groomed, a fact which at once inspired respect in Claire Grahame for her sense of values. She had a bland voice which lagged and speeded until it produced a sense of rhythm. She indulged in no preliminaries but plunged at once into her subject:

"Fellow Townswomen:
We have talked largely about what we would do if we were given equal civic opportunity with our husbands and fathers and brothers and friends of the male persuasion. Our opportunity has come. During the second week of November—little more than fourteen days away—at a special Town Meeting, we are to elect a selectman to fill the vacancy on the Board. We have no intention of maligning or undervaluing the present candidate, but, we feel that he is a too recent resident, in spite of the fact that he lived here until he was nineteen, to know the needs and sympathize with the traditions of our community. He frankly boasts that he will make this a boom town. Do we want a boom town? He will be elected—if he is elected—because no other man has interest enough to make him fight for the office. Why shouldn't we women put forward our own candidate? Why not a selectwoman?"

An instant of hushed silence was followed by a tumult of applause. The speaker proceeded:

"There are numerous phases of town government which require the same careful attention to detail as housekeeping, the same administration of thrift. Most of us women have to consider the dollar. We are trained to that much more than are men. There is criticism of the few women who are filling political offices in the country. Is there any reason why the woman whom we propose couldn't make good? Let's elect her and see that she does make good. If we do nothing else we'll set the political blood of the men to circulating. They are lethargic now. Will they be if we put a woman on the ticket where no woman's name has ever before been printed? Try it and see. No man but one at present will consider the office. No man but one feels that he has time to devote to it. Perhaps all those others haven't the time. They are unused to doing everything there is to be done as is a homemaker. I predict that if you decide this afternoon to support a woman candidate we'll have every male voter on tip-toe to beat her. Fine. A much more healthy condition than the present one. The men may like the woman—as a woman. They may admire her. But—they won't want her in office. A few of us have formed a nominating Committee. We have a candidate to propose. Four generations of her family have been citizens of this town. Always they have stood for the best, for church, for home, for respect for law, for community spirit, as does she. She was educated in our own schools until she went to college. She—I will let her speak for herself. You all know her. Rose Grahame."

Claire could have sworn that the jump of her heart forever dislocated it from its supporting cartilage. Rose? Her Rose? Impossible. Yet, there she was on the platform, flushed, smiling, perfectly poised. She herself, wouldn't have been able to speak her name had she been standing in her daughter's place. Girls were trained now to express themselves in public. Why not when they were being trained also to think on public questions?

Not too hearty applause greeted the candidate's appearance. There was a hint of "We-don't-think-much-of-this-but-we'll-hear-what-you-have-to-say," constraint in the audience. How lovely she was, Claire thought, with tender pride. Who had suggested this to her? Anthony? Never. What would he think? Mark? Of course. He and Rose had seemed inseparable after office hours. She had wondered how Anthony, loving her as he did, had borne it. He had been so sure that he could end the farce with Daphne Tennant. She had heard nothing of a broken engagement there. He had grown thinner and whiter, but, that might be accounted for by the miserable mess into which Nap Long had plunged the business by hiring away the pickers.

Nap Long. Rose out to contest his candidacy! How unwise. But she must listen. Her daughter, her own daughter was speaking. She was charming in her smart little *bois de rose* frock and hat. How well the color suited her. Did she know that her mother was listening? She was unaffected. Undisturbed by the hundreds of eyes gazing up at her, the majority no doubt, with cold appraisal in their depths. Claire bristled maternally. They would be lucky, these critical women, if Rose consented to give time to what undoubtedly would be a losing fight. She must pay attention. She picked up the thread of her daughter's talk:

"Since making the breath-snatching suggestion to your Chairman that we put a woman in office at the Town Meeting in November I have been investigating the duties of the Board. Not too onerous. Not too difficult for a woman. There are many questions coming up for decision in the town. If we women are represented on the Board, won't our opinions and judgment have more weight when it comes to the question of, do we or do we not need more schoolhouses? The children growing up are our greatest asset. We ought to have a zoning law. There are permits to be granted for new streets, let's see to it that they are fairly distributed. If I am elected I shall recommend and urge that the Board sponsor a Budget exhibition so that the townspeople may know how every cent of the money they pay in taxes is spent. I saw one in New York. It was fascinating. Every department supported by the city's money was represented and illustrated, every slightest detail was listed and explained. We aren't New York but we spend money. Why not know how much and why our town housekeeping costs as it does?"

The girl's dimples flashed as she added:

"In the bright lexicon of youth there's no such word as 'fail,' but, if there has to be in ours, if we go down to defeat, I predict that it will be because we have stirred up the male political pot until it has boiled over. Never again shall we hear the excuse, 'I haven't the time.' "

The applause was soul-satisfying. Continuous. Woman turned to woman, eyes snapping, cheeks excitement red. Claire Grahame knew how a hen feels when her duckling for the first time swims away. Rose, her Rose, talking with such ease and assurance. Incredible. There could be no doubt but that the female political pot was bubbling lustily. It boiled over into breathless questions:

"Can it be done? Can we elect a woman to such an office in this conservative old New England town?"

Rose had made no mention of her opponent. She had rested her case on the advisability of electing a woman to the Board of Selectmen, not on the merit of Long for the office. What would he do? If he resented the Grahame attitude on the labor and box matters what would he say to this, the girl's mother wondered.

She slipped away before the question came to a vote. She was not needed. She felt as though her traditions and inhibitions had been pulled up by the roots. She would rather not hear comments.

Nicholas Cort was in the living room at White Pillars when she entered. He looked up quickly, expectantly:

"How did it go?" he demanded.

"You knew?"

"Of course. How did it go?"

"Go! The women are wild with approval."

He laid her coat and gloves on the couch.

"Was Rose nervous?"

"Nervous! She doesn't know the first letter of the word. Ring for tea, Nick. I feel as though I had been through an earthquake and had just been dragged out of a crack. Who put Rose up to this? It couldn't have been Anthony?"

"Mark Hamilton, with a few prods from me. It seems that Rose heard Long threaten Anthony. He blustered that if the Grahame outfit didn't hire the labor he recommended and order his boxes, when he was selectman he'd grant himself a permit to build another factory on the land adjoining the White Pillars' boundary—you know we haven't a zoning ordinance in this town—more's the pity."

"Rose spoke of that this afternoon."

"She told Mark of Long's threat and he suggested that she try for the office of which Nap was so sure. She took it as his nonsense at first. Then she remembered that I had made the same suggestion. She came to me to talk it over. I advised her to consult some of the town mothers. She won't win, this time, the men in town won't stand for it, but, she'll stir them up. There will be a man candidate in opposition to Long, the men will realize that the women won't vote for Long now—and he'll win. But, the experience won't hurt Rose. What did you think when she appeared on the platform?"

"I didn't think. I just felt. When the buzzing in my ears subsided I realized that I was as puffed with pride as a turkey gobbler. You know how opposed I have been to women in public life, Nick. I confess that seeing my daughter on that platform did queer things to my prejudices. She was so unaffected, so girlish, so—so altogether charming. She made no attack on her opponent. No apology for her youth. Assumed that they realized her inexperience. It was as though she said:

" 'Here I am to serve you. Take me or leave me. If you nominate me, I promise you my best.'

"Whatever the faults of the younger generation—what younger generation hasn't had them—the girls are being trained to express themselves in public. I should have been stiff with terror had I been in her place. I wonder what Anthony will say."

"Rose did not want him to know until the women had decided either to support or discourage her candidacy. How did they vote?"

"Vote? I don't know. I didn't stay for that. I was in such a state of mental upheaval that after Rose spoke I slipped away. Here she comes. Now we'll know." Too excited to remain seated, she rose as her daughter entered the room. The girl was flushed and smiling and noticeably excited. Her eyes were anxious as she asked:

"Mother, I saw you go out. Were you disgusted?"

"No, dear, no. Tremendously surprised but proud, very proud of my daughter. I didn't wait. I was too thrilled to talk with anyone. How did the vote go?"

"Unanimous to support my candidacy. This is only the beginning. I'll have to work to make good."

"Won't it be too much with your office work?"

"No, I'll love it. I'm going campaigning evenings and . . ." She broke off the sentence to answer the ring of the telephone:

"Rose Grahame speaking. . . . Of course it's true. Why shouldn't I? . . . Will you? That's showing the proper spirit. . . . Thanks. Good-bye." As she hung up the receiver she answered the question in her mother's eyes:

"One of the girls having tea at the Country Club had just heard the news. She said that they would all back me and . . ."

The telephone bell.

"This is Rose Grahame speaking. . . . Of course it's true. . . . Am glad you think so. . . . No. No! Don't give me a luncheon until I'm elected. Then it will have to be a dinner. I'm a working woman. Thanks lots. Good-bye."

"Polly Carter wants to entertain the new candidate and . . ." She picked up the receiver in answer to a shrill call:

"Rose Grahame speaking. . . . I'll say I am. . . . Why not? . . . Won't I make as good a one as Nap Long? . . . Why didn't you step into the ring? . . . Well, I've made the time. Good-bye."

"Good heavens, is this what my life is to be for the next few weeks." With a little grimace at the telephone she answered the bell:

"Rose Grahame speaking. . . . How are you, Billy? . . . Yes, it's true. . . . You don't like politics for girls. . . . Sorry . . . I'll try not to let it spoil me. . . . Oh, some time. Not tonight . . ." her voice rippled with laughter.

"I shall be busy writing my campaign speech. . . . Good. . . . He's rung off." Rose hung the receiver on the hook. "That was Billy Jarvis and he's furiously opposed to my candidacy. Thinks that it will spoil me for matrimony and . . ."

"Candidacy for what?" demanded Anthony Hamilton from the threshold.

Emotion tugged at Claire Grahame's lips as she regarded him. The lines in his face were tense. His riding leggins were splashed, a tiny dab of mud on one cheekbone accentuated the whiteness of his face. He had been working early and late in the orchards. Had he known how constantly Rose and his brother had been together? Was the knowledge partly responsible for the smoldering passion in his eyes? She herself had told him to move cautiously in his courtship. Had that been wise counsel? Should he have swept the girl into his arms by the ardor of his love? How much should one advise another? Never again would she do it. She watched his eyes as her daughter slipped her arm within his and answered his question:

"Candidacy for selectwoman."

"You!"

She bobbed him the little curtsy of her dancing-school days.

"I. Little Rose Grahame."

"You, in opposition to Nap Long. I won't have it. What does your mother say?"

"Mother approves, don't you, Mummy?"

"Yes. Could you have seen her on the platform, you would have approved, Anthony."

"Well, I don't. It's outrageous for her to get into this mix-up with Long. His threat sent you into it, didn't it?" he demanded.

"At first, Tony. Now I am tremendously interested. I am sure that I can make good in office if I get the chance. Don't scowl at me. Let me take that blotch of mud from your cheek. It makes you look about as friendly as the giant in 'Jack and the Beanstalk.' "

"Don't touch me," he protested and left the room.

Rose looked after him in indignant surprise.

"He needn't have snapped my head off."

Claire Grahame understood.

"Anthony is carrying a tremendous burden, dear. Don't tease him."

"Tease him! Do you think I'd worry Tony for one minute? Tony—wait!"

Her mother saw him slip his arm about the girl's shoulders as she ran up to him in the hall, saw him draw her into the office. She heard Rose's eager voice in explanation before Juno, the cook, pushing the tea-wagon blocked the sound. The woman was as black as a teak-wood god, black as to skin, eye pupils, gown. White as to eyeballs, teeth, hosiery and an enveloping apron.

"M's. Claire. Jup'ter's up yondah dressin' when yo' rung de bell. He'll be runnin' backuds an fawids fer de nex' fifteen minutes tryin' to fin' his clo'es wat he put away hisself. So I come. Whar yo' was all day, Honey-Chile?" she demanded as Rose returned to the room. "Yuh eyes, dey shinin' like lamps. Tell yuh Mammy wat yo's been doin'."

She lingered beside the tea-wagon. Claire Grahame smiled. Juno delighted in serving tea. She and Jupiter knew everyone who came to White Pillars and, she suspected, knew more of their family histories than did she. The servants had two classes into which they pigeonholed humanity, "quality," "no quality." They had a maddening way of being supercilious with family friends and acquaintances of whom they disapproved. But, they were devoted and loyal and, in this age of independent labor, loyalty counted tremendously.

Juno presented plate and cup to Rose.

"Hyar yo' are, Honey-Chile. I mak' dem scones jes' fer yo'. Now yo' tell yuh Mammy whar yo' been."

"Trying to get nominated for selectwoman, Mammy Juno."

"Lawd, yo' don' say, Honey-Chile! Well, I'm a ooman wat b'lieves in de on-comin' of ma sex. Jup'ter an' me say 'twas a shame fo' Gawd dat dat no quality Long boy wat used to bring groceries here from his Pa's store goin' ter be 'lected ter boss dis village. He sure ain't fit to step into de fron' door of dis house."

Rose's eyes danced with laughter.

"I'm glad that you approve, Mammy. Mr. Tony

doesn't," she added as Anthony Hamilton entered the room. Juno bustled over to him with cup and plate.

"Now yo' set righ' dere, Mars Tony. Yo' sho' jes' tired to def. Yo's been workin' an' workin' on dem ole apples all day. Tak' a scone, Honey." She looked about to see that all were served before she left the room. At the door she turned:

"Don' yo' let no pusson d'scourage yo', Honey-Chile." She visibly swelled with importance, " 'Member, yo' Mammy's presiden' ob de Society ob de Folded Han's. I'll stimmalashun dat orga'zashun an' get out every member to Town Meeting. I sho' will."

She began to hum in the hall. As the distance increased between her and the living room her voice floated back melodiously:

> " 'O whah yuh goin' Angel,
> Wid yo' wings all dipped in gol'?
> Gwine down to de rivuh Jurden
> Fo' to res' mah weary soul.' "

Rose laughed as she dropped to the piano bench. Her fingers made a soft rippling accompaniment to the song Juno had been singing as she talked:

"If I have the Society of the Folded Hands behind me I'm elected. Uncle Nick, we'll attend one of their meetings. We'll—what's coming next," she wondered aloud as Jupiter crossed the hall to answer a ring at the front door. Idly, as people will, the four in the living room held their breaths to listen.

"She not at home."

Claire Grahame's eyes sought her daughter's. There were only two "shes" in the house and they were at home. What did Jupiter mean? His voice was insufferably overbearing as he insisted:

"I tell yo', Missy Rose she not at home. W'en yo' come to dis yere house again, Napoleon Bonypart Long, yo' come de bac' do' de way yo' uster. De fron' do's fer quality, I'm tellin' yo'."

Before the listeners could recover from their horrified amazement the door had banged shut and Jupiter was on his way ell-ward muttering to himself. Rose sprang to her feet with a shocked:

"Jupiter!"

Anthony Hamilton's laugh was brittle. He dropped his head to the back of his chair and blew smoke-rings into the air above him.

"After that—the deluge," he misquoted cryptically.

## Chapter X

ROSE in a red-brown frock and coat that were the color of the foliage on the banks dipped her paddle noiselessly into the river. She kept as near the shore as possible without swishing through the brown rushes. Sumac and swamp maple drooped over the water line. Cautiously she turned her head. Far up river she could see a gigantic spider-web which was the bridge. Nearer loomed the dark bulk of the cedar boathouse. Faintly from its interior drifted Rusto's infuriated protest. She had felt as though she were insulting a dearly beloved when she shut him in, but she couldn't have him at her heels this afternoon. For the last few weeks he had dogged her footsteps. Curious that he had transferred his attention from the boys to her. Tony was immersed in business and Peter was away except over week-ends, which facts might account for his devotion.

Saturday again and a half holiday. Less than a week had passed since she had been proclaimed a candidate for selectwoman. Outside of office hours she had made calls, talked at house-meetings. Nicholas Cort had been right in his prophecy. A man candidate had appeared in opposition to her and Long. In fact, six had flung hats into the ring but the six had agreed upon one of their number.

The situation was thrilling. The town was buzzing like a planing mill throwing off chips of conjecture, approbation, advice, discouragement, backbiting, not so much of that, though.

If only Tony were in sympathy with her. He didn't like her candidacy, she knew. For the first time since she had seen them together he had been furiously angry with his brother. As though Mark were responsible for what she did. He had suggested and helped but she had a mind of her own. She had gone into the fray first in an attempt to checkmate Nap Long. Now she was thoroughly imbued with the thought of the service she could render.

At luncheon today Tony had suggested that they two drive somewhere for supper and a dance. He had added:

"We'd better make the most of this September weather in November. The Weather Man warns that there is a curious disturbance due."

Emotion had forced the tears thick in her eyes when he had asked her. It had been ages since they two had been together. He was so changed. Was Daphne responsible? Her mother was still seriously ill but she might manage to see Tony. She shouldn't complain. He would have taken his fiancée this afternoon instead of his sister, had she been available. She had told him that she would be ready at exactly four o'clock. His smile had done curious things to her heart, which fact only went to show how much one could care for a brother, she reasoned.

Would he have smiled had he known her plan? He would have locked her up. Two hours ago the airplane had dropped to the top of Headless Hill. Since Mark had read her the editorial about the bootlegging of aliens, she had been obsessed with the idea that that plane might be on some such business. Tony had made no reference to it since she had confided the suspicion to him. Doubtless he thought that her scenario-complex had grabbed the bit again. But a number of foreigners had applied at the orchard office for work. Had Nap Long sent them?

She had planned to investigate the old wood-path up the Hill. Suppose—just suppose that the airplane and the aliens were one of Napoleon Bonaparte Long's money-making schemes? Silly, to suspect such a thing! Would he dare defy the government? Nap would dare anything. The greater the risk the greater the thrill—and—the greater the punishment if he failed. If she could get proof of his law-breaking, his interference with the Grahame employees, his plan of a box-factory snug against the White Pillars' line would be checked with a smash which would bring the billions of white hot suns—commonly called stars—in the milky way into high visibility for him. As a possible official and citizen she should be concerned because of the breaking of the government's prestige and morale, but, to her shame be it known, her overwhelming purpose was to show up Nap Long.

Silently she paddled into the mouth of a silver creek. She fastened the canoe to an overhanging alder. Neither branch nor twig snapped as she followed a worn trail in company with which the creek curved and vanished and swerved again into sight. She heard the chug of an approaching flivver. She plunged into waist-high bushes. She was nearer than she had supposed to the road which girdled the Hill. She would wait until the car passed before she crossed it to make her way up the rocky trail. Was it stopping? She crouched in a jungle of bushes. Snakes? Ooch! She wriggled. She admonished herself sternly.

"Silly! Whoever saw a snake in November?"

In answer she tucked her feet securely under her skirt. There might be a reptilian keen for the cold-air cure. She consulted her wrist watch. Three o'clock! How the time had flown! She peered through the dusky greenness netted with sunlight and intricate shadow. She held her breath as the chug-chug of the engine obliterated every other sound. The flivver stopped. She could see the top. The driver—could it be—it was! Santa Anna! The butler at La Mancha *sans* his theatrical trappings.

A bird-note! An echo. A signal? Rose had the sensation as of myriad angle-worms looping their stiff-jointed way up her spinal cord with every cylinder hitting. Into what maze had her suspicions pitched her? She remembered the figure which had started up from the shadow on this very road the night of Mrs. Hamilton's dinner. She sat back on her heels and smiled into space. What a night that had been! To have Tony all to herself—there was no one like him—Mark was great fun but he lacked Tony's fineness—never would he whirl with "inimitable dexterity" to face temptation, he'd fall off his horse—a voice?

"*Bueno!* Where's dat . . ."

"*Dios! Pronto!*"

A door banged. The engine picked up. The flivver backed. Turning? Rose dared not move. The hood of the machine nosed into the bushes between her and the road. Would she be crushed? Would she be seen? She didn't dare call a warning. Better take her chance with the wheels than with the men in the car if one of them were a smuggled alien. The flivver backed into the road, advanced on the bushes again at a slightly different angle. Reversed. Advanced. Backed. Chugged off.

She would wait a few moments then make her way to the top of the Hill, Rose decided. She would look around to see what traces of the airplane landing she could see and then race down. It wouldn't take long for her to dress. She would be waiting for Tony promptly at four.

She listened. There was no sound save the soft voice of the sky-pointing pine and the wistful whisper of the silver creek as it glided over stones and moss, through brakes to the terminal green of the river. Her chance.

She climbed rapidly. At the end of the trail she stopped for breath. She had forgotten the extent of the plateau. It was a soft sward, russet-colored now. Hardly a bush broke the level sweep. Had Nap Long reduced it to this tame state for a landing field? At one end was a hangar.

She crossed the pleateau humming as she went. There was something eerie about that closed door. It was like a Jack-in-the-Box from which anything might spring. Silly for her heart to pound. Hadn't she seen the men ride away? She—

The door swung wide. For an instant Rose contemplated flight. No, that would look too much like guilt. She stood quite still as Long appeared in the opening. She was near enough to hear his low exclamation, hear his voice as he flung an order over his shoulder. She hadn't seen him since Jupiter had repulsed him at the door. She was sorry about that. This would be a good time to tell him so.

She could see the ugly set to his mouth, the angry color in his cheeks as he approached her. His Napoleonic lock gave emphasis to his sinister voice as he demanded:

"What are you doing here?"

His manner infuriated her.

"Have you bought this Hill, too?" she inquired suggestively. Then realizing that he had just cause for anger she added:

"I am glad to meet you, Nap. I want to tell you how sorry we are about—about the other night. Jupiter didn't realize that we were at home—that we would have been glad . . ." her apology died away under the fury of his eyes.

"Would you? Queer! As I have reminded you before neither you nor your mother nor Hamilton ever asked me to come."

"I will ask you now. Come to White Pillars sometime."

"Don't worry. I'm coming. Why do you think I came back to this dead town? Why do you think I bought La Mancha. Why do you think I'm putting my time which is worth a dollar a minute into this selectman business?"

He caught her wrist in a grip which crushed. He drew her toward him. She had but an instant to wonder wildly if he had gone suddenly mad when a voice from the hangar called:

"Bus is ready, Mr. Long."

With a low imprecation he dropped her wrist. Rose looked toward the hangar. An airplane was being trundled out. As the machine came to a stop a man dodged back into the building.

"Sam Hardy!"

Rose was unconscious that she had spoken. Long laughed.

"You recognize the last deserter from the Grahame forces, I see. I'll get them all in time. Won't you come for a ride?"

"In the plane? No, I thank you. I have an engagement." She looked at her wrist watch. "I shall be late. I must hurry."

"You haven't told me yet why you came here?"

"To the top of the Hill, do you mean? Oh, just in a spirit of investigation. When I'm selectwoman I want to be thoroughly posted on all public land." Her voice was tinged with mockery.

"When you're selectwoman? My girl . . ."

Hardy came to the door and called:

"You won't make it if you don't start at once, Mr. Long."

"I'm coming. Having made your investigations, I suggest that you keep away from this Hill," Long advised and turned away.

Rose dashed across the field as though pursued by de-

mons, frightened, eager to escape from the stare of those
black eyes. At the opening of the down trail she stopped
for breath. As though hypnotized she turned. Long with
his back toward her was getting into his leather jacket.
Hardy was watching her. He made an imperceptible mo-
tion of his hand for her to go on.

Always she felt as though she had stepped into a cloud
of mystery when she saw Sam Hardy, she thought, as
she picked her way cautiously down the stony trail. Deserter! Tony had believed in him, trusted him. He couldn't
be all bad. Twice he had called when his employer was
becoming decidedly unpleasant. Both times couldn't have
been coincidence. What had Nap meant by his impas-
sioned demand:

"Why do you think I came back to this dead town?
Why do you think I bought La Mancha?"

As though she cared why he had come or why he had
bought the place. If only he would depart again. She
wasn't timid but she hadn't cared for that meeting with
him on the top of Headless Hill. He had boasted that he
would get all the Grahame employees in time. Would he?
Not if her suspicion of that visiting airplane was correct.

She crossed the road and entered the trail which led
to the river. The roar of a propeller, the zoom of a plane
came from above. She listened till the throb of the engine
diminished in the distance. Thank heaven, Nap was out of
the way for the present. She went on. Suddenly she
stopped. Someone was approaching from below. Had she
been seen by the men in the flivver? Had they set a trap for
her? As an excuse for her presence she dropped to her
knees and began to gather reddish-brown oak leaves. She
almost broke her fingers twisting the tough branches.

A snapped twig! She hadn't been mistaken. Someone
was coming. Softly. Very softly. Her heart thumped heav-
ily. How silly to have turned her back to the trail. She'd
better not move now. Nearer. Nearer. If the sinister thing
would only pounce or make some betraying move. Something touched the back of her neck. Something cold. She
tumbled round on her knees.

"Rusto! You old scout! How did you get here?"

She hugged the dog's tawny head, dodged his rough
tongue on her cheek. Quickly she released him.

"You're dripping! Did you swim across the river? Bad boy, not to mind Rose." She hugged him again by way of emphasizing the reproof. "Come on! We'll go. There is no need of caution now."

When they reached the mouth of the creek the dog took his place forward in the canoe. From the stern the girl sent the frail craft ahead with long sure strokes. She hadn't much time to waste. It was four o'clock now and she had told Tony that she would be ready at four. It would be dark soon. How short the days were getting. As she pulled up alongside the float the dog sat like a graven image. His master had trained him to that.

"Out!"

At the sharp command he sprang to the platform. She pulled the canoe to the float before, with Rusto at her heels, she raced toward the house. Juno and Jupiter were in the vegetable garden. The two small black dogs fell upon her with shrill yelps of welcome.

"Down, boys! Down! Juno . . ."

The black woman braced her hands on her capacious hips.

"Wat yo' mean, Honey-Chile, bein' so late? Hyah Mars Tony he bin runnin' roun' dis house backuds an' fawids fer de las' fifteen minutes tryin' fin' where yo' is?"

"Where is he now?"

"Wat I'm tellin' yo'. He wen' up yondah to de Club. Thought yo' might have made a mistake an' think he tole yo' to meet him dere. Mus' think yo' a little girl. I tole Jup'ter ma Honey-Chile could be late if she wanted. Ain't yo' free, w'ite an' twenty-one? Dat's wat Peter says w'en I tells him to keep out der cookie-jar. Whar yo' been? Yo' look like yo' gwine to sprout wid all dem dry leaves stickin' out."

"I'm a sight, Mammy Juno. I'm terribly late. Come and help me. Jupiter, look after Rusto. You know he's been running away."

In her own room Rose pulled off her coat and soft hat and flung them to the bed.

"Get out my rose-color georgette, Mammy, and my big black hat. The coat with the gray fur collar and cuffs," she directed as she slipped out of her frock.

Juno bent to straighten the large hooked rug on the old

pine floor as she grunted assent. She stopped on her way
to the closet and, with arms akimbo, surveyed the gilt
and crystal clock on the mantel. Rose's eyes followed hers
for an instant. Juno was rigid with admiration before the
timepiece which was to Rose always like a false note in
a musical composition otherwise perfect. Its swinging
pendulum, a great circle of enormous brilliants, was so
out of period among the Windsor chairs and Sheraton
dresser and the mahogany four-poster. A friend of her
mother had willed the clock to her and she had kept it
on the mantel because of sentiment.

The colored woman drew a long breath:

"Honey-Chile, yo' jes' ought to tak' dem swingin' di-
'monds off dat ole clock an' wear 'em danglin' on yuh
bosom w'en yo' go to dances. Jes' wasted w'ere dey are.
De res' de ladies dey be 'flicted wid jealousy. Yassen'deed."

Rose, before the mirror patting her black hair into
order, chuckled. She visualized herself arrayed for con-
quest with the rhinestone pendulum dangling as a
pendant. She slipped into her frock to the accompaniment
of the colored woman's croon:

> " 'O whar yuh goin' Angel,
>     Wid yo' wings all dipped in gol'?
> Gwine down to de rivuh Jurden
>     Fo' to res' mah weary soul.' "

"Rose!" shouted a voice from the hall below.

"It's Mr. Tony, Juno. Quick! My hat! My coat! My
bag! Not that one! The beaded bag. That's right. Thanks
lots. Com—ing, Tony! This room looks as though a
cyclone had struck it. Put my things away like an old
dear, will you, Mammy Juno? Com—ing," she called in
answer to another shout.

Half way down the stairs she met Anthony Hamilton
coming up. His eyes were flames. His face was white. He
caught her in his arms.

"Tony! What has happened? Mother? Peter?"

"Where have you been?"

His vehement question, his eyes, sent the blood rioting
through her veins. She put her hand to her heart to still
the curious pounding. Was it Tony looking at her like

that? She shivered. He loosed his hold. His wonderful smile. It stilled the tumult in her heart. It flooded her with a warm sense of security.

"Did I frighten you, dear? You had promised to be here at four. You are never late. I waited and waited. I 'phoned round the neighborhood. Someone said he had seen you on the river. Then—for a minute or two my imagination went mad. That's the trouble with being a prompt person. You are not allowed a moment's latitude. Come on, the roadster's at the door."

As Rose settled into the seat beside him he met her eyes and smiled. She reproached:

"Tony, you said that at last you realized that I had grown up. You take a queer way of showing it."

"Were you trying out the new canoe?"

She smothered a laugh at the assumed impersonality of the question. He was too absurd. Why didn't he admit at once that he wanted to know what she had been doing? His tempestuous "Where have you been?" the expression of his eyes set her body on fire when she thought of them. She thrust the disturbing memory aside as she evaded tormentingly:

"I had business on the river. It took me longer than I thought."

"Business?"

"Business."

He was too absorbed in his diplomatic cross-examination to notice the ripple in the repetition.

"Were you alone?"

The ripple developed into an able-bodied gurgle.

"No—not all the time."

"Who was with you?"

"A gentleman."

"Mark?"

Another ripple. He usually was so cool that she reveled in his evident exasperation.

"Not this afternoon."

"Who?"

The expression in the eyes which looked down into hers tangled her breath. What was this subtle thing which was coming between her and Tony she wondered before she parried:

"A most chivalrous gentleman. Dashing! Romantic! He swam the river to my rescue."

"To your rescue! Rose!"

She maternally patted his hand on the wheel.

"Silly, don't you know when I'm teasing you? For all your dignity and sternness. Tony, you are a boy at times."

"Who was this most chivalrous gentleman?"

"Rusto. I shut him in the boathouse before I started. He must have jumped through the window to follow."

"Will you tell me why you went on the river when you had a date with me?"

His dictorial tone set off a little rocket of temper.

"No, I won't. Just because you are a few years older than I, Tony Hamilton you have no right to cross-examine me as though I were a prisoner in a witness box." She looked at him from the corner of her eye. She laughed as she compromised:

"Now, having disciplined you I will tell you what I discovered. Sam Hardy is working for Nap Long."

"I knew that."

"You did! Why didn't you tell me?"

"How did you find out?"

Rose settled deeper into her seat.

"Listen carefully, Tony, while I relate my afternoon adventure."

# Chapter XI

DUSK was stealing up. A few lights twinkled into brilliance along the road. The red eyes of speeding automobiles ahead suggested a swarm of prehistoric bugs. With a sigh of relaxation Rose Grahame settled back against the deep cushions of Mark Hamilton's luxurious roadster. She felt his eyes on her as he asked:

"Tired? Was the meeting a frost?"

"No-o, but there was no enthusiasm. The women aren't ready to elect a woman for town office, particularly an inexperienced girl like myself."

"Going to call it off?"

"Call it off? I should say not. If I can't beat Nap Long the other candidate will."

"That's the stuff. How is the office work going?"

"Like a breeze. I love it."

"Apples all picked?"

"Yes. The men who remained loyal have worked like Trojans. But anyone would work under Tony. Tomorrow they commence setting out the new orchards at the old Allen place. They will take the trees from the nursery we can look down upon from the office. I shall be tempted to sit at the window and watch. I love to see work going on."

"Let's go somewhere for dinner?"

"I can't. Juno and Jupiter have the evening off to attend the monthly meeting of the Society of the Folded Hands. I always help with the dishes. Don't talk. I want to think over what I said at the meeting or the brillant things I might have said when I answered the questions while they are still fresh in my mind. I'll incorporate those in the next speech."

Absorbed in reflection she settled back in the corner of the broad seat. A startled pheasant flew across the road. The whir of a bird's wings roused her from her revery.

What was that curious sound? She strained her ears. She touched her companion's arm. Unconsciously she lowered her voice to a whisper:

"Stop, Mark! Shut off the engine. Do you hear that sound as of sawing? Isn't it late in the day for that?"

"I hear it. Probably some poor apron-tied devil sneaked off for golf or tennis this afternoon and forgot the wood supply. Friend wife is now applying the thumb screws."

"Perhaps. Listen!"

The rush of the river, a distant motor horn, the shrill of a last optimistic tree toad were the only sounds audible. Even those drifted toward them as though smothered beneath the soft garment of on-stealing night. Rose settled back in the seat again.

"I don't hear it now. Let's go!"

As Mark Hamilton slipped in the clutch he asked with an evident effort to control his voice:

"Rose, will you marry me?"

The girl sat stiffly erect in shocked surprise.

"No! Oh, no!"

"Why?"

"Why—why—I don't love you."

"Any other reason? That's not insurmountable. Haven't I been a model of behavior these last weeks?"

"You have, and oh, how I like and respect you for it. You've made a great fight, Mark."

"You did it. Keep on—make me over."

For a fleeting instant the girl wondered if it were her duty. The tenderness in his voice made it so like Tony's when he said, "Dear," that her heart went out to him. Common sense administered a sharp shake. The reminder crisped her voice as she protested:

"I don't want a man who needs making over. I want a ready-to-be-depended-on man."

"You expect perfection?"

"Don't waste sarcasm on me, Mark. Why should I expect perfection? Haven't I a nice bunch of maddening traits myself? But I do want a man—I really don't want one at all, I'm perfectly content with my brother—who is master of himself, one whose hand I could clutch tight over rough places knowing that his foot wouldn't slip."

"You are an enigma to me, Rose-Pomona."

"That's why I'm so nice," she teased in an effort to swerve the conversation into less emotional channels. He ignored the lure.

"When you are with Tony you are absurdly young and naive for your age. When you're not your ideas are more suited to a woman of fifty."

"Tony won't let me grow up." She remembered Anthony's "My little girl has gone," and amended:

"That is, he wouldn't. I think that my strict attention to business plus my French frocks has made a slight dent in his consciousness."

"I suppose you think that Tony's foot wouldn't slip?" She ignored the bitterness in his voice.

"I know that it wouldn't."

"Then, why don't you marry Tony," Mark Hamilton snapped as he sent the car ahead with a spurt. Rose snatched at her scarf as the breeze lifted it from her shoulders.

"M—Marry Tony?" she repeated indignantly. "I don't care for your brand of humor, Mark. Tony is the same as a brother."

He muttered something under his breath. It sounded like "—my tongue!" She maintained an aloof silence till they reached the porte-cochere at White Pillars. As she looked at the lights in the old house the shocked sense of outrage eased. The windows in one of the lower rooms suddenly flared with light.

"God's in His heaven and Tony's in his office," she paraphrased to herself happily.

The sense of security softened her voice as she held out her hand to the silent man in the car:

"Good-night, Mark. Thank you for bringing me home. I seem always to be sermonetting at you. I'm sorry. Don't think that I don't appreciate your—your asking me to . . ."

"To marry me," supplied Mark Hamilton gravely.

"If I didn't like you very, very much I wouldn't care what you did, would I?"

"I'll turn that 'like' into something warmer. Goodnight."

She watched the red light of the roadster till it disappeared. Mark was mighty sweet-natured not to hate her for her frankness. She just couldn't bear to see him degenerate into a pulpy mass of irresistance without making an effort to rouse him. As she put her hand on the door a soft breeze tapped satin finger-tips on her cheek. She turned. Listened. Curious. Sawing? The wind came from the direction of the nursery next the office building. Could it be possible . . .

With her heart thumping in her throat she dashed into the house. In the hall she collided with Jupiter. He rolled his eyes as he expostulated with the warmth and freedom of long service:

"Chile, I sho' am enjoyin' mah life. Fo' wat yo' go knockin' it outen me? I jes' lightin' de fire in Mars Tony's room an . . ."

"Hasn't he come home yet?"

"I tell yo', Chile, I don't know nothin' 'bout de whare 'bouts of him."

"Where's Mother?"

"M's Claire? She prob'a'ly at one of her Clubs. She don't stop goin' from mornin' till night. Jes' sure she sits down at home somebody comes intuhrup'in' her."

"The moment she comes in, the moment Mr. Tony comes tell them that I've gone to the tree nursery near the office building. Remember!" Rose flung the last word over her shoulder as she ran out of the house. She heard Jupiter's excited protest:

"Chile, don't yo' go alone!"

Alone! Who would go with her, the girl demanded of herself as she ran along the drive. Doubtless her scenario-complex, as Tony called it, was working overtime but there had been something sinister in that sound of sawing. If only Tony . . . Mark's suggestion blazed into her mind. "Why don't you marry Tony? Why don't you marry Tony?" The words kept time with her heart-beats.

She increased speed as though to run away from the rhythmic repetition. The western sky was brilliant with afterglow. In a crimson sea floated magical isles of violet cloud, rifts of lemon yellow, beguiling streamers of rosy pink. The river was a sash of iridescent tinsel with every contributing creek a ribbon of burnished color. The glory steadied the girl's pounding heart. Mark had been too absurd about Tony. Why, why couldn't she force the suggestion from her mind? She had much better think of business or town politics or—or anything else. Had she started out on a fool errand? Who would dare attack the trees? Why should anyone want to?

A roaring young blade of a breeze tugged at her short skirt, snatched at the rose-colored scarf about her throat. The morning weather report had prophesied high winds after sunset, she remembered. They were coming. She crushed her soft hat more firmly on her head. She had no time to chase that. Lucky this blow came after the apples had been picked. Otherwise it would have brought down bushels of good fruit which would have to be sold as windfalls. Orcharding certainly was just one catastrophe after another.

She stopped running as she neared the wind-break which protected the nursery. Barely breathing she stole from the shadow of one tree to another. She stopped under a great spruce, from which she could see the highway. She listened. Except for the soft swish of leaves and branches there was no sound. Evidently she had been suffering from an acute attack of imagination. If she had no one should ever know. Peter would revel in the fact that she had set out single-handed to stalk nursery marauders. Mark had been right. A repentant golf-husband had been cutting firewood for friend wife. She would go home by the road . . .

The sound again. Sawing! Near the river. The young MacIntosh Reds were there. The trees which were to be removed tomorrow. If only she could see. She bent far forward. A gay young breeze whistled with triumph as it snatched the scarf from her shoulders. She took an indignant step in pursuit then shrank back against the ample trunk of the spruce as a full grown wind gave chase to the youngster. Let the scarf go. It might lodge against a tree and then . . . what had happened? Was she dreaming? She brushed her hand across her eyes. She looked again. As the wind swept the nursery alternate trees bent flat before it. They cracked and groaned with protest as they went. What a wind to bend them like that. Why didn't they stand up? Why? Why? *Why?*

The question caught in a strangled sob. Sawed through. Of course. The sound she had heard. Someone had waited for a high wind. Years of Tony's work gone. She choked back a cry of realization. She must not make a sound. Whoever had wrecked the nursery might still be within hearing. Clever crooks! They had left the rows next the highway standing. No one would suspect the devastation beyond. She would steal back to the road, hold up the first automobile she met and get home. Tony and Tim must know at once. There still might be time to catch the vandal.

She took a quick stealthy step forward. She almost lost her balance. Something tightened about her arms. A rope jerked her back against the tree.

Rose heard heavy breathing behind her. She twisted in a vain attempt to see her captor. She opened her lips to remonstrate. Instantly a dirty bandana was drawn across her mouth and chin. Sinister silence! If only the wretch would speak! Give her some clue to his identity!

With a sound which was a cross between a snort and a grunt the presence behind jerked the bandana into another knot.

Had he gone? Rose strained her ears for the sound of footsteps. She bent as far forward as her bonds permitted. Her heart turned turtle. A figure! Among the fallen trees! Creeping! Toward the office. More damage there? If only, if only she could break away!

She twisted her hands, her body. She turned her neck till it ached unbearably from strained muscles. She sagged against the tree. She relaxed for strength to make another try for freedom. Stay here indefinitely with that tree slayer at large? Not if she knew herself.

An automobile! On the highway! Tony's! She knew the sound. She had listened for it often enough. Where was he going? To the office? He and Tim had a way of wandering about the plant after dark. She had teasingly accused him of tucking in his possessions for the night.

She craned her neck. It was Tony's car. She could see the little light on the wheel guard. She tried to call. Nightmare! Couldn't she make him feel her predicament? Thought transference was a joke if she couldn't make the person she loved almost more than anyone in the world realize that she needed him. She shut her eyes tight. She shouted in her mind:

"Tony! Tony! It's Rose calling!"

The car was slowing down! He had heard! He had heard!

"Tony! It's Rose! I need you, Tony!"

Could it be? Yes, the car had started again. She made another frantic effort to reach his spirit across space:

"Tony, dear! Don't go! Oh, *please*—don't go!"

Through tear-drenched eyes the girl saw the small light shoot forward. It disappeared up the road.

# Chapter XII

ANTHONY HAMILTON stopped his roadster at the door of his foreman's cottage.

"Get the men to the nursery early tomorrow, Tim. We must make quick work of setting the trees. Never know when Long will pick off more of our helpers. This is a wicked wind but if the sky is a true prophet it will go down before morning."

"I'll have 'em there early. Trust little Eddie Timmins for that. Routing out my squad was the best thing I did in the army. The apples are picked in spite of Nap Long. Now we'll set the plantations. Don't you worry, Cap'n. It's a pity we had to lose Hardy. Where do you suppose he went?"

"He's probably one of those restless beggars who can't stick to one place. Good-night, Tim."

"Good-night, Cap'n."

"Wiser not to tell him that we are having Hardy watched," Anthony thought as he drove on. When there was sleuthing to be done each interested person who didn't know of it reduced just so much the danger of betrayal. How reckless but how characteristic of Rose to go to Headless Hill to investigate the reason of the landing of the strange airplane. Could there be ground for her suspicion that the alleged Spanish servants at La Mancha were smuggling aliens? It seemed unbelievable but, any more so than that authenticated magazine article? Rose was inclined to suspect Nap Long but, Long wouldn't stoop to that. Why should he? Apparently he had more money than he could spend. He was eager to establish himself socially. He was making headway. Door after door in the town had opened to him. He had seen him leaving the Tennant house. Had he been admitted? What did it mean when Daphne had refused to see the man to whom she had been so eager to become engaged?

Days had passed and he was still caught in the mesh of that entanglement. Into his mind flashed the memory of his defiant reply to Claire Grahame on the night he had discovered that he loved Rose.

"The farce between Daphne and me will end tomorrow," he had declared and she had asked:

"Dear—are you sure?"

"Sure! What could stop me?"

Daphne had stopped him most effectually. Meanwhile Rose and Mark were together constantly out of office hours. Her candidacy for selectwoman made an excellent excuse but was she learning to love him? Her influence would steady him, had already. There was no doubt that he loved her—at present. Should he step aside and let his brother win her if he could?

Never! A right-living man was entitled to the woman he loved if he could get her. Besides, of what enduring stuff were these new resolutions of Mark's? Even if he himself cared for Rose only as a sister he would put up a stiff fight to prevent her marrying his brother, until he had proved his worth. Rose and Mark? No, a thousand times, no.

Had he been weak to allow Daphne to evade him? He could have demanded an interview but, with her mother seriously ill he had bided his time. He could have broken his promise and told Rose the truth but, a promise was a promise, and when he opened the subject with her he wanted to be quite free to say a few things that were in his mind. Of course he was free now but . . .

Was that Daphne ahead? Walking and alone. His chance. His roadster shot along the sunset crimsoned highway and stopped abruptly beside the girl.

"Jump in, Daphne, I'll take you home."

She opened her lips to protest.

"Don't argue. Get in. I want to talk with you."

She shrugged and stepped into the car. He eased in the clutch. As the roadster slid smoothly forward he announced without preamble:

"Daphne, I have told you once before, I tell you again, this farce of an engagement between you and me must end. Now."

"Just a few days longer, Tony."

"Not a day. Not an hour. The deception has been a matter of convenience to you. It has become an immense inconvenience—to express it mildly—to me. I have heard that your mother is much better, that she goes out every day. Tell her that you were mistaken in your feeling for me. Give any reason you like for the break. If I don't hear from you by telephone this evening that you have done so, I shall spread the glad tidings myself before morning. Take your choice."

"And you have the reputation of being a knight errant."

"Where do you get that nonsense? Choose."

"I will tell mother tonight. She will send an announcement to the local paper. Will that be sufficiently final?"

He ignored the bitter question.

"Remember, that if she doesn't, I will."

She maintained a sullen silence. Anthony kept his eyes on the road while his thoughts raced. How real was this illness of Mrs. Tennant's? It might be part of the scheme. Actual or simulated it would no longer influence his life. He was free. Of course he had been really, but, now Rose could know. Why had he allowed himself to make that fool promise not to tell her the truth about the engagement? Why waste a moment on the past? The future was unmortgaged.

He glanced at the girl beside him. Was she still angry? Her face was white. Why talk? What more was there to be said? As he stopped the car in front of her home, through the window he saw her mother, saw Mrs. Tennant's hand resting on the arm of a wing chair beside a table. Often he had seen her sitting like that as he drove by. Daphne's eyes followed his. He sensed her shiver before she stepped to the ground.

"Good-night," she called over her shoulder and ran along the path.

He waited until he heard the door close behind her. As he drove on the village clock struck five. The days were shortening. Thanks to the brilliant afterglow it was still light enough to see distinctly. He would have time to go to the office before he returned to White Pillars. Would Rose be at home this evening? He would cajole her into staying and when that telephone message came from

Daphne it would make an excellent opening for him to
tell the girl he loved the truth about one or two matters.

As he approached the wind-break which sheltered the
young trees in the nursery adjacent to the office he cut
out the engine. Should he take another look at the Mac-
Intosh Reds and Baldwins which Tim had selected for
transplanting? What foolishness! He must begin to let
others take responsibility.

With the decision the car shot ahead. He looked back.
A curious urge that had been to stop. As the packing,
shipping, office plant loomed a dusky blur against a vivid
sky he remembered that he had ordered some special
planting boards. They were to be notched to give greater
distance between the trees. An experiment. He'd better
make sure that they were where Timmins could find them
in the morning. He would want them early.

The afterglow had turned the windows of the building
to burnished brass as he stopped the car before it. His
key grated uncannily in the lock. A flippant breeze
snatched the door from his hand and clanged it shut
behind him. The silence was ghoulish. He fought an impulse to tread softly. He pursed his lips to whistle,
thought better of it and approached his office as though
on moccasined feet. He opened the door. Lingered on the
threshold. Had he heard a curious chatter or was his
imagination tricking him?

As he flung the door wide he tried to fling with it a
smothering sense of mystery. Had the annoyance and anxiety of these last weeks begun to fray nerves which he
had thought were steel? He felt as might a one-eyed man
trying to watch a three-ring circus. As soon as the planting was over he and Mrs. Grahame and Rose would take
a holiday. A trip somewhere to get back his sense of
balance. If . . .

Was that a man at his desk? A head and shoulders
were bent far forward as though searching for something.
With his eyes on the still figure Anthony reached for a
planting board upright against the wall beside him. His
touch sent a bunch of them clattering to the floor. The
sound echoed and reechoed through the building. The
figure at the desk remained still. Uncannily still. Unconsciously he shivered. Chills. Millions of them cavort-

ing up and down his spine. He clutched the board and crossed the room. He gripped the shoulder of the man huddled over the desk.

"What are you doing here?"

No response. Not so much as a quiver of the muscles under his hand. The portions of a man's cheek and neck visible were crimsoned by the afterglow. One blood-red hand gripped the telephone base. The hair on the back of the head was matted where a blow had been struck. Who was it? One of his men or a stranger? With gentle force Anthony drew the bent figure back against the chair. The head rolled weakly.

"Sam Hardy!"

The shocked exclamation bounded and bounced into space.

"Sam Hardy!" the walls echoed. The corridor outside picked up the name:

"Sam Hardy! Sam Hardy!"

Anthony laid his hand over the man's heart. It was beating! Feebly. But it was beating. Carefully he lowered the bruised head to the out-flung arm. He picked up the telephone instrument on the other desk. As he waited for an answer to his call his mind reacted to normal. What had brought Hardy back to the plant? How had he entered? He must have retained the key he had while employed on the place. Tim had been asleep at the switch not to have asked for it when he paid off the man.

Suppose Timmins were not at his cottage? He must be. He hadn't had time to get his supper since he had left him at his door. Good Lord, but the operator was slow! Anthony Hamilton's eyes roamed about the room looking for clues to the mystery. They widened in startled unbelief. Was that a monkey on top the filing-case or was it another phase of nightmare?

The creature was real. It was the very monkey which had made the spectacular raid upon the living room at White Pillars, the monkey who, he was convinced had left the red-ink warning. He was here with Sam Hardy! Had Hardy sent that sketch of the lopped rose-bush? He couldn't be mistaken. There couldn't be two poilu caps like that. The tri-colored cockade tipped profligately over one ear, a large red apple was gripped tightly in two scrawny, long-nailed claws. As the creature's snapping eyes met those of the man watching him he dropped the fruit. His face wrinkled into grotesquerie like an India rubber mask in the hands of a small boy. He looked as though he were about to burst into tears. He whimpered like a senile old person as he looked toward the man huddled at the desk. Anthony spoke to him, glad of an excuse to break the uncanny stillness in the room.

"How the dickens did you get here? Were you a party to or a witness of the assualt? Either way we'll keep you prisoner till . . . Tim?" Eagerly he answered the voice at the other end of the wire. "Thank the Lord! Come to the office in the storage plant at once. . . . Never mind what's up! . . . Bring the Ford truck. Put on the curtains before you start. . . . Don't stop to ask questions. Come!"

As he hung up the receiver Anthony thoughtfully regarded the motionless figure at the desk. The afterglow had turned to dusky pink. Better not light up. Hardy's assailant might be in hiding in the building. The first thing to be done was to get the injured man where he could be cared for. White Pillars? Yes. If his whereabouts were kept secret the reason of the attack and the identity of the assailant could be more easily investigated. Could Hardy satisfactorily explain his presence here in the office? In spite of the evidence piling up against the man he still liked and believed in him, Anthony assured himself stubbornly.

With tender skill he lifted the inert figure and laid it flat on the floor. The stiff lips moved. He bent his head to catch the faint whisper:

"That's better!"

The murmur reached the monkey. Chattering, shivering, he swung down from the filing-case. Impatiently he yanked his cap into place before he ran along the floor with his curled tail dragging. He wriggled his body under the stiff arm and with a whimper laid his head against the injured man's breast. Hamilton was conscious of an uncomfortable constriction of the throat.

"So-o, you're Hardy's buddy, are you?"

The beady eyes watched him as he filled a glass with water from the cooler. Would the beast attack him if he touched his master, he wondered? He carefully lifted

Hardy till his head rested against his shoulder and put
the glass to his lips. But the monkey only looked on with
a ludicrous expression of concern wrinkling his century-old
face. The man touched his lips to the glass. His face
turned gray.

"Down—quick!"

Anthony rubbed his wrists till the deadly pallor passed.
As a faint tinge of color stole into his lips Hardy whispered with strained effort:

"Get rid—of—the monk. Turn—him—loose."

His head dropped back. With eyes on the prostrate
figure Anthony picked up the telephone. It seemed as
though he waited an eternity before an answer came to
his call:

"Judge Cort? This is Hamilton—Anthony. Get Doctor
Carter to White Pillars . . . No. *No,* nothing wrong with the
family. Wait for Timmins and me at the side door. Get
everybody out of the way if you can. . . . No, don't
let Jupiter know. He'll be easy to dodge. He and Juno
are going out this evening, they'll be too absorbed rush-
ing dinner ahead to notice anything outside the kitchen
and dining room. . . . All right. Good-bye."

"Thank heaven for Nicholas Cort," he murmured as
he hung the receiver on the hook. He must have had one
horrible moment when he thought that one of the Grahames was ill or injured. He had believed in Hardy. What
would he think when he learned that the man had been
investigating his late employer's desk, in the dusk, after
office hours?

"For the love of Mike, Cap'n! Whosis?" whispered
Timmins at the door. As he dropped to his knees beside
the still figure and slipped his hand under the injured
man's shirt the monkey sprang to the top of the typewriter.

"Where'd you find Hardy?"

"Bent over my desk. We must get him away."

"Why didn't you send for the hospital ambulance?"

"We'll take him to White Pillars."

"You're crazy, Cap'n."

"I think not. Hardy was attacked here. If the victim
suddenly and mysteriously disappears the assailant . . ."

"Will go nutty with anxiety to know what's become of him! I get you."

"And unless I miss my guess, at the same time we will get a line on the man who is responsible for the fruit thefts. Is the truck ready?"

"Yes, Cap'n."

"Go down and run my car into the shed. Brace something against the entrance door to hold it open. This wind is raising the dickens. No lights. Someone may be watching."

"What'll we do with the monk?"

"Hardy came to long enough to tell me to let him go. I thought at first I'd keep him for a witness, he looked so infernally human, but we'll turn him loose."

Shutters clattered, beams creaked in the heavy wind. The door of the building crashed shut behind them as they lifted the inert body into the truck. Anthony sat on the floor and eased the bruised head against his arm. Timmins took the wheel. He whispered into the blackness behind him:

"The monk has beat it down the road. All set?"

"Go on! Drive carefully."

Nicholas Cort was waiting when the truck stopped at the service entrance to White Pillars. With immense effort they carried Hardy to the third floor. Anthony breathed a sigh of relief as he nodded to the doctor. So far so good. He left Timmins in charge. Nicholas Cort followed him into his home office and closed the door.

"What happened, Anthony?"

"The last hour seems a nightmare. I don't know what to make of it. Perhaps you will." Rapidly he told the story.

"You should have turned him over to the authorities. This fight against you is growing."

"I'll buck it without help for a while longer, at least until we get the information we've sent for. Tomorrow I will take *Madre* into my confidence and we'll plan a way to keep Hardy's presence here a secret until we have caught his assailant. Thank heaven she and Rose were in their rooms when we gum-shoed upstairs. They were, weren't they?" he demanded as Nicholas Cort made an inarticulate denial.

"No. Neither of them. Rose has not come home."

"What do you mean? She left the office early to speak at a meeting. Mark took her in his car. My God! He hasn't . . ."

"No. He brought her home safely. Jupiter told me that she dashed down the drive calling over her shoulder:

"Tell them I have gone to the tree nursery near the office building!"

Anthony's face whitened.

"The nursery—Hardy at my desk—trying to telephone —I understand now! What is it, Tim?" he demanded as the door was cautiously opened.

Eddie Timmins held out a rose-colored scarf.

"I found this jammed in Hardy's pocket, Cap'n."

# Chapter XIII

ANTHONY stared at the filmy bit of color in his foreman's hand. He made a desperate effort to pull himself together. For an instant no sound but the sputter and snap of logs in the broad fireplace broke the silence. Then he commanded:

"Tim, find Rusto! Cort, see that no one gets in touch with Hardy. Keep the doctor here if you have to tie him. Tell *Madre* . . ."

"Tell Mother! Mother's dining at the Club," announced Peter Grahame mysteriously from the threshold. "It will knock your teeth in when I tell you with whom. Mr. Napoleon Bonaparte Long."

"Long!"

Cort and Hamilton echoed the name in characteristic tones of unbelief.

"The same. Mother was being paged at the Club and I answered for her. Nap's a smooth geezer. First he palavered with a lot of apologies about it's being five— as though every clock in the house wasn't striking at that minute—then he explained that he had just been notified that he had been elected to the Club. Mrs. Hamilton was to dine with him to celebrate the event and he wanted Mrs. Grahame to join them. For a minute his nerve knocked my thinker into a cocked hat—then, just as I was about to roar: 'No, she won't!' up came mother and . . ."

"She accepted?"

"Keep perfectly cool, Tony. She did. Asked me to tell Rose . . ."

"Rose! Good Lord, why are we wasting time here! Tim, we'll start after her . . ."

"No need of that, Tony. She's here."

Not until he heard the girl's voice and saw her in the doorway did Anthony Hamilton realize the extent of his

127

fears for her safety, realize how that red-ink warning popped up like a little demon at every untoward happening. For a moment he was limp with relief. Then he took a quick step forward. His apprehensions had not been without foundation. What had happened to her? Her short fur coat was torn. Hatless! Red welts on her cheeks. Smudges on chin and lips. Her black hair which usually waved close to her head drooped to her shoulders. Hands scratched. Nails broken! Peter was the first to recover from the surprise her appearance created:

"Boy! Rose! You're all dirt!"

"Am I? I thought I was powdered with star-dust. Don't I look as though I had been playing with the angels?" Her satirical voice caught in a choked breath.

Anthony put his arm about her shoulders. His lips were white as he smiled down into her eyes:

"Steady, darling. Who, who is responsible for this?"

"The gentleman didn't give his name."

Peter snickered nervously.

"Attaboy. You're getting yours, Tony."

"Dear . . ."

"Tony—Tony—don't ask me questions—yet. I'm so mad I've got to—cry. I . . ."

She pressed her head close against his shoulder. There was no sound in the room for a moment but the girl's choked sobs. Anthony bent his lips to the soft hair. He tightened his arm about the shaking shoulders:

"Dear," he comforted. "Dear."

"Let her cry it out, Anthony," suggested Nicholas Cort, practically, from his position on the hearth-rug. Rose lifted her head. Tears had made little rivers through the smudges. Anthony smiled at her as he dried her eyes with his handkerchief:

"Better?"

"All right now, Tony. You'll have to admit you haven't seen me cry many times Good heavens, what a sight," she ejaculated as she caught a glimpse of herself in the mirror. She looked around the room. Timmins was stuffing something into his pocket. Nicholas Cort was frowning at her. Peter was dumb with surprise. She laughed as she sank into the big chair near the fire:

"You look as stunned as though a prehistoric monster

had landed from the Lost World. I'm all right now except that I'm perishing for a drink of water."

Peter was off and back with a glass. His eyes were wet as he choked:

"You hold it for her, Tony. To see Rose like this. . . ."

"I'll hold it myself, thank you. I'm perfectly all right. I was breathless when I arrived and so—so furious I couldn't see but now . . ." She drank thirstily. As she returned the glass to Peter she made a wry face:

"Horrors! I forgot. That dirty bandana on my mouth . . ."

"Bandana!" chorused the four men as they closed in about her.

The girl patted the hand gripping her shoulder.

"Get the color back into your face Tony, then I'll tell you what happened. Ugh!" she shivered uncontrollably.

"Wait until you're rested."

"Rested! I'm not tired. I'm furious. Someone has cut down our young trees!"

"Never mind that, dear. Are you hurt?"

"Only in my pride, Tony. You'll accuse me of a scenario-complex this time. But this really happened."

She told of standing on the porch at White Pillars, of her uneasy impression that there was something sinister in the sound of a saw . . . Of the breeze which had snatched her scarf . . . The fire snapped. The wind rattled the vines against the window. When Rose described the figure creeping through the nursery Hamilton's eyes met Timmins'. His lips formed the word,

"Hardy!"

She told of Anthony's stop at the top of the rise. Her effort to broadcast a thought to him. Her sense of frustration when he started on. She leaned her head against his arm as she confessed:

"When you turned away, Tony, for an instant I lost faith in God—in everything."

He laid his hand on her hair:

"And then?"

Rose sat erect. Her eyes sparkled with laughter:

"And then, why then, I caught up Old Gloom, stuffed him in a chest and sat on the lid. Fearless but feminine again. I relaxed. Thought. As I sagged against the tree it

seemed as though the rope which bound my hands slipped.
I moved cautiously. Eureka! It had. Hardly daring to
breathe for fear someone was watching, I waited. I wriggled one hand free. The other. I snatched the dirty thing
from my face. Scrubbed my mouth with nice fresh, clean
earth. Hence, this painted Indian effect."

"How did you get here?"

"I cut across fields, Uncle Nick. I didn't dare go by the
road for fear I might get caught again."

The notes of a Japanese gong chimed musically through
the house. Rose sprang to her feet.

"Dinner? I won't stop to dress. I'll remove the marks of
conflict and be with you before you can say 'Jack Robinson.' "

"Do you feel equal to it?"

"Equal to it! I'm ravenous. Don't treat me as though I
had had a fit of sickness just because I turned sob sister
for a minute, Tony. Where's Mother?"

"Dining at the Club."

"Mother! At the Club. Her men here! *Mirabile dictu!*
She is broadening. I'll be with you in a minute."

The four men watched her as she crossed the hall. Timmins pulled the scarf from his pocket and dropped it to
the desk.

"I'll leave it to you, Cap'n, to find out how that came
in Hardy's pocket."

Peter bristled.

"What's Sam doing with Rose's scarf, Tony?"

"I'll explain later. You'd better go back upstairs, Tim.
I'll bring you some dinner."

As Timmins departed Peter demanded:

"What's the mystery? Why should Tim dine upstairs
and what's happened that you offer to do Jupiter's work?"

"That is part of the explanation."

In the living room after dinner Anthony told Peter of
his experience at the office.

"Boy! Is Hardy much hurt?"

"He will be all right in twenty-four hours. Just a nasty
crack on the head."

"What will you do with him?"

"Keep him a prisoner until he explains what he was

doing at my desk. Undoubtedly the man or men who sawed the trees . . ."

"Then you don't think Hardy did it? You're easy! That scarf in his pocket is evidence against him. It blew away while Rose was under the trees, didn't it?"

"Hardy may have been spying on the vandal. I won't suspect him for that yet. But, I'll keep him here until he tells me just what he's doing in this neighborhood after leaving us because he had to move on."

"Go to it, Tony. Going out tonight?"

"No. Why?"

"You wouldn't like to loan a poor, but hard-working law student your roadster, would you?"

"What's the matter with the flivver?"

"Laws, Mars Tony, ain't dis de night of de meetin' of de Soc'ty ob de Folded Han's?"

Peter mimicked Juno to a tone.

Anthony laughed.

"Take the roadster, I had planned to go for your mother . . ."

Nicholas Cort flung his cigar into the fire.

"I'll bring the lady of the house home, Tony. She knew that I was to dine here. I'd like an explanation of her absence."

As he slipped into his topcoat in the hall Rose came through the door which opened from the ell. Her tone was a blend of laughter and perplexity as she commented:

"Never before has Juno failed to encourage me to wipe all the dishes on her evening off. This time she fairly hustled me out of the china closet with the observation:

" 'A candy-date fo' selectooman hasn't got no bus'ness to be fussin' roun' dishes, no mam.' I wonder what was behind the consideration? They're off. I hear the flivver. Home so early, Uncle Nick?"

"I'm going to the Club for your mother. I can't understand her acceptance of Nap Long's invitation."

"I can. It's just like her. She felt so badly about Jupiter's impertinence that she has gone to make it up to his victim. One of Mother's obsessions is the fear that she may be considered a snob. Between you and me, that fear is just about half of Nap's pull for election. The towns-people remembering what he came from are afraid that they'll be accused of snobbery if they don't elect him."

"How is the battle going?"

"Fairly well. I may be wrong, but I feel some of the women backsliding. Friend husbands are getting in their work. You'll come in with Mother, Uncle Nick, so I won't say good-night. I'll change my gown, Tony, I hate to keep on my out-door clothes in the house—then you and I will have a long, lovely evening together."

Anthony closed the door upon Nicholas Cort and backed against it. He could hear Rose upstairs moving about humming softly. The best little sport in the world. Apparently she was none the worse for the afternoon's experience. Had the red-ink warning been sent to prepare him for just this sort of thing? He and Timmins had done their best to prevent her going anywhere alone. He had taken Mark into his confidence in regard to the sketch of the lopped rose-bush. His brother had insisted that it was a joke but—he had put aside every other interest that he might be free to take the girl wherever she wanted to go.

The mystery of the stolen apples, of the warning, would be, must be cleared up soon. He and Nicholas Cort had had Hardy watched, now they had him where he couldn't get away. The Spanish servants at La Mancha were under expert observation. If they were proved to be law-breakers Long would be involved. If he were discredited he wouldn't remain twenty-four hours in the village. Sometimes the sky cleared suddenly and completely in almost a flash. Perhaps his problems would vanish like that. One would. Daphne was to telephone tonight. He would be free to tell Rose—how should he tell her?

"Tony! Tony!"

The whispered call roused him to a realization that he still leaned against the hall door, still gazed unseeingly at the stairs. He took the steps two at a time. Half way up the girl met him. She had changed to a filmy frock figured with gorgeous pink roses. She was breathless:

"The clock on my mantel has gone!"

"Gone! What do you mean?"

"I mean that it was there before dinner and now it isn't."

"Probably your mother sent it to be cleaned. You are so accustomed to it that you only think you saw it before dinner."

"Could I enter the room without missing that blazing pendulum? It is so out of character with the other furnishings that it jumps at me every time I step over the threshold. Come up and see for yourself."

As they entered the room Rose persisted:

"Could I miss noticing that space on the mantel? The clock and the candlesticks are the only things I have there. Nothing else seems to have been touched."

The room was in exquisite order. The tester, curtains, and valance of snowy net on the four-poster were undisturbed, the candlewick spread was creaseless, the chintz slip-covers on the chair were unwrinkled, the big hooked rug had not been disarranged by so much as an inch.

"You see, Tony, the clock has gone."

"Anything else missing?"

"All my beads and doo-dads are here. I have nothing of value. Orcharding doesn't provide much of a margin for jewelry. Look!"

She emptied a box upon the net befrilled dressing table. Beads in colorful variety, earrings of decorative rather than monetary value, rings—several of them—of the "costume" type, a pin or two. As Anthony glanced down at the array he visualized the Hamilton pearls. With dark, unseeing eyes he watched the girl as she replaced the trinkets. He caught up a ring and slipped it into his waistcoat pocket. His lips flashed into a smile as he explained:

"I'll keep this for the size. Cheer up! Apple prices for this year are higher than ever before. We may be able to squeeze a ring for you out of the profits."

"A ring for me! Tony, I'd love it but—but now that you've spoken of it yourself I'll tell you something. The girls are wondering why you haven't given Daphne a ring. I know that it is none of my business but I just can't bear to have them think that you—you are stingy."

"What does Daphne say about it?"

"I'll have to acknowledge that she's a good sport—about that. It must be horribly embarrassing for her. She says that you have sent for a rare oval stone. She's nicer than I would be, Tony Hamilton, if the man to whom I became engaged didn't care enough to have a ring waiting for me."

So that was the explanation his fiancée *pro tem* was giving, Hamilton thought. With self-control which brought dark color to his temples he refrained from catching Rose in his arms and assuring her that a ring would be waiting for her. He crushed his hands hard in his pockets. He'd keep his promise to Daphne but tomorrow—His sense of approaching freedom was reflected in his voice as he teased:

"I'll give the man to whom you become engaged a tip to have one ready. Let's rummage on the first floor. Your mother may have told Jupiter to take the clock down."

They investigated closets, shelves, even the kitchen, but the clock had disappeared as completely as a vanished dream.

"Curious. We'll have to wait until Mother comes, Tony. She may be able to clear up the mystery. Must you work tonight?"

"I ought to but I won't. I'm drafting a set of laws for state regulation of apple selling. I am to present them at a conference of the New England governors."

"I ought to encourage you to work on them, but I won't. Put out the light. Let's sit in the dark and watch the fire," Rose suggested as she curled up in a corner of the davenport. Anthony complied with her request:

"I had much rather look at you."

"I'm a sight. Tony, you're positively radiant tonight. You twinkle, twinkle. I hate to dim your brilliance but now that my nerves have stopped twanging I think we ought to talk about the trees. What will you do about them?"

"What can I do? You said they were flat to the ground."

"I don't mean that. I mean do something to ferret out the enemy of our orchards. It's the hateful, hectoring sort of thing Nap Long would do, isn't it?"

"No. For a moment I suspected that he was getting back at us for Jupiter's insult the other night and your candidacy for town office. But, it is too obvious a revenge.

By his own admission he buys off his opponents, he doesn't fight them."

"He buys them." The girl's tone and eyes were reflective as she gazed into the fire. "I wonder—I wonder what he will offer me?"

"He will have to begin soon to bargain. How is your candidacy coming on?"

"Sometimes I wonder if it is coming on at all. Juno gave me an idea when she boasted that she could turn the Society of the Folded Hands in my direction. Group leadership. I have heard the theory discussed, now I'm trying it out. Juno and Jupiter are influential in the colored population, the others follow their lead. I am making friends with the daughter of the Italian fruit-dealer, quite a constituency there; I've been calling on the wives of farmers in outlying districts of the town, they are as clannish as any social set; there are three churches here. I have presented our point of view to the leading woman in each."

"Why haven't you told me before what you were doing?"

"Because I know that you disapprove of my trying for the office. Cross-your-heart-an'-hope-to-die, you do, don't you?"

"For you, yes."

"Why for me especially?"

"I am afraid that public life will fascinate you. That you won't want to marry."

"The consistency of man! Last June you were afraid that I would marry before I had seen the world."

"That was when I thought you a little girl."

"And you don't now?" Rose's tone was jubilant.

Shining, kindling, disturbing, his eyes met hers. His voice was low, amused:

"I don't now."

Flame under snow. Lightning slashing a cool sky. Volcanic warning within a green hill. Rose had the smothering sense of life closing in about them—about Tony and herself—shutting out all the world. She sprang to her feet. Quite unconsciously she put one hand to her throat to still the pulse that was beating wildly.

"Tony, you are different tonight. You seem so—so—I can't express it."

"Don't you like me so—so—inexpressible?"

The amused inquiry sent the girl back to the corner of the davenport.

"I love you anyway, Tony, but—but you caught my breath for a moment. What weighty matter was under discussion?" she inquired with attempted insouciance.

"The lure of public life."

"Don't fear it for me. I am immensely interested in this contest. Two men against a girl. If I am elected I will give the town the best there is in me—there is a new idea for bettering conditions here born every minute—but occasionally I slump. The bottom drops out. Am I a quitter?"

"No."

"Why aren't politics more satisfying? Struggle. Battle. Petty personalities. Round and round in a circle."

"You are tired, dear, you have been doing too much."

"Nonsense. I am frightened. I sense election day rumbling forward with the sinister inevitability of a dripping juggernaut. Will it roll me flat?"

The sound of a bell echoed through the quiet house.

"Someone to spoil our talk-fest? You'll have to go to the door, Tony. You and I are all the servants in my mother's house and all the family too," she paraphrased gaily.

She heard him open the front door. Voices in argument. She slipped into the hall. Santa Anna, the butler from La Mancha, blocked the doorway. Beneath his poncho she glimpsed the red of his sash. His dark hair drooped to his brows. Narrowed lids accentuated the glitter of his black eyes. His thin lips bared perfect teeth. He bowed low as he explained his errand.

"I tell *Señor* Hamilton something happen to make my seester, Carmencita, you know her, she parlor-maid at La Mancha—ver' sober. For ver' long time she hav' monkey. Thees mornin' he run away. *Nombre de Dios!* She cry much."

"I repeat, the monkey is not here."

*"Si, Señor.* But Senorita Grahame, she see him p'raps?"

"I have not seen the monkey. Have you inquired in the village?"

"I come here firs'. You tell at dinner at La Mancha how monkey bounced into living room at White Pillars. Tonight, w'en my seester cry, 'He ees los'!' I t'ink of here. He p'raps come again. Yes?"

"He is not here."

"Wal, p'raps eet ees the judgment of God he go. He queer feller. *Adios!*"

His glinting black eyes seemed to rake the hall as he backed out of the doorway. He straightened in rigid surprise.

"W'aal, w'at you know 'bout that?" he demanded.

Rose and Anthony wheeled in the direction his finger pointed. Tobogganing down the banister rail in Peter's most approved style, with his poilu hat dangling over one ear, shot the monkey.

## Chapter XIV

THE MONKEY jerked himself erect on the newel post and pulled off his cap with the red, white and blue cockade. He fumbled in its lining, blinked as though in profound thought, scratched his head and replaced the cap thereon. He settled into unwinking inspection of the trio beforè him.

How had the creature entered the house, Anthony wondered. Tim had turned him loose when they left the office. Had he been with Hardy? Santa Anna was the first of the surprised three to speak:

"*Dios!* An' you say you not know where he ees!"

The man's tone sent the color to Anthony's face.

"I did not know. Take him and get out. Quick!"

But the monkey had views. As the butler stepped toward him he jumped to the floor and dashed into the living room. The top of the old clock. Sanctuary! Anthony Hamilton's voice was edged as he suggested:

"Are you sure that that is your sister's monkey, Santa Anna? He doesn't seem overwhelmingly anxious to go with you."

"It ees Carmencita's monk. *Americano* gif him to her. I do not like heem. That why he not come to me. You not know he ees here? How then he get in? He have *amigo* here—p'raps?"

That last question? Had the man come for the monkey or was he trailing an accomplice? Anthony regarded him thoughtfully as he answered:

"*Amigo* means friend, doesn't it? If you refer to the colored servants, no. They are afraid of him. The monkey won't descend till he's good and ready. We can't poke him off without endangering the clock. You'd better go. We'll coax him down when you are out of sight. I'll have him locked in the garage and you can get him in the morning."

"*Si*. The *muchado* ees right. I go. *Adios*."

Hat sweeping in a low curve he backed out. As the outer door closed Rose breathed a little sigh of relief:

"He is too theatrical to be real, Tony. But, I suppose that is the Latin temperament. To whom does that monkey belong, I wonder."

"I suspect to Sam Hardy who is upstairs. Injured."

"Injured! Upstairs! How did he get there?"

"Tim and I brought him here. I found him at my office unconscious. The monkey was there also."

"At what time?"

"Soon after five."

"You were going to the office then when I tried to make you hear me. Is he alone?"

"Tim is with him."

"I wondered what Eddie Timmins was doing here but I was too engrossed with my own experience to wonder long. Did Sam Hardy saw the trees?"

"I am sure that he did not. When he left our employ he told me that he was after somone who had had him sent to prison to get him out of the way. I know that he went from us to Long, but I still trust him. Santa Anna confided that an American had given the monkey to Carmencita. I am convinced that Hardy was the man. Perhaps he was on the trail of that monkey? Perhaps the creature deserted the girl when he found his former master was in the neighborhood."

"I hated the butler's eyes when he said:

" 'He have *amigo* here, p'raps?' "

"I suspect that Santa Anna was more interested in a missing man than in a missing monkey. Why are we standing here in the hall? Come into the living room."

He drew her with him by an arm across her shoulders. He held her lightly while he snapped on the light.

"Tony, I feel up to my knees in mystery. Every way I turn—" She gripped his hand on her shoulder. She whispered close to his ear:

"L—look!"

She nodded toward the Coromandel screen. As his startled eyes met hers she barely breathed:

"That moved!"

His arm tightened about her shoulders as he watched

the brilliant screen. Drip! Drip! tinkled the fountain. Tick-tock! Tick-tock! intoned the clock. On the top of the old timepiece the monkey chattered with excitement. The screen shivered. Anthony released the girl and motioned toward the hall. She shook her head. She was behind him with the poker as he caught one brilliant panel and jerked it aside. The man and girl stared in unbelief:

"Juno!" they chorused.

The colored woman's face was bleached by fright. Her hands were crossed tightly on her chest in the attitude of prayer. The sash banded low about her ample purple hips was as red as the screen beside her. Anthony stared for a stunned instant before he shouted with laughter. Rose dropped to the couch. Indignation and hysterics fought for supremacy as she demanded:

"Juno, what do you mean by gum-shoeing into the house like this? Why aren't you at the meeting of the Folded Hands?"

The woman's eyes rolled like black and white glassies in action. Her voice spurted in gasps as she answered:

"Chile, I jes' been hu—humiliated to de groun'. Jes' we started doin' Step-on-de-Puppy-tail at the ball dat Jup'ter grabbed holt mah ahm an' made me come home. Jes's though I wan't a good cittazun wif de priv'lidge injoyin' mah own life."

"Jupiter made you come home, Juno?"

"Umph-umph! He did. Comin' home he tried to mak up. Did dat give me cawnsolashun fer bein' ashamed 'fore all dem s'ciety colored folks? He 'sulted me."

Anthony dropped his head on his arm extended on the mantel and shook with laughter. Juno looked at him and sniffed. Rose choked back a giggle. The woman turned on her wrathfully:

"Yuh laff, Honey-Chile. How'd yo' like it w'en yo' all dressed up if yuh own man say to yo' 'fore a room full of folks:

" 'Yo' sinnuh ooman, where'd yo' git dat thing on yuh nec'? Yo' come right back home! Don't yo' go sportin' no jewels dat yo' ain't got no right to. D'ye' think dese people don' know Jupiter can't buy yo' dat? I'm gwine experditious to git dat flivver an' home we go.' "

"Jewels?"

"I jes' took um from yuh room, Honey-Chile. Yo' wouldn't min' yuh ol' Mammy takin' dese, would yo'?" she wheedled, as she removed her clasped hands from her breast. Pendant from her neck on a huge brass chain glittered the clock pendulum of rhinestones.

Anthony laughed immoderately. Rose buried her face in the couch pillows to smother her emotions. The woman regarded her in aggrieved indignation. Scintillating. Rainbow gemmed. The gorgeous circle on her breast rose and fell with each agitated breath. Anthony's voice choked as he demanded:

"Why the dickens did you steal into the house, Juno? Why didn't you come in the back door?"

"We wen' dere. Dat Eddie Timmins he settin' on de steps smokin'. Jup'ter says I bettah not let de fam'ly see me, dey hav' a policeman grab me sho. Dey was someone talkin' at de fron' do'. No light in dis room so I tried de gahden room do'. I thot, Mars Tony, yo' were off cortin' an' mah chile somewhere dancin' her little silver shoes off. All de trouble comes fro' me settin' too much store fer de van'ties of life. All de same, 'twas a shame 'fo' God de way dem folks laffed an' laffed w'en Jup'ter shouted at mah."

Rose emerged from the pillows and wiped her eyes.

"Put the clock back in my room, Juno. Don't try to replace the pendulum. Mr. Tony will do that."

"I tell yo' right now, Chile, I ain' nevuh goin' to touch dat clock no mo' after I get it on yuh mantel piece. How yo' 'spect I evah goin' recover from dis hu-humil-'ashun? All dem pussons at de ball goin' to 'member I was 'cused of ondecen' behayviuh. An' I goin' roun' gettin' votes fer yo', too. I ain' nevuh done a thing but sing de Lawd's praises and cook for M's Claire." She sniffed violently and wiped her eyes. Rose laid a comforting arm about her shoulders and pressed her soft magnolia-tinted cheek against the black one:

"Forget it, Mammy Juno. I don't mind. I'm glad you wore the jew—jewels." She steadied her voice. "They were simply stunning with that purple gown."

"Yo' mah honey-lamb, Chile. Yo' knows quality w'en yo' sees it. I'll go tell dat ole Jup'ter w'at yo' says."

She stalked out like an avenging Nemesis. From the hall

drifted her rich voice, slightly mournful and prophetic as befitted a Nemesis:

> " 'I'm on mah way to heaven
>     An' I don't wan' stop,
> I don' wan' be
>     No stumbelin' block.' "

A door closed. Silence. Rose's voice rippled as she asked:

"Did you ever see any—thing funnier than that pendulum on Juno? Now I know why she wouldn't let me help with the dishes. She wanted to get that clock out." She indulged in a little gust of laughter before she went on: "What a day! I feel as though I had lived a century or two."

"You must be tired. I ought to send you to bed—but—"

"I shouldn't go. Do you want to get rid of me so that you can work?"

"Work! No. I'm expecting a telephone call and then—" he stooped to poke the fire.

"From Daphne? Forgive me, I shouldn't have asked that question but, but I'm troubled about you, Tony. I don't think she's giving you a square deal."

"My dear—girl. If I were to tell you—" A timbre in his voice released a phonograph record in her mind:

"Why don't you marry Tony? Why don't you marry Tony?" It ground on and on. The refrain was suddenly submerged in the sound of ripping branches and a dull thud. Inside a shout, a crash.

"Fo' de Lawd! Mars Tony! Chile!"

Juno avalanched down the stairs. Rose and Anthony met her in the hall. Her eyes rolled. The pendulum blazed. Her chin shook. She pointed to the ceiling; words gurgled forth:

"Man . . . bandit . . . gallery."

Anthony caught her by the shoulder.

"Get your breath. Now. What did you see?"

Juno's breast labored like a ship in a heavy sea.

"I wus jes' goin' to put back de clock, Mars Tony, w'en I heard a soun' on de upper stairs an'—"

"Don't stop to gulp," prodded Rose.

"Lawd, Chile. I jes' got to git mah breaf, isn't I? I saw a shadder creep by yo' do'. I wus jes' carbonized wid fright an' I yelled an' I dropped de clock an'—"

"Tim! Tim!" Anthony shouted and started up the stairs. Eddie Timmins appeared at the ell door.

"Patient's asleep," he advised in a confidential whisper which might have been heard at the storage plant. "Went out for a smoke—" his startled eyes followed Anthony as he disappeared from the upper landing. He was still staring at the spot when his employer ran lightly down the stairs.

"He's gone," he flung over his shoulder and made a spectacular exit from the front door. Timmins followed. After him streaked the monkey.

As the men disappeared Juno drew a long, gratified breath.

"I guess 'twas lucky I took dem di'monds, Chile. Ef I hadn't I wouldn't hev jes' been puttin' de clock back in yuh room an' yo' never would hev known dere wus a thief in de house. Yuh done ketch him, Mars Tony?" she asked breathlessly as Anthony entered the hall. "I jes' cayn't tink ob goin' ter bed wid dat strange pusson roamin' roun', I cayn't."

"He has gone, Juno. Be sure and lock up the back of the house. Good-night."

"I jes' go pick up dat clock first, it didn't break, it jes' crackled," she rolled her eyes apprehensively in the direction of Rose, but the girl was apparently indifferent to the fate of the jeweled timepiece. She had caught the lapel of Hamilton's coat. As the door closed behind the colored woman she demanded:

"Was there a man, Tony?"

He brushed the soft hair back from her brow. What would happen if he kissed her smotheringly, possessively till—the thought set his heart to pounding deafeningly. Was he losing his mind? He put his hands hard in his pockets and smiled down into her troubled eyes:

"Hardy has made his get-away. Out of the hall door to the balcony and down the big tree. We found a broken branch, must have given way and let him down. When

Tim left him upstairs, he was apparently sleeping as peacefully as a baby."

"He couldn't have been as badly hurt as you thought. It looks as though he knew something about the destruction of those young trees. Otherwise why should he run away?"

"Why should he have been at my desk trying to telephone? I am convinced now that that was why he was there. I still believe in him. I suspect also that the Spanish butler was trailing him and not the monkey tonight." He caught both her hands in his. "Let's not talk any more about our problems. I refuse to have this evening clouded."

"There you go again, Tony, every little while you blaze as though you were gorgeously happy."

"I am."

"Why? Have you seen Daphne?" Rose demanded with jealous suspicion.

"Yes. I met her on the road and took her home on my way to the plant."

"Has she anything to do with your happiness?"

"Yes." With a jubilant laugh he pressed his lips to the pink palms of the hands he held. Rose snatched them away and clenched them behind her back.

"You needn't spill your happiness over on me," she protested angrily. Then as she met his eyes tears rushed to hers. She caught the lapels of his coat with both hands and hid her face against his shoulder:

"Don't get married, Tony."

He laid his cheek against her dark hair as he answered with caressing unevenness in his low voice:

"But I want to marry, dear."

Rose twisted away from him. Humiliated, furious with herself she put her hands to her hot cheeks. Because she had clung to him Tony had had to tell her that he wanted to marry Daphne. It was quite time that she went to her room. She started for the stairs. Anthony caught her shoulder:

"Dear—"

The front door opened. The sound of a car speeding away rushed in with a blast of cold air. So also came Claire Grahame. Her eyes sparkled. Her color was high.

Her voice registered excitement repressed as she inquired gaily:

"Why are you two children standing in the hall?"

Rose was grateful for the diversion. She hovered over her mother in the living room. As Anthony took her coat and hat to the hall the girl perched on the arm of the wing-chair opposite the davenport on which Claire Grahame was seated and commanded:

"Lady, step into the witness-box. Why did you accept Nap Long's invitation? Uncle Nick was savage with resentment."

The laughter in her daughter's voice deepened Claire's color.

"He was rather wrought up, wasn't he? He isn't consistent. A few weeks ago he accused me of being narrow. I value his judgment, so, when opportunity presented to step from the beaten track, I stepped. He resents it. But that was only one reason for dining with Nap. I was glad of the chance to atone in some degree for Jupiter's inexcusable rudeness the other night."

"Did you enjoy the evening?"

"Your voice is horrified, Rose. I did. Nap is crude in many ways but he has had interesting experiences and he knows how to relate them. He's pompous, arrogant, as moneyed men with no background sometimes are, but, he appeared to excellent advantage as a host."

"Did he say anything about my candidacy?"

"He said that you and he would have to get together before Town Meeting. That he had a proposition to make to you. He was casual, and slightly amused."

"Oh, he was? I suppose it's a proposition to buy me off. He won't be so amused next week," prophesied the girl wrathfully. "Did people at the Club speak to him?"

"Our table was surrounded most of the time. Your mother has a train of admirers, Anthony. All the Club beaux hovered over her. She is two years older than I. I kept her pace fairly well tonight."

Her eyes were brilliant with laughter. Her zest for life, her glowing charm made one realize that youth was not the greatest of woman's attractions, Rose thought for the first time in her young life. No wonder that Nicholas Cort loved her. She regarded her mother with puzzled eyes as she queried:

"Do you care about being attractive?"

"Care! Of course I care. Do you think that I don't care for lovely frocks? That I don't care when a man's eyes flash into interest when he looks at me? When I cease to care the real me will be gone though this body of mine lives on."

"Mother!"

"Don't be frightened, dear. I shan't bob my hair. I shan't acquire the cigarette habit. I just refuse to be considered a back-number by—by anybody. That's all."

She was all motherly concern as she looked at her daughter.

"Nicholas told me that you had had an adventure. My mind was full of it as I entered but something started me on that rebellious tirade. Come and tell your gay old mother what happened?"

"My gay young mother, you mean. I feel in the sere and yellow leaf when I look at you. Don't you, Tony? This afternoon—Peter, what's happened now?" Rose demanded as her brother appeared at the door. His face was white. His usually smooth and shining hair was ruffled. His eyes were abnormally large as he echoed:

"Happened! Boy!"

Anthony caught his shoulder.

"Steady, Peter. You are frightening your mother. Get your breath."

"You'll have it knocked out of you when I tell you. Mrs. Tennant is—has gone."

"Gone!"

"Dead!"

"Peter!"

"When Daphne went home this afternoon she saw her mother sitting in the big chair as usual—that's her story —when she went up to her she was as lifeless as a stone Buddha."

"At what time?"

"It was half-past five when she roused the neighborhood."

"I left her at her gate at a little before five."

"Better not make any statements yet, Tony."

"What do you mean?"

"I've been trying to break it to you gently. They think some one chloroformed her."

"Peter!"

"That's the talk in the village, Mother."

Mrs. Grahame started to her feet.

"Poor little Daphne! She must be terrified. Anthony, we must go to her at once."

Peter looked from one to the other.

"You'd better. You see—they think she did it."

# Chapter XV

ROSE GRAHAME stood at the window of the loggia at La Mancha looking down upon the river. A fine rain was falling. Not a cheerful outlook. Unconsciously she clutched the tawny ear of Rusto who sat on his haunches beside her. She had not intended to bring him in but he had bared his teeth and growled with such abandon at the servant who had appeared to take her sedan to the garage that she had not dared leave him. She spoke to the dog:

"Tony made me promise not to drive about the country without you, Rusto, but I doubt if he intended me to take you to tea. Remember, at parties you are expected to behave like a gentleman. You are not to growl at the butler as though you were about to detach a nice, juicy cutlet from his leg."

She glanced about the loggia. What atoms she and Rusto seemed beneath the vaulted blue ceiling. The coffee-colored stone floor with its black marble squares suggested a gigantic chessboard. A depressing place because of its immensity in spite of the gay furniture.

Had there been a sinister glitter in the butler's eyes when he admitted her? He had waited while the maid had taken her coat. Almost as though he distrusted the girl in the fanciful costume. Perhaps she had imagined it. Why should Santa Anna's eyes glitter when he looked at her? Did he think that she and Tony had deliberately tried to conceal the fact of the presence of the monkey at White Pillars? How he disliked Rusto! He had kept one wary eye on the dog who had growled an accompaniment to their progress through the great hall. The growl might have been inspired by Santa Anna, possibly by the symphony from the radio in one of the ornate balconies. Rusto always felt called upon to broadcast his voice when he heard music.

Not a week had passed since the tragedy at the Tennants' yet it seemed aeons ago. For a few days the village had seethed with excitement. It was quieting down now. Poor Daphne! Wasn't it hard enough to lose her mother without being suspected of harming her? Why should she break open a locked drawer in Mrs. Tennants's room and rifle it? She had had numberless opportunities to search it had she wanted them. But the difficulty lay in the fact that the neighbor to whom the girl had rushed for help had admitted under cross-examination that Daphne had kept saying over and over:

"I'm glad I did it! I'm glad I did it!"

Incontrovertible evidence it would be to many but Nicholas Cort was attorney for the county and he had insisted upon handling the case in his own way. Apparently his way was to allow Daphne to go on as though nothing had happened, to prepare to administer her mother's estate.

Tony had testified that he had left her at the gate a little before five o'clock. She herself could confirm that. Hadn't she seen him on the way to his office? She had reason to remember. She had been trussed to a tree with that dirty old bandana over her mouth as she counted the strokes. One more anxiety for her solitary horseman. Why, oh why, did he have to get engaged?

Her face scorched. Why did she still ask that question after Tony had told her that he wanted to be married? She burned up from embarrassment every time she thought of his answer. She forced her attention to her surroundings.

All this gorgeousness belonged to Nap Long. Unbelievable when one remembered the ragged, dirty, overgrown boy who had been the pest and tormentor of the younger children. He had been extraordinarily clever in school. He had led all his classes. Where had he acquired his surface polish? He had lived in his sordid home until he was nearly nineteen. One never could tell till the polls closed but it seemed as though the keen edge of community interest in his campaign for selectman had been dulled. He had told her mother that he had a proposition to make to his opponent. He would better hurry. Town Meeting would be day after tomorrow.

Rusto thrust his cold nose into her hand. She smiled down at him. He appeared inexpressibly bored. He wasn't the only one who hated being at La Mancha. Why had Mrs. Hamilton sent for her? To question her about Tony and Daphne? She had nothing to tell. The day of the sad occurrence at the Tennants' had been a hectic day for herself. The incident which led to the flight to the nursery was burned into her mind. The burning process had commenced earlier than that. When Mark had said:

"Then why don't you marry Tony?"

If only she could forget that absurd question. It seemed indecent that it whisked in and out of her mind continually. Tony would be furious with his brother if he knew of the suggestion. The words flared like an electric light sign whenever her eyes met his. She was becoming absurdly self-conscious when she was with him. She would avoid him until the memory faded.

Mark was a problem. The moment one grew up life presented one hard nut after another to crack. A smile tugged at her lips. Wouldn't he resent being compared to a nut? The laughter left her eyes. Mark was worth liking. He had stopped doing the thing she so hated. He had been a tower of strength since she had stepped into the political arena. He had helped, scolded, bantered, encouraged her. If she detested some of his ideas gleaned while living in an older civilization she liked one of them. He did not judge a woman by her age but by her intellect and attractiveness. He was as charming and attentive to her mother as he was to her. So was Tony. But—Tony was one in a million.

All roads led back to him. Absurd to plan to avoid him. She rarely saw him. The shortage of labor and untrained helpers kept him in the orchards or in the shipping house from early morning until late. The rest of the time he probably devoted to Daphne. These last two days he had been in New York. She hadn't talked with him since the night Juno had appeared with the blazing pendulum swinging from her neck. How he had laughed. He had fairly shouted. Rose laughed aloud at the memory. Rusto sympathized with a bark and rubbed his cold nose against her wrist.

"Tell me what you find so amusing, Miss Grahame.

Anything to brighten this gloomy day. How I loathe your New England weather," complained Flora Hamilton as she approached.

She extended her hand in languid greeting and waved a long green enameled cigarette holder in the direction of a capacious chair. The light from curious lanterns overhead softened her hard eyes. Her frock shimmered into bronze and green as she moved. "Serpent!" the girl thought before she answered:

"I was laughing at the memory of something our funny old cook did. It wouldn't interest you. Thank you, I don't smoke. Rusto, be still!" she commanded as the dog growled at the butler who entered, attended by a red-sashed supernumerary laden with tea-paraphernalia.

"My appologies for bringing Rusto, Mrs. Hamilton, but he seemed so unfriendly that I didn't dare have him go to the garage. I have promised Tony that I won't drive about these country roads without him."

Did Santa Anna prick up his ears or was her scenario-complex getting busy again, Rose wondered. He seemed unduly solicitous about the arrangement of the great silver tray.

"A wise precaution these hectic days. Santa Anna, we will serve ourselves." As the servants backed out of the room Flora Hamilton observed crisply:

"Mark says that you are one of the most direct persons he ever knew, Miss Grahame, so I will proceed at once with my reason for asking you to come this afternoon. I want Anthony."

Surprise and indefinable fear sent Rose's heart to her throat. In spite of its pounding she bit experimentally into a curious concoction of Spanish peppers and anchovy sandwiched between crisp golden-brown wafers of toast before she inquired:

"Why send for me?"

"Because you can help, if you will. First, I want to get him away from Daphne Tennant. Surely you agree with me in thinking that a most unsuitable engagement."

"Does my opinion count? Poor Daphne!"

"It would be just like Tony to marry her at once thinking that he could help her better that way. He would fling

himself and his future into the breach as he did ten years
ago."

"Now what do you mean by that?" Rose wondered as
she caught the glint of green eyes under drooping lids.
Had she referred to Tony's coming to White Pillars as
manager? Why speak of it as though it were tinged with
mystery? The girl looked down at the black and orange
squares in the floor which she had compared to a gigantic
chessboard. Was Mrs. Hamilton attempting to use her as
a pawn?

"You know your own son well enough to realize that
neither I nor anyone else can influence him against what
he considers right."

"He's quixotic. We offered your mother money. Why
should he give himself? Why support her family all these
years?"

"Offered Mother money? Support our family? What
do you mean?"

"Sit down, Miss Grahame . . ."

"I won't sit down. Go on!"

"As you like. It seems unbelievable that you do not
know why Anthony took on the management of the Grahame orchards, why he was as wax in the grip of his
conscience."

Curt. Caustic. Cold. She related the events of a decade
before. Rose clenched her hands behind her. She thought
that she had loved Tony before—now, there was no one
like him in all the world. Why—why couldn't he have
begun life with a real mother? Flora Hamilton's voice
tightened as she ended her recital with the observation:

"I hope that you agree with me when I claim that he
has paid his debt to the Grahames. Because your brother
Peter has chosen to study law instead of orcharding is no
reason why Anthony should continue to bury himself in
this country village, continue to slave over those trees. I
am going back to France and I want him to go with me,"
and then, as though for full measure, she added:

"It is a wonder to me that he has not felt it his duty
to marry you. It would be so like him."

Rose whitened. Flushed an angry crimson. She drew on
her gloves, as she replied crisply:

"Tony is—Tony. No one can decide for him. Why

should he want to go with you? What have you ever done to make him love you? As to feeling it his duty to marry me—come, Rusto. Good-night."

She had had to make that abrupt departure, she told herself, as she ran down the short stairs with their fine *reja* into the great hall. The dark-eyed maid appeared as by magic with her coat. A scarlet-sashed man-servant materialized from nowhere. He swung open the massive grilled door. Rose went out, her mind in a tumult. Her car was at the door. Perfection of service. Everything functioned as by magic. There was a suggestion of sleet in the fine mist. She didn't wonder that Mrs. Hamilton objected to this weather. Lucky she had taken the sedan.

With Rusto's long nose resting on her shoulder Rose drove on. Her thoughts were in a ferment. Mrs. Hamilton's bitter suggestion went on and on in her mind:

"It is a wonder to me he has not felt it his duty to marry you."

She set her teeth in her lips until she winced from pain. She would not think of that, she would not. Had there been any truth in Mrs. Hamilton's explanation of the coming of Tony to White Pillars? He had told her that his heart had been skinned alive. Had he paid her mother money? Had he supported her family all these years? It wasn't true. It wasn't. She must know the facts. Who would tell her? Her mother? Why pull her heart up by the roots by reviving the old agony? To whom could she go for the truth? Not Tony, she couldn't talk with him about it. Nicholas Cort? Why hadn't she thought of him first?

With a stern admonition to Rusto to be quiet she parked her car at the side of the drive of the old Cort mansion. A motorcycle was half hidden among the skeleton vines at the side door which she and Peter used when they came to see the man who had been as tender as a father with them. A client perhaps. Although he had retired from practise, the Judge, as everyone called him, though he wasn't a judge at all, occasionally took cases. She rang at the front door. A Japanese man answered.

"Good-afternoon, Toto. Is Mr. Cort busy?"

The servant beamed till his yellow skin crackled like parchment. He ducked his head with a funny little bow:

"Come in, Mees Grahame. His Excellency feverishly return from departure an hour before."

Rose smothered a laugh as she followed him down a long hall. Toto strung words on a sentence as he might string a motley lot of beads without regard to size or appropriateness. He knocked deferentially at the library door. There was a moment of silence, the indeterminate sound as of a door closing softly on the other side of the barrier, before a gruff voice inquired:

"Who is it?"

"It is I, Uncle Nick."

Nicholas Cort flung open the door.

"My dear child. Come in."

Had she interrupted a conference, the girl wondered, as she entered the lofty-ceilinged, book-lined, book-stacked room. The air was heavy with tobacco smoke and impalpably heavy with significance. A heaped-up ash tray rested on the arm of the deep chair Nicholas Cort usually occupied. The fine lines about his eyes crinkled into a smile as he held out his hand:

"This seems like old times when you and Peter used this as a confessional when you had been naughty. What has happened?" he demanded as the excitement she had been restraining caught at her breath in a sob.

The smile which shone through her tears was like the shining of sun through rain.

"Nothing has happened, Uncle Nick. I—I was told a story today. I can trust you to tell me if it is true. Why did Tony come to us ten years ago?"

"Don't you know?"

"I didn't. I have been an ostrich. I realize now that I suspected something out of the ordinary but—I didn't want to know. I dug my head into the sand if anyone approached the subject."

"Then why—now?"

"Mrs. Hamilton sent for me today. She told me. I want your version."

Nicholas Cort flung the contents of the laden ashtray into the fire. He patted the back of the deep chair:

"Sit here."

Rose perched on the broad arm of it and shook her head:

"No. I should be lost in it. Go on. Please."

With hands clenched in her lap she listened while Nicholas Cort gave her unvarnished facts. She looked up through wet lashes:

"Dear mother. What a soldier she has been."

"She has been a wonder. She has hoped that you and Peter would never know how David went. She has faced difficulties—and they've been legion—with head up and smiling lips."

Into the girl's mind flashed a vision of Scott's solitary horseman:

" 'Who without quitting his ground presented his front constantly to the enemy,' " she quoted softly.

"Who are you talking about?"

"A friend. Uncle Nick, did we accept money because of the accident to Davie?"

"No. Anthony gave himself."

"And his money hasn't taken care of us all these years?"

"I should say not. Your mother invested all she had in the orchards. He has worked like a galley-slave to make them pay. He has shared your fortunes. He has . . ."

"You needn't go on. I realize what Tony has done for us. I wish I had known all this. I might have been more helpful, more tender."

"Tenderness comes with age, child."

"Tony didn't have to wait for age. I must go. Thank you, Uncle Nick."

"Wait for tea. Toto will be 'desolated exceeding' if you don't."

"I had tea at La Mancha. It is a wonder it didn't choke me. I must get back to White Pillars. I left the office early. Tony ought to be back from New York, he will have a posse out looking for me. He and Eddie Timmins watch me as though they expected one of the gods from Mt. Olympus to swoop down out of a cloud and carry me off. Mark is just as bad."

"We can't run any risks with our candidate. How goes the battle?"

"There isn't any battle. Each candidate is busy stalking voters. Is there anything new about Daphne?"

"She refuses to see me."

"You won't give her up, will you, Uncle Nick?"

"No. I shall hold on for Tony's sake if not for hers."

"I don't want to be disloyal but—but do you think that Tony really loves Daphne?"

"Even if he doesn't, could he desert her, Rose? If that engagement were to be broken now the fact might be construed into his distrust of her. Keep that in mind, child."

"I will. If only the mystery could be solved."

"Forget it. The sooner the town forgets it the quicker the case will be cleared up. There was no tragedy. Papers were stolen. We are sure that the handkerchief was a blind. We are sure also that Daphne is shielding someone. Her mother's heart was weak. Fright may have stopped it. It may have been too tired to keep on. Is there to be a dance at the Club tonight?"

"Yes. Mark asked me to go with him."

"Then go."

"Do you think I ought when Tony's fiancée . . . he is the same as my brother, you know."

"Go. The sooner the townspeople get back to normalcy the better. Do you like Mark?"

"Am I on the witness stand, your Honor?"

"I'm not attempting to cross-examine you. I just don't want you to be too kind."

"Uncle Nick, should a girl marry a man if she thinks—is sure that he will be a better man with her?"

"Any man is a better man to marry the woman he loves, but if you mean marry him to reform him, no, a thousand times no. Don't let that Victorian idea take root in your mind. I know you Grahames if once you are obsessed with the idea that a thing is 'right.' Child, the man who won't live cleanly and temperately out of self-respect, won't change permanently—after marriage. Love may pull him up, but unless he has in his right hand love and in his left hand self-respect, it won't hold him up. Self-respect thrives mightily after it sends out a root or two, thank God."

"Uncle Nick, you are white with earnestness. I won't marry a man to reform him, I promise. I am not quite so simple. Good-night and thank you for everything, even the sermon," she added saucily.

Rusto greeted her with a reproachful snuffle. She

dropped a repentant kiss on his ear as she stepped into her car.

"Hungry, old dear? We'll be at home before you can bark 'Jack Robinson.' "

A motor-cycle shot ahead of the sedan. The rider's face was illumined for a moment by the headlights. Sam Hardy! Had he been her predecessor in Nicholas Cort's library? As he swerved into the highway he barely escaped collision with a roadster. Instinctively Rose jammed on the brakes. She stalled her engine. The man in the roadster had stopped his car to look at the rider vanishing in the mist. The lights from the lamps of the two cars created a zone of golden mist. Rose jumped from the sedan to lift the hood. What had happened that she couldn't start the car, she wondered. Fortunately she was not far from the house. Toto would be 'joyful exceeding' to help her.

"Engine trouble?" queried a suave voice behind her.

Nap Long! Rose resisted an impulse to burrow into the department of the interior. She responded gaily without lifting her head:

"Oh, no. I just wanted to see the wheels go round."

"Don't try to be funny, Rose. Who was that on the motor-cycle?"

"How should I know?"

"You must have left the house at about the same time. I am sure that it was my man, Sam Hardy," he laughed, "the man I hired away from your manager."

Rose ignored the last sentence.

"The man who takes care of your plane?"

"When he isn't taking care of my rooms at the Lodge. I wonder . . ." she could see his eyes contract to pinpoints of light, they seemed to bore into hers as he went on, "I wonder what he was doing at Cort's."

"Why don't you ask him?"

She stepped into the sedan and pressed the switch. The engine responded. Rusto rumbled a warning. He displayed a set of sharp teeth in perfect biting form as Long laid his hand on the door. The man ignored him. He must have faith in his "star" not to quail before those jaws, the girl thought with a tinge of approval.

"I want to talk with you about Town Meeting, Rose."

"Then come to White Pillars."

"After my last experience?"

"Both mother and I have assured you that we regret Jupiter's rudeness."

"If you really are sorry, prove it. Have tea with me at the Club tomorrow."

"No!"

"What a snob you are."

"I am not a snob. In one breath you boast of luring away our men—in the next you ask me to have tea with you. I have apologized for Jupiter's impertinence, that is enough!"

"You're afraid to be seen at the Club with me. You're afraid that the fact that you have recognized me socially may influence some of the old conservatives to vote for me!"

"Nap! How can you accuse me of anything so small?"

"It's easy enough to prove me mistaken. Have tea with me."

"Rusto, be quiet! I can't hear myself think. Your argument is silly, Nap, but I'll be at the Club tomorrow at four-thirty. Good-night!"

She sent her car ahead. Tea with Nap Long at the Club! Ugh, how she hated the thought. It wasn't because of what he had come from—she met a number of men whom she had liked who had had quite as humble beginnings—it was what she felt he was, because of his hectoring way of picking off their men. He had twisted her refusal into political opposition. Darn! Oh well, one tea wouldn't hurt her. What had he to say to her? Late in the day to buy her off.

She left car and dog at the garage. Mr. Anthony had not yet returned, the man in charge told her. Lucky. She had half expected to find him on the steps waiting for her. She stopped for a few moments before the living room fire. The air had been penetrating, full of ice. She was half way upstairs when she heard Anthony close the front door. He ought to know that Sam Hardy was now domiciled at the Lodge. Why had the man been at Nicholas Cort's?

"Curiouser and curiouser," he quoted from "Alice" as she turned and ran down to the hall. How tired Tony looked. His eyes seemed to burn into hers. She tucked her hand under his arm:

"Tony, it's wonderful to have you back. I . . ."

She felt the muscles under her fingers tighten.

"Stop leaning against me!"

Rose backed away. She stared at him in unbelief. His eyes were black. His lips tense. The color flooded to her hair. His mother's words echoed through her mind:

"It is a wonder to me that he hasn't felt that he ought to marry you."

Was that what was the matter with him now? Did he think that she expected him to . . . oh, no! No. No. Anger rushed to her rescue:

"Ogre! I don't want to lean against your old arm! I had something to tell you. Something very important. I'll never, never come near you again!"

She raced up the stairs. She disregarded his stern:

"Rose! Come here!"

She heard steps behind her. She slammed and locked her door. Refuge! She leaned against it breathing hard.

"Rose!"

She remained mute and immovable.

"Rose! Open the door. If you don't I'll break it."

Melodrama. Her sense of humor threatened her dignity. She felt an overpowering desire to laugh. The door creaked. She knew Tony. He made no idle threats. She would not listen to an excuse for that snub. He just hadn't wanted her near him. Could he explain away that fact? Daphne was winning him away from the Grahames. Could she escape? She looked toward the French window which opened on the balcony, at her short skirt. It had been a number of years since she had slid down the old tree trunk, but wet as it was she could do it. She tiptoed across the room to the accompaniment of an imperious voice demanding:

"Rose!"

Softly she pulled open the long window. A wet wind swung the hangings into the room. She listened. Quiet in the hall. Had Tony gone for a battering ram? She laughed at the thought. Her resentment was oozing. She never could remain angry with him. She blew a kiss from her finger-tips in the direction of the hall door before she turned to step out on the balcony. The smile stiffened on her lips. Illumined by the glow from the room behind her Anthony Hamilton leaned against the wrought-iron rail. Amusement lighted the gravity of his face as he reminded—

"There are other windows. Did you think that I had forgotten your old stunt, Miss Grahame?" He caught her close as with a swift change of voice he challenged:

"Don't think that you can escape from me—ever."

## Chapter XVI

ROSE GRAHAME sat opposite Long at a small table at the Country Club. They were the only occupants of the room except the Club cat. A heap of tawny fur with pale gold paws tucked beneath her fluffy breast, she regarded the tea party through expressionless green slits.

Outside a fine sleet was descending, coating ground and trees and shrubs with ice. Inside the blaze from enormous logs roared up the chimney of the huge fireplace. On the hearth coals blinked red-hot eyes. The room was dotted with small tables lighted by candles the bouffant shades of which gave the impression of miniature, headless ballet dancers standing on one foot.

Rose regarded Nap Long speculatively as he wrote the order. He had lured her here by his absurd suspicion as to her motive in refusing to take tea with him. Now, what did he want? Did his hand shake or was it the flickering light which made it seem unsteady? His swarthy skin had a washed-out look, his black eyes were furtive; usually they challenged the world. Was the election getting on his nerves? Was he frightened? Frightened? Nap? With his belief in "Long's star"? Her imagination again. Between memories of the information thrust upon her by Mrs. Hamilton, Tony's snub, the tenderness of his voice, the feel of his arms as he had caught her close on the balcony, she hadn't slept much last night. She drew an uneven breath.

"Why are you sighing like a furnace? Getting fed up on being a candidate for office?" demanded Long, sarcastically.

"I? Sighing? Absurd. I love being a candidate for office."

"So much that you couldn't be induced to chuck it?" Rose's eyes met his.

"Are you about to attempt to buy off this opponent, Nap? Is it for that you invited me to tea?"

His black eyes were no longer furtive. They were disconcertingly bold.

"Not entirely. I'm realizing one of my boyhood ambitions, almost the biggest. I'll tell you of that later. I'm in this Club as a member with you sitting across the table from me. I am getting a greater thrill from that than from any adventure of my life, and I've had 'em good and plenty. There has never been any other girl who counted. Just you."

Rose pushed back her chair with an instinctive desire to escape.

"Nap, please, don't."

"Sit still. I won't say anything more about that at present. Only remember, that poor, dirty, ragged boys sometimes have social ambitions. You can't realize what it means to stand on the outside looking in."

"You are in now."

"I am. I mean to stay in. If . . ." The ghost of an emotion flitted through his eyes. Was it fright, Rose wondered. Why did the absurd suspicion that the invincible Long was frightened persist?

"I want you to give up this selectwoman business, my girl."

His tone set the color burning in her cheeks. Her voice was stormy as she objected:

"Don't call me—my girl, Nap, in that tone. It is like a villain in the movies. It isn't done in polite society. Having that off my mind I will proceed to business. I shall not withdraw my candidacy."

He waited until the maid had arranged the tea-things and departed. He thrust his hand in his pocket. He answered the question in Rose's eyes as she raised the teapot:

"I take mine strong. I am like the old woman in Mother Goose. Trying to realize that I am really I. That you are pouring tea for me . . ."

"Nap!"

"All right, it will keep."

He laid a velvet case before her on the table and snapped it open. Diamonds from a broad band of links blinked a thousand brilliant eyes in the candlelight. Rose set down her cup in haste. She was conscious that members were filling the other tables. What would they think if they saw that gorgeous thing? Long tapped the bracelet lightly:

"Give up the selectwoman farce and you get this."

Anger choked her for an instant before she answered in a tone of suppressed fury:

"You can't buy me ever with anything. Put that out of sight. Quick! If you don't I will leave the room. There are others here. My abrupt departure might be commented on."

With a muttered protest he snapped the case shut and dropped it into his pocket.

"You'll get that later—with a lot more. Just now, we'll talk terms. If you won't take the bracelet, we'll trade."

"Trade! You have nothing I want."

"Perhaps something you don't want. Suppose I shake out and air the reason why Anthony Hamilton came to White Pillars?"

The room rocked and settled into place. Rose caught her lips between her teeth to steady them. Bring up that old story? What difference would it make? Everyone in town knew and loved Tony. And yet—yet it would hurt him. Hurt her mother. What ought she to do? Let a personal controversy influence her public service? The town would buzz. There wasn't much chance of her election. Perhaps she would better give up and close Nap's mouth. Was honor a sliding scale when applied to politics? No, a situation was honorable or not honorable. And keeping a political pledge was a matter of honor. Long's voice was super-suave as he interrupted her thoughts:

"From your expression I judge that you have concluded to withdraw from this fight."

Rose became absorbed in the design of a silver spoon she held in finger forced to steadiness.

"I thought you didn't fight your opponents."

"I don't. This is a trade. Do you withdraw or don't you?"

"Don't you want to win on merit? Not because you bought off the other candidate? If I give up you will still have an opponent."

"I am not afraid of him. Yes or no?"

Rose arranged and re-arranged a few crumbs of cin-

namon toast on the table. Suppose her conscience allowed
her to desert the women backing her, would Tony want
her to shield him? Never! He would "whirl with inimitable
dexterity" to meet this attack. If only she could think of
a way to checkmate the arrogant Nap. She had her suspicions, but . . .

One! Two! Three! Four! Five! chimed a clock. Just as
a long-sought letter sometimes is flung into the empty
square in a cross-word puzzle by the subconscious, so
into Rose's mind slipped Peter's description of Nap's invitation to her mother to dine at the Club the very night
she had been tied to the tree. She had been waiting in the
hall to get her breath after cutting madly across fields
when she heard him say:

"Nap's a smooth geezer. First he palavered with a lot
of apologies about its being just five, as though every
clock in the Clubhouse wasn't striking at that minute."

Why should Nap have been so eager to impress the
exact hour on Peter's mind? It had been but a short time
later that Daphne had discovered the tragedy at home.
Could Nap have known of it before she did? An absurd
suspicion, and yet if there was nothing in it why should
it have flashed into her mind with the striking of the
clock? It had been like an instant's illumination of the
dark. Why not follow the gleam? It might develop into
an arc light.

"Yes or no?" urged Long impatiently.

"No."

"You mean that? You don't care if that old story . . ."

"That dramatic pause is packed with significance and
threat but it leaves me quite unshaken. Everyone knows
that old story. If you feel that it is worth dragging into
the limelight I'll do a little dragging too. Where were you
on a certain fateful afternoon shortly before five o'clock?"

"What do you mean? Didn't I 'phone your mother at
just five?"

Bull's eye! Why else should Nap think that her remark
had referred to the day of Mrs. Tennant's passing? Could
he hear her heart pound?

"Curious that you should understand at once to which
afternoon I referred."

Long hastened to repair damages.

"Don't you realize, my girl . . ."

"Don't call me that again, Nap!"

"My mistake! Why shouldn't I remember the day your mother dined with me here? To be recognized by her was another of my ambitions. Now that I'm in socially . . ."

"You would better not risk being thrown out."

"Thrown out! That's a joke."

"Nap, you are magnificent. You ruffle like a turkey cock at the mere suggestion that you may be dragged from from your high estate."

"Stop talking like a book."

"Someone ought to open your eyes. Do you think the townspeople have altogether forgotten that poor, dirty, ragged boy to whom you referred a while ago? The boy who tormented the younger children at school? You are attempting to bully me now, Nap, as you bullied when you shot Annabel Lee."

"Shot who?"

"Annabel Lee."

"Rose, you're crazy. Who the devil was Annabel Lee?"

"My doll. And the bracelet you just produced—striped candy. You have managed to gild that boy, Nap, but the gold paint chips off when you get excited. Attempt to annoy Anthony Hamilton, who has lived in this town and worked for it for ten years, and see what happens."

"Anthony Hamilton again! Gosh, but you're in love with him, aren't you?"

"In love with Tony! Nap! Tony is . . ." Derision. Anger. Illumination. Realization. Desire. Fright. Emotions in succession flashed and fused into one another like rainbow colors from a spot-light off stage as into the girl's mind crashed the knowledge of the quality of her love for the man whom she had regarded as a brother. When, when had it changed from sisterly affection? She caught a satisfied gleam in the eyes of her companion. He had turned the trick. He was jubilating in the successful sidetracking of her query in regard to a certain afternoon. She forced back the discovery battering at her heart for recognition and reminded:

"Shall I start an inquiry as to what you were doing that afternoon—and what you know of the airplane which lands on Headless Hill every Saturday? Yes or no?" she mimicked.

"You are mad to defy me like this."

"A movie line. Defy you? 'The coward dies a hundred deaths, the brave man dies but once.' Yes or no?"

"We'll leave the matter as it is. There is a possibility, a bare possibility, that I may be called out of town to-morrow. If I am—I have another plan for removing your name from the ticket which would be even more satis-factory."

"How mysterious. I must go. What was that?" she de-manded as a dull thud shook the building.

"Sounds like a tree falling. It is a fierce storm. I'll take you home. I'm driving the Rolls Royce."

"Thank you, but I prefer to take the Club taxi. Here's Mark," she rejoiced as the elder Hamilton appeared in the doorway. She sensed his amazed regard of her and her companion as he demanded:

"Why are you out in this sleet-storm?"

"Call a taxi for me, will you, Mark?"

"A taxi! You will go with me. Did you hear that tree crash? The world is coated with ice."

"Let's start at once. We probably won't meet again till one of us has been elected or both of us defeated, Nap."

"You may see me before that. You never can tell."

Mark Hamilton frowningly regarded Long as he turned away.

"What the dickens did he mean by that cryptic plati-tude?"

"Forget him. Let's go. Mother will be anxious if I don't get back soon."

Safe within the haven of the closed car Rose looked through the fast crystallizing windshield upon a fast crys-tallizing world. Click! Clock! Clack! went the chains on the wheels. The light from the lamps set shrubs and trees ablaze with prismatic colors. Mark's face was white. He drove cautiously, head forward, eyes intent on the road ahead. The storm whistled and crashed and thundered a fitting accompaniment to the tumult of the girl's thoughts.

That bracelet! Outrageous! But how characteristic of Nap Long to offer it. What a mad conjecture that he had inside knowledge of the occurrence at Mrs. Tennant's. And yet, when she had flung the insinuation at him, he had promptly backed down on his threat to drag up that old story about Tony. He had been a somewhat constant caller at the Tennants', Mark had said. What had been the attraction? Daphne? His interest in the girl had waxed after the evening of Mrs. Hamilton's dinner—he had taken her home—he had said something about friends in Texas and immediately she had accepted his escort— there had been a hint of coercion in his voice, she remembered. She remembered also how enraged she herself had been at Daphne's treatment of Tony—Tony! Nap had said:

"Gosh, but you are in love with him, aren't you?"

"Oh-o-o!"

She put her hand to her lips to smother the hurt cry but Mark had heard:

"Don't be frightened. We're safe enough."

"I am not frightened," she answered before her thoughts surged on.

Did she love Tony—differently? She tried to evade her own question but brought herself sternly back to it. She must look her heart in the face. Was that why she had so resented his engagement? Nap's caustic comment had knocked down a wall between her mind and heart and let in a blinding light. Why hadn't she known? How could a girl of her age and education be so simple? Why hadn't she realized how she cared when every pulse in her body had responded when Tony had caught her in his arms? One might think that never had she heard of love between man and woman. She had read "frank" novels. Not many, she hated them. Always they produced the hotly embarrassed sense of having opened a bedroom door by mistake. She loved Tony. Tony loved Daphne, else why the engagement? No wonder he had snapped at her when she had leaned against his arm. He must have realized that she loved him. Had he been trying to make her understand?

The fury and tumult of the storm raged outside and inside her heart. What should she do? She must set a barrier between Tony and herself which she could not cross. After his unselfish devotion to the Grahame in-

terests it would be the last straw to fear that the daughter
of the house was in love with him. If only she could rest
her head against his shoulder and talk it over. Silly! That
sort of thing was at an end forever.

The car skidded, executed an isosceles triangle and returned to the road.

"Have patience, Rose. We are almost home."

"I am not frightened, Mark."

Little she cared if she were permanently smashed, she
told herself. She would be saved a lot of suffering. Common sense slapped her smartly. Wicked. Morbid, Sob-
sister stuff, Peter would call it. She had a whole life ahead
in which to accomplish. If she were elected to office she
would infuse so much energy into the town that it would
resort to sedatives to quiet its old nerves. If Nap Long
won, would he build that factory next the White Pillars'
line? He would not. She had talked zoning ordinance to
the town mothers till they were avid for it. What was
back of Nap's consternation when she had mentioned
Mrs. Tennant? He hadn't cared for her reference to the
visiting airplane. Gleams! She would follow them.

She must do something to keep her mind from dwelling
on the revelation of her feeling for Tony. When had it begun, this change? She thought back over the weeks since
her return from Europe. From the time when he had
realized that she was grown up! She had been so eager
to supplant the memory of the little girl who had slipped
her hand into his. She had succeeded. Pandora's box.
From that success subtle, disturbing, heart-shaking emotions had escaped.

"Thank God! We've made it!"

Mark Hamilton's fervent exclamation brought Rose's
thoughts back to her surroundings. Had she traveled
billions of miles since she left the Club? Had she lived
through several generations? She felt centuries old. Mark
caught her arm and steadied her as she slipped on the icy
steps.

"What a night! Don't try to go to La Mancha, Mark.
Stay here. Take the car to the garage."

"That car will park where it is for a while. I lived
through Dante's frozen Hell getting here. If anything had
happened to you . . ." his voice broke. With an effort he

added lightly, "you might not have been able to testify that I was sober and in my right mind."

"Mark, dear, did you think of that? What a pity, when we all know what a fight you have made and how magnificently you are winning."

"You have done it, Rose."

His eyes, so like his brother's, met hers. A sudden thought caught her breath. A way out! Mark loved her. Tony loved Daphne. She loved Tony and he knew it. His mother had taunted:

"It is a wonder to me that he has not felt it his duty to marry you. It would be so like him."

The suggestion was unbearable. She could remove that worry from his mind. Should she? She would be helping Mark. She liked him. She respected him. She touched his arm with the tips of her fingers:

"Have I really helped?"

"Helped! Rose, I thought I loved you before, but as the car crept along and I realized your danger . . ."

"Do you care so much, Mark?"

"Care!"

"Then I will try to care too. No! No! No!" she protested frantically as he caught her in his arms and bent his head to hers. "Not that—yet. I said that I would try."

"Now that you have reached the stage of trying do you think I can't make you love me?" he exulted. "You're mine! May I tell your mother? Tony?"

"Perhaps—sometime."

"Let me tell them tonight, after dinner. It will make you seem so much more mine, make it seem so real."

"Real? Will it? Then tell them tonight, Mark."

## Chapter XVII

"COME in here, *Madre*."

Anthony drew Claire Grahame into his office at White Pillars and closed the door. He rested his arm on the mantel and looked down upon her seated in the large chair.

"Thank you for getting Daphne here tonight. How did you manage it? She has so steadily refused to leave home."

"She didn't need much urging. The storm terrified her. Isn't it frightful? I have run from window to window at every crash trying to see which of our old trees had gone. It has been a sickening experience. Now that Daphne is here we will keep her. Why did you want her tonight especially?"

"Nicholas Cort is coming if he can get here. She must tell what she knows about her mother's death. Of course we know now that the wild story Peter burst in with the night it happened was an instance of village imaginations let loose. That Mrs. Tennant's heart stopped. That the handkerchief was camouflage—but, why? Who took the missing papers? The situation is deplorable for Daphne, it is playing the mischief with my life. Was Rose at the Club with Mark this afternoon?"

"No, but he brought her home. She had tea with Nap Long. Anthony, dear, why not tell her the truth about your engagement to Daphne?"

"Nicholas says, 'Not yet.' He fears that the fact of the deception might leak out. The townspeople persist in thinking that in some way Daphne is responsible for the rifled secretary. I'm paying and paying for my weakness in consenting to that fake engagement."

"Don't blame yourself. I can't bear it. You did it out of kindness."

"Kindness! What good can come of a lie? Rose and Mark . . ."

"A word to her, Tony."

"What word? She regards me as a brother. Suppose I show her that I love her? I am engaged to another girl. She would despise me. Send Daphne here, will you?"

With her hand on the knob of the door Claire Grahame paused:

"Make Rose realize that you love her, Anthony."

As the door closed he rested his head on his outstretched arm and stared down into the fire.

"Make Rose realize that you love her."

The words clamored in his mind. Should he? Had she begun to love Mark? There had been a curious restraint between the two at dinner. Rose had changed. Her eyes no longer met his. The boyish charm of her lips had vanished. They were the lips of a woman. Was Mark responsible for the change? He was making a fight to live up to Rose's ideals. Would it last? Who could know until he was put to the test by disappointment or sorrow? It was easy to ride a tricky horse on a good road. If he were making the effort merely to win the girl the regeneration wouldn't last. Unless he believed in the enduring satisfaction of her principles he would slip back as soon as he gained his point. Well, stand or fall, he shouldn't have her. She was his.

He opened the door in response to a knock. Like a frail black shadow Daphne Tennant slipped into the room.

"Mrs. Grahame sent me, Tony."

"Sit down. I want to talk to you."

He drew the large chair nearer the fire. She looked blue and cold. Her eyes were set in smudges in her white face. She twisted a bit of black-bordered linen in trembling fingers. A pathetic little figure. Anthony cloaked his pity in gruffness:

"The situation can't remain as it is, Daphne. You are shielding someone. With a wave of crime surging over the country the townspeople are clamoring to have the mystery cleared up. Who rifled that locked drawer?"

"I do not know."

"If you don't know you suspect someone. Don't deny it. You may have the right to wreck your life by your silence but you shan't drag mine down with it. We can't tell the truth about this fake engagement until the mystery is solved. Come in," he called in answer to a knock.

As Nicholas Cort entered and closed the door behind him Daphne sprang to her feet and took refuge behind the chair. Her eyes were frankly terrified as she clenched her hands on her breast. Cort warmed his hands before the blaze.

"Good-evening, Miss Tennant. Do you two snug and warm here realize what a storm it is? My car turned completely round three times coming over. A bad night for the trees, Anthony."

"Yes. Tim is in the orchards. He is to report to me later."

"I hope that you won't have to go out." He turned quickly to the girl: "Don't be afraid of me, Miss Tennant. I am here to help you. Sit down again. Answer my questions. Think of Anthony and me as friends, not as inquisitors."

Daphne huddled back in the chair.

"Why do you suspect that Sam Hardy broke open that locked drawer?"

"Sam Hardy! Why—why—who is Sam Hardy?"

"I hoped that you would trust me, Miss Tennant. Do you remember your shocked surprise the evening at Mrs. Hamilton's when you learned that I had been in Texas? I knew then that you knew Hardy."

"Had he told you?"

"No. Not then."

"Has he told you since?"

"Yes."

"What?"

"Not much. He said that information as to the acquaintance must come from you."

"Where is he?"

"It is better for you not to know at present. Now, will you tell us why you suspect that he was in the room when your mother—when her heart stilled? Sam has trusted me. Why can't you? He told me of the early morning visit you made to the old Allen place."

Color flooded the girl's white face.

"Did he say why I went?"

"You knew that he had a gun. You feared . . ."

"Feared! I was in terror of what he might do. He had been so unbearably cheated. I was watching Sam's monkey, with an apple clutched tight under one arm, disappear through the roof when I stubbed my toe, and brought down that lean-to, Tony." She dropped her head back against the chair and closed her eyes for a moment as she capitulated wearily:

"I will tell you all I know about that afternoon."

"Then we will clear him from your suspicion."

"You don't think he did it?" There was a rising note of hope in the eager question.

"No."

"Then who did?"

"Please, Miss Tennant. Time is flying. Tell me what happened when you found your mother—gone."

Daphne leaned back in the chair, hands listlessly resting on the arms. Her voice was toneless as though all her vitality were needed for composure.

"Mother and I came here a year ago when I knew that Sam had been freed. He had been my friend, a friend of whom mother disapproved. I believed in him even when he was sentenced. I knew that he was innocent of the charge against him."

"How did you know?"

"How does any woman sense certain qualities in the man she loves? Sometime, Tony, I hope you'll forgive me for taking advantage of your . . ."

"Go on, Daphne," prompted Anthony Hamilton gently.

"I knew that he had been reckless. I knew that he had bootlegged some. That seemed not so disreputable when I considered that my friends encouraged him by patronage. I couldn't see much difference in his culpability and theirs, unless theirs was the greater. At first to me he was only a college man who had had hard luck."

"You came to this village at his suggestion?"

"Yes, Judge Cort. Someone told mother that the climate in this valley was exceptionally beneficial for a weak heart. It was easy to get her here after that. Sam wrote me that the trail he was following led here. He had heard that he could get work in the Grahame orchards."

"Have you met him since he came?"

"Yes."

"Did your mother know?"

"She never knew that he was in the neighborhood. She had been opposed to our friendship from the first. One can't blame her, of course. If she had been kinder, I could have talked with her, but when she was able she was immersed in her own interests. She was socially ambitious for me. Poor mother, position and background meant so much to her. Perhaps because she never had had them herself. She was kinder after my engagement to you, Tony. She said for the first time in her life she was realizing an ambition."

Anthony looked away from the eyes which met his with apology in their depths. He thought of the girl's appraisal of her mother. Mothers! What a difference in the three who touched his own life most closely at the moment. His own, Claire Grahame, Mrs. Tennant. All three had fed and clothed and educated their children, with what varying results. Claire Grahame had had a sense of moral responsibility, she had put the best of herself into hers, and they in turn, were standing for the best. His mother had thought only of herself. Mrs. Tennant had failed somewhere or Daphne would have trusted her. Nicholas Cort's voice interrupted his comparisons:

"Tell me of the last time you spoke to your mother."

"It was the first afternoon I had been out in days and days. She was better. I left her reading. The maid had promised to be within call. I know now that she 'only ran in next door to borrow an egg.' I remember that I thought as I went out:

" 'Perhaps you and I will be more in sympathy as we grow older, Mother.'

"On my return from the village I met Tony. He insisted that the farce of our engagement must end. I had avoided him, thwarted him, because I hoped that I would get by without mother's knowing the truth. The doctor had said that the end might come at any time. I promised Tony that I would tell mother the truth that evening. How I dreaded it. I knew that there would be a terrific row. Through the window I saw her hand on the arm of the chair. Seated as I had left her. Still reading. I argued:

" 'I won't disturb her now, I will tell her after dinner.'

"I ran softly up the stairs so that she would not hear me. On the landing I found this."

She produced a twisted slip of paper from her black, beaded bag. Against the white background lay a few wisps of red, white and blue bristles.

"Had the monkey brought you messages before?"

"Are you a wizard, Judge Cort?"

"Had he?"

"Once. One evening just as I was starting to go to dinner at Mrs. Hamilton's."

Into Anthony's mind flashed a vision of the great hall at La Mancha; he saw himself bending to retrieve the blue enamel case, saw again the tri-color bristles caught in the gold lace of Daphne's frock. The girl hurried on:

"I knew that that meant a message from Sam. I fairly ran to my room. I found a note the monkey had left on the sill of the window. When I went out I always left it open so that he could get in. Mother never came upstairs. Her bedroom opened from the living room. Sam had written:

" 'Have found my man. Tonight I'll face your mother.' "

"Was that all?"

A faint color tinged the pallor of the girl's face.

"All that had to do with mother."

"What next?"

"For the first time in years I was happy. Sam's name would be cleared. Somehow we would reconcile mother. Every good thing seemed possible. I forgot you, Tony. Forgot my promise. I hummed as I changed my frock. As I passed my work-table I looked down at the pile of white handkerchiefs I had that day finished initialing for Sam. I had left them in a neat pile. They had been pulled this way and that. The mischievous monkey, I thought. As I put them in order I saw a drop of blue wax on the snowy linen. Curious. Blue! I looked toward my dressing table. One of the candles which stood beside the mirror was gone. Feverishly I counted the handkerchiefs. One missing!

"My heart stopped. Could Sam have taken it? Had he come already? Had he talked with mother? I must know. I ran downstairs. I dashed into the living room. I looked toward her chair . . ."

Daphne put both hands over her eyes. Nicholas Cort waited. Anthony's eyes misted. The fire snapped. Icy vines tapped ghostly fingers against the windows. The banjo clock ticked off the seconds in stolid disregard of human tragedy. The girl clenched her hands tight and went on:

"Her head rested against the back of the chair. A white cloth was tightly drawn across her face. I crept closer. A faint odor. I lifted the white thing. The missing handkerchief. The face under it was beautiful. The lines of worry, querulousness, disillusionment had been erased. Her lips were curved in a slight, enigmatic smile as though she were in possession of a secret past my understanding."

The girl turned so white that Anthony took a step forward. She held up a protesting hand.

"Don't touch me, Tony. Let me finish. I was numb with terror. My first thought was for Sam. He had been there! He had done this terrible thing! What should I do? The handkerchief! Initialed! I seized the scissors and cut out the betraying corner. Flung it into the fire. I didn't dare dispose of the whole thing. Then I rushed for help justifying myself over and over in my mind:

" 'I'm glad I did it! I'm glad I did it!' "

"Unfortunately you didn't confine it to your mind. You said it aloud."

The girl brushed her hand wearily across her forehead.

"Did I? What difference does it make?"

"None, we hope. Have you had word from Sam Hardy since?"

"No."

Nicholas Cort's question brought back to Anthony's memory the figure of the man sprawled upon his desk in the late afternoon glow. It must have been at about that time that Daphne had dashed in upon her mother. Had Hardy been guilty he could not have made the distance from the Tennant home to the nursery, then to the office in that short time.

"Would the papers which were stolen be of use to Hardy?"

"Not unless he wanted the mass of documents mother had collected during the farce of his trial. Determined to convince me of his worthlessness she employed a detective that she might supply evidence if the state didn't," the girl explained bitterly.

"And he found. . . ."

"I refused to listen to what he found. She was determined that I should be prejudiced. I think she kept the papers to use in case Sam appeared."

"And those are the missing papers?"

"Y—yes."

"Your mother and Nap Long had become friends, had they not?"

"Yes. From the moment he learned that we had come from Texas he was untiring in his devotion to her. He brought her birds, flowers. I was shiveringly sure that he had a sinister motive. I kept out of his way. Once as I entered the room unexpectedly, I heard her say:

" 'As soon as I am equal to looking them over I will give you those papers.'

"Long was too suave. As he rose to place a chair for me he explained:

" 'Your mother has a bit of land in Texas which I think I may be able to sell for her.'

"I remember thinking, 'So that accounts for your interest? You want our land.' "

"Thank you, Miss Tennant. We won't keep you longer. Stay at White Pillars until this mystery is cleared up. You shouldn't be so much alone."

"Thank you for your kindness, Judge Cort. Tony, you are quite free. Tell the truth about that silly engagement. When mother assumed that night—she knew that you hadn't asked me to marry you—that you cared for me, I seized it as a shield. It would protect me from the thrusts of her suspicions in regard to Sam. I'm sorry."

"The truth is not to be told until tomorrow." supplemented Nicholas Cort. As the door closed upon the girl he added:

"I'm sorry Anthony to keep you in this miserable entanglement a moment longer, but, we must let it stand for the present."

"Do you think she told the truth?"

"Part of it. In Texas I got hold of the very detective employed by Mrs. Tennant. After producing my credentials he confided that the evidence he had looked up had completely exonerated the man who at present calls himself Hardy from the charge of smuggling aliens. That acting upon it he had been able to free him. Apparently Mrs. Tennant never told her daughter. I suppose she was afraid she would marry him."

"Had the man in Texas views as to who was the guilty party?"

"No. All he could do was to prove that Hardy wasn't."

"Sam told Daphne that the trail he was following led here. What trail?"

"The monkey. He had trained it and had given it to Carmencita the daughter of the Mexican woman where he had his room. When they pounced upon him for smuggling, girl and monkey were spirited away. He knew then that the power which had caused his arrest had removed her. Her testimony would exonerate him. When Hardy was released he heard that the monkey had been seen traveling north. He trailed him from place to place until he located him at La Mancha with Carmencita."

"The night Santa Anna came here hunting for his 'seester's monk' I suspected that he was more interested in Hardy's whereabouts than he was in the monkey's. Only one or two more knots to untangle, Nick, and we can draw a long breath."

"Let's forget the knots tonight, Anthony." Cort tried to peer through the icy pane. "What a night! Whose car is that?"

"Mark's. He ought to take it to the garage. He brought Rose home from the Club."

"Brought Rose home? He has been faithful and steady through her campaigning, but—don't let him have her, Anthony."

"He'll get her only over my dead body. Will I ever break away from this infernal engagement? Rose thinks that I'm tense with anxiety over Daphne and her troubles. You know, anyone must know that I love her. I have camouflaged fearing to repel her by a sudden change from brother to lover. The strain is turning me into a savage."

"Patience for a few hours more, Anthony. Who's coming."

The boards of the veranda creaked and cracked under a heavy foot. The door was flung open with a bang. Peter blinked at the two men regarding him in amazement. He was glazed from glinting cap to glinting overshoes. He slammed the door and advanced to the fire. He flung hat and gloves to the floor. He blew on his red hands:

"Boy, what a night! I walked from the station. I'd rather take a chance on my feet than in a car. I came in this way so as not to drip over the hall rugs. Mother doesn't care what happens here."

"Why did you come?"

"Come! Isn't tomorrow Town Meeting? Do you think I'd miss voting for my sister? Not a chance."

As he peeled off his coat the telephone rang. Anthony answered.

"Hamilton speaking. . . . He is. . . . Where is he now. . . . You did? . . . keep him there . . . someone of us will. . . . What's that. . . . Hardy! Hardy! . . ."

With the receiver still at his ear Anthony covered the mouthpiece with his other hand.

"That was Sam Hardy. He said that Long was packing up at the Lodge. His voice was so low I had difficulty in hearing him. Said that he had told Eddie Timmins the whole story. Had a hunch that someone would better know. Then came a crash and I couldn't get him." He pressed the hook up and down. "No, there is no answer. What do you suppose happened?"

"Ice brought the line down, probably."

Peter who had been looking from one to the other with slowly widening eyes burst out:

"What's the mystery?"

There was a joyous rat-tat-tat at the door to the hall. Anthony flung it wide. Rose and Mark! His heart stopped. The girl's face was white, her eyes brilliant. His brother announced triumphantly:

"We have come for your blessing, Tony."

## Chapter XVIII

ROSE felt Anthony's eyes scorching like red-hot coals down, down to the very bottom of her heart. How they burned. What had she done? She dragged back her assurance. She had set a barrier between them, so that he should not suspect that she loved the man who had been a brother to her, from his point of view, only a brother for ten years.

"Come here, dear."

At the tenderness of his voice her heart winged straight to him. She resisted the impulse to follow. She withdrew her hand from Mark's and barricaded herself behind the large chair.

"I—I would rather stay her, Tony."

"Are you afraid of me?"

"A little—when you look like that."

Anthony took a step toward her. She could see how the skin strained over the knuckles of his clenched hands as he crossed his arms over his breast.

"Don't you know that all I care about is your happiness? Don't you know that I won't consent to your marrying Mark until he has proved . . ."

"Look here, Tony, if Rose is satisfied, what business is it of yours what I do? You are not her legal guardian. She is of age. She can do as she pleases."

"Do you think that I don't want her to do as she pleases? I want to be sure that she knows. Dear . . ."

"If he calls me dear once more in that voice I shall fling myself into his arms," the girl thought passionately, even as she answered woodenly:

"What is it, Tony?"

"I want you to promise not to consent to even an engagement to Mark, yet. Make him earn you. Make him prove that he can live up to your ideas and ideals for a year—at least."

His brother took a protesting step forward.

"Tony, play fair. Don't take advantage of what you have done for Rose to . . ."

"What I have done for Rose! Mark, you're crazy. I have done nothing for her, nothing for her family in comparison to what they have given me. Promise, dear."

"Don't promise, Rose."

The girl looked from one white-faced brother to the other. She shook her head.

"I shan't promise, Tony."

"Hear that Dictator!" Mark jubilated. He caught the girl by an arm about her shoulders. She twisted away from him.

"I won't promise Tony, but, I won't have our engagement announced until after the new year." Mark's brows met in annoyed incredulity as he echoed:

"The new year! We'll be married and off for France by that time."

"You have forgotten. I may be elected selectwoman tomorrow. It would be slightly inconvenient to commute from France for the meetings."

"Resign."

"That from you who urged me on?"

"Circumstances alter judgements. I've got to get back to France. I . . ."

Claire Grahame appeared at the open door.

"Are you all asleep or deaf that you can't hear the telephone? Your mother wants to speak to you, Mark. Peter! When did you come?"

The boy put his arm about her shoulders. His eyes met Anthony's.

"Anything to eat, Mother? I'm starving."

"Come to the dining room. Never mind if you are wet. What do I care about the rugs if I have you at home a night like this." As they left the room Mark picked up the instrument on his brother's desk.

"Take the message in the living room. This is a different line," Anthony explained curtly. Rose saw his eyes flash to Nicholas Cort. The elder man nodded and followed Mark from the room. Rose's heart went into a nose-dive as the door closed. She clutched the back of the big chair. Her knees wobbled treacherously. She must meet Tony's eyes sometime. Why, why should she feel like a criminal? If she were to carry out her program she should be radiant, gay. She tried to smile as she protested:

"Tony, when you look at me like that, 'I'm jes' carbonized wid fright.' "

His laugh sent a ripple of fire through her veins.

"Come out from behind that chair. No? Then I'll come to you." He caught her by the shoulders gently as he demanded:

"Do you love Mark?"

This was a moment to proclaim her freedom but words would not come.

"Has he—kissed you?"

"No, oh no!"

Something in the exultant blaze in his eyes sent her backing away from him. He seized her two hands in one of his and held them behind her back. He caught her in his free arm and bent his head to hers. He kissed her smotheringly, possessively, thoroughly. Throat, hair, mouth. For an instant the girl surrendered then, she twisted away, and faced him scornfully:

"And you, engaged to Daphne Tennant!"

A smile lighted his dark eyes as he demanded:

"Do you know whether you love Mark, now?"

With a little sob the girl sank into the large chair.

"Dear . . ."

The infinite tenderness in his voice changed to a sharp command:

"Come in! Oh, you, Mark?"

He struck a match on the mantel and prepared to light his pipe. His brother glanced from him to the girl in the chair.

"Look here, Tony. Have you been making Rose cry?"

"Ask her."

"Have you been crying, Rose?"

"No, Mark, no. Of course not. Did you answer your mother's call?"

"Yes and I've got to go at once. She's frightened."

"Frightened?" Anthony thrust his pipe into his pocket. "What has happened?"

"She says that the servants are behaving strangely. It's

the ice-storm, getting on their nerves and hers, I suppose. I told her that I would come at once."

Rose was on her feet, her own emotions forgotten.

"Can you get there, Mark?"

"I must. Fortunately it isn't more than a quarter of a mile from this door to that."

"Try out your engine, Mark. I'll join you as soon as I can get hold of Tim."

"Tony, must you go? Think of the trees crashing along the road."

Mark turned and regarded Rose curiously. His lips were quite white as he smiled:

"You didn't think of danger for me?"

Color crept into her white face.

"Because it seemed as though there were nothing to do but go to your mother when she wanted you, Mark."

He lifted her hand and pressed his lips to it.

"Thank you for that vote of confidence. I don't really need you, Tony."

"Go and try out the engine, Mark. Of course I'm going. If there is trouble at La Mancha do you think I'd let you go into it alone. Curious I can't get central."

He rattled the receiver.

"It's dead. I must get hold of Tim—here he comes," he interjected as the veranda cracked under a heavy step. He flung open the door. The clothing of the man who confronted him glistened like the apparel of a somewhat shabby ice-king. His eyelashes were a fringe of ice. In one mittened hand he gripped a bunch of straps from which hung metal prongs which clinked as he moved.

"Come in, Tim!"

"I'd better stay here, Cap'n. I'll melt all over the rug."

"Never mind the rug! Come in. Rose, tell them in the kitchen to make a big pot of coffee. Have it hot and very strong. I know how you like it, Tim. Have Jupiter bring it here when it's ready. Start the engine, Mark. Tell Peter to pile the ropes in the shed into the back of the car. We don't know what we may need going even that short distance."

Rose met Mark as she ran back from the kitchen. He started to speak, then with a wave of his hand hurried out. As she entered the office Timmins was standing on the hearth-rug with his garments steaming like a hot-spring in the Yellowstone. Quite unconsciously she slipped her hand through Anthony's arm as she listened to what he was saying:

"I've been through all the orchards. Ice. Ice. Ice. The old trees are standing up under it, but two hundred of the young ones are flat. Split and broken to the ground. For the love of Mike, it about broke my heart when I saw those youngsters you and I have nursed and cherished as though they were babies smashed to splinters. Isn't there anything we can do, Cap'n?"

"Build low fires between the rows of those prize Mc-Intosh Reds. It will scorch some of them to death but the heat may keep ice off others. Can you get hold of the men?"

"All those who are stock-holders are out. Looking after their property."

"Then get wood from the house and start the fires. Peter and Jupiter will help. I will join you as soon as I can. I'm going to La Mancha with Mark."

Timmins pointed to the bunch of straps and iron he had dropped to the rug.

"Take those ice-creepers along. You can't go a foot without them."

Anthony selected three pair before he put on his shaggy coat. His brother appeared in the doorway.

"Engine's doing its work like a trump. The ropes are in the car. Jupiter added the pulley by which he lifts the trunks to the attic. Nicholas Cort insists upon going with us. I tried to get mother on the 'phone to reassure her but the line must be down."

"Even in this storm it won't take us long to get there. Don't leave until you get that coffee, Tim. Peter's getting out the wood. Dear . . ." the caressing tenderness of Anthony's voice warmed and stimulated the girl's fright-ened heart, "see that he obeys orders. Come on, Mark."

Rose followed them to the hall.

"Be very, very careful, To—boys," she admonished softly.

Mark Hamilton's eyes met hers steadily as he answered:

"I'll bring him back safe, Rose-Pomona."

The girl pondered his words and tone as she returned to

the office. Had he as well as Tony discovered whom she loved? What had Tony meant when he had caught her in his arms and. . . . The remembrance of his lips on hers caught at her breath. She couldn't bear it. This storm was working havoc with them all. Mrs. Hamilton terrified at La Mancha; Daphne like a frightened white wraith; the black servants shuddering. Only her mother had kept her serenity. She had encouraged and soothed Juno and Jupiter, she had tried to infuse Daphne with her own vitality; she had hovered over Nicholas Cort with solicitude and hot coffee when he arrived. How he had basked in her unusual tenderness. Jupiter came in with a tray. Rose's thoughts flew back to the man by the fire. She placed a teapot in front of Timmins.

"Don't get up," she protested as he struggled from the chair in which he had been half asleep. He rubbed the back of a painfully red hand over his eyes.

"I must have dozed. The change from cold to heat, I suppose. I'll bet this coffee's good," he sniffed. "Curls my eyelashes up tight just to smell it."

"Will the fires save the trees?"

"There's a chance."

He poured himself another cup of coffee. He drank it to the last drop.

"Great stuff! Don't worry, Miss Rose, we'll save some of those pets of the Cap'n's."

"Tim, do you think that there is anything wrong at La Mancha?"

"Wrong?"

He regarded the silver coffee service, filled his cup and drank the steaming contents.

"Danger, I mean."

"From that gang of red-sashed greasers? There's something phoney going on there. Sheriff closes in on La Mancha tonight. Sam Hardy told me. He and Judge Cort have camped on the trail of the man who had him sent to prison. Suspected Santa Anna. Got a job to take care of Long's plane. Headless Hill. Strange airplane. Strange men. Smuggled. Watched Long. Too much at Tennant's. Carmencita discovered Santa Anna was sending the monkey into the orchard to steal fruit. Sam took the monk with him to old Allen house. Lost him the day you and the Cap'n had tea by the river. Mex girl told Sam that the butler had orders to kidnap you. Sam sent the monkey with red-ink warning. Didn't dare let the Cap'n know where it came from for fear he would block his man-hunt. The greasers sawed the trees. Sam crawled to office to warn us. Someone beaned him. Came to long enough to tell us to turn the monk loose. Was afraid Santa Anna would trace him. Don't know if Long's in deal. Sam married to Tennant girl. Mother dead against it. She. . . ."

"Daphne married!"

At Rose's shocked exclamation Timmins glared wildly round as though he had been roused from a dream:

"For the love of Mike, what've I been saying? I promised Sam I wouldn't tell. Coffee-jag! Excuse!"

Before she could realize that he was going he had bundled himself into still wet outer garments and slammed the veranda door behind him. She heard the crunch! crunch! of his heavy tread. She could see nothing from the window. She dropped into the chair before the fire. A coffee-jag! She laughed until she had to clear the tears from her eyes. Tim had delivered a full-length novel in tabloid form. About seventy-four thousand nine hundred and seventy-five words saved. Daphne married! Was the intricate maze in which they all had been caught to be untangled at last? Had Tony known all the time? He had crashed through barriers of reserve tonight.

She couldn't face the thought. She must do something to help. She wouldn't sit still and wait for word from La Mancha. Word! No word could come. The lines were down!

She breathed on the window and rubbed a little spot clear. They had started the fires in the nursery. She could see a faint-red light. She could tend a fire. Juno and Jupiter could make coffee, gallons of it while she was dressing. Somehow, someway she'd get it to the men. Peter was with them. She crossed the hall to the living room. Daphne was curled up in the wing-chair, white and pathetic. Dreaming or half asleep? Married! Incredible! Mrs. Grahame was peering out of the garden room window. She spoke over her shoulder:

"An awful night for those three men to go over the road, Rose, just to quiet a shallow woman's nerves."

That from her mother who was always the most tender, tolerant of women. She must be anxious. Rose tucked her arm within hers:

"Let's you and I get busy then we won't think of danger. Tell Juno and Jupiter to make gallons of coffee, to get together everything we have in the house for sandwiches for the men in the nurseries."

"My dear child, how will we get it there? Peter is with them."

"I'll see to that. Tell Jupiter to pack it in the clothes basket and I'll push it down the hill."

"Rose, you shall not go out in this storm."

"It isn't so bad. Come on, Mummy, be a sport. Help. Eddie Timmins is trying to save the young MacIntosh Reds."

"Help. Of course, I'll help, Child. But to let my little girl . . ."

Rose tucked her arm within her mother's. Her eyes shone with excitement as she echoed theatrically:

"Your little girl! Your selectwoman apparent, you mean."

## Chapter XIX

"FO' de Lawd. Honey-chile, w'at yo' doin' in dem close?" demanded Juno as Rose appeared in the kitchen in a winter sports costume of brown mixed wool cloth. The coat with its furry cuffs and high upstanding collar of kolinsky came well below the hips over breeches of the same material. Dark brown khaki wrapped leggins above Russian calf shoes matched the khaki-colored wool cap and mittens. She held a ski-pole. Rusto sniffed at her hands.

"Everything ready? I will take the coffee and sandwiches to the men working in the orchard. I hope you've made gallons."

"We done did it. Jes' so fotunate we hav a w'ole big ham cooked an' we made san'wiches an'—"

"Ham! Juno! The men will die of thirst." Rose's mouth and throat dried to a crackle at the thought.

"I jes' guess dey'll be glad to git somefin' widout bein' so fussy. De coffee's in de preserve boiler, de tin cups yo' all use fer de picknic is packed wid it in de big close basket jes' yuh ma tole us. San'wiches dey all tucked in roun'. Jup'ter he pulled de basket outen de do', jes M's Claire say. But I guess Mars Tony lambas' Jup'ter an' me good an' plenty 'cause we let yo' go out," she grumbled.

Jupiter blew in on a blast of sleety air. He was greatcoated, overshoed, muffled to the tops of his ears. His black eyes rolled between his icy cap and collar top. His teeth of a recent vintage shook like castanets. He chafed his hands:

"Chile, yo' sho crazy to go outen dis storm. All de ghosts eber been in de worl' walkin' tonight. Wha's that?"

His voice was lost in a crash which shook the house. The lights went out. Rose felt the color leave her face. She pulled a flash-light from her pocket.

"Stop howling, you two, Jupiter, go and help mother

188

find some candles. Juno, light that oil lamp over the sink."

The black woman shuddered as she obeyed orders. She was almost white in the flickering light.

"Honey-chile, dis is shore de wors' storm since Mr. Noah an' his sons did commission de ark." She turned coffee into a cup. "I's frightened outen' ma teef, but yo' isn't goin' out till you's had somefin' hot to drink.' She poured cream with a liberal hand.

"Juno, I can't wait. Those men must be freezing. You should have seen Tim. He looked like an animated icicle."

"Dey won't be any more icicler 'cause yo' get somefin' hot into yuh stomick, chile. Drink it! If yuh ma wil let yo' do sech foolishness as to go, yo've got to min' yuh ole Mammy. Take it." She held out a tin cup full of golden liquid. Hot. Steaming. Fragrant. Aromatic. The girl drank the last drop. The heat and flavor set her spirit and courage on tiptoe. After all, life was a glorious adventure. Was she to be beaten because she loved a man who did not love her? Didn't he? She felt again his arms about her, his lips on hers.

"Fo' w'at yo' sain' o-o-o-o, Honey-chile jes' though yo' wus frightened," queried Juno. "If yo' scared don' yo' go nigh dem orchards. 'Taint no place fo' de candy-date fo' selectooman, noway."

"It was the coffee, Mammy. Oh, so strong. Tim said it curled his eyelashes up tight just to smell it. I'm off. Did you get the candles for mother, Jupiter?"

"M's Claire, she don' need me. She say fo' me to come an' help you."

"Come on!"

As they crackled down the back steps Rose smothered a shocked exclamation. A great limb of the oak before her window lay across the service drive. A giant felled.

The girl shivered. Rusto whined at her heels. The fires in the nursery between house and river illumined a magic world. All about her birch trees swung and clashed softly like crystal pendants of an old-time chandelier. Junipers bent plumed heads upon their breasts, the glittering crowns they bore too heavy to hold erect. Oaks, chestnuts and maples cracked and creaked beneath a coating of ice. Detonations in the distance. It was like war. A horrible

war in which Nature stood behind the guns and pushed
home the shells. Crash followed crash. For an instant the
racket ceased. A breeze sprang up. The world seemed
stirred by a mighty orchestra. Icy branches clashed like
castanets. Rubbing twigs sighed like wind instruments.
Grasses and shrubs were tinkling cymbals. Telegraph
and electric light wires along the road were ropes of glass
fringed with innumerable tiny spikes of ice which clicked.
The guns again!

A wild night. A terrifying night. Had Tony and Mark
reached La Mancha? The road was lined on either side
with massive trees. Rusto nosed her hand. Jupiter unbent
his stiff back from over the basket:

"I'se tied a lon' rope to dis, Chile. Yo' put it roun' yuh
wais' then it can't run away from yo'."

"I'll put it across my shoulders. I have my ski-pole to
keep me from slipping. Now, give the basket a push. Heel,
Rusto," she commanded as the dog started down the icy
slope. "I should send you home but you're such wonderful
company, you old dear. I'm off. Go back and help mother,
Jupiter."

The man shouted an answer above the wind and thun-
der of falling trees. Rose made her way cautiously. Between the glittering fringes which were her eyelashes she
could see icy figures flitting about in the rose-color light
form the fires. She pushed and retarded the laden basket.
As she neared the nursery she could see the steam from
the men's clothing as they approached the fires. It seemed
ages before she was near enough to them to call through
cupped hands:

"Coffee! Hot cof—fee!"

She recognized Eddie Timmins from his stodgy mo-
tions. Had he recovered from his attack of garrulity or
was the coffee still doing its perfect work. He had heard
her call. He beckoned to two men. She heard the crust
crack under their ice-creepers as the three hastened toward her.

"Thank heaven, I've arrived. Take the rope off my
shoulders, will you Tim? Thanks. There are sandwiches
and piping hot coffee in that basket. What can I do to
help?"

"Help? Go home."

"No. I'll tend a fire. Which one?"

"Cap'n'll break my neck."

"No, he won't Tim. I'm warm and dry and perfectly able to do my share. Where's Peter?"

"Gone for wood. He'll be back. If you're set on staying, feed that fire. Don't let it blaze. Three hundred trees gone. Save some. Perhaps."

With Rusto, a shaggy ice-dog following her every step, the girl tended the fire. Her clothes steamed. Her eyes smarted from smoke. Within the radius of the heat the limbs of the young trees glistened wet and bare. Beyond, the world was like a pantomine stage-set. Ice grottoes. Prism of glorious color. Swaying stalactites crimson tipped. Glistening actors against a glittering back-drop. Young stock prostrate. The vandal who had sawed their trees might have saved his energy, the girl thought. Would Tony abandon orcharding after this? She piled on wood. The flame roared heavenward.

"Hey there! Not so high," shouted a voice.

She could smell the scorch of her woolen suit as she tried to scatter the fire. Her eyes smarted unendurably. Rusto sneezed and backed away. She retreated into the icy shadow to get her breath. She looked toward the house. Dim lights made spots which were windows. A sudden glare illuminated the icy stretch of ground. An automobile. Tony and Mark had returned. She must know that they were safe and unharmed.

"Tim!" she shouted. "I'm going to the house!"

"Righto!"

She plunged her ski-pole into the glassy slope and struggled up. Coming down had been far easier. Why hadn't she thought to put on creepers. She brushed the sleet from her lashes. How cold it was now that she was away from the fire. Bitter. Penetrating. The dog slipped and slid beside her. She stuck her hells into glare ice. Once she fell. For a few feet she crawled. She pulled herself up by a tree. She must get to the house. Crash! Another giant gone. She was spent when she reached the portico of White Pillars. The front door slammed. Someone crept cautiously down the steps.

"Tony," she called.

With a shocked exclamation the man stepped into the light.

"Nap!" she whispered. "Why, why are you out a night like this?" As he remained silent she peered into his face which was ashen in the dim light. "Nap, why—why are you here? Has anything happened to—to Tony?"

She caught his sleeve in her mittened hand. She saw his eyes flash curiously in the light before they narrowed:

"Don't be frightened, Rose. I came—I came to take you to him."

"Take me to him! Where is he? Where, Nap?"

"At La Mancha."

"Is he hurt? Oh Nap, don't be so slow! Tell me."

"I don't think it's serious. He wants to see you."

Already she was in his car.

"Get in, quick. Let's take the short cut."

Long bent to the wheel.

"We can't. Trees down on that road."

"Let's walk."

"Walk! You'd never get there."

"I know it. How are you going?"

"I can't tell yet. Depends upon the roads."

"Tony wasn't caught under. . . ."

"No. A nasty crack on the head. Made him—kind of crazy. Insists on seeing you."

"Hurry, Nap!"

"Hurry a night like this? My God, if I only could."

Rose watched the rhythmic swing of the windshield cleaner. The car was blissfully warm. She could feel little rivulets of water from melted ice run down under her clothing. She tried to peer out of the window. It was ice-coated. Nap was bent forward his eyes glued to the small cleared space of glass. He drove almost as well as Tony, she thought. Tony! She shut her teeth into her lips. She mustn't think of him or she would get out and run.

"Where are we now, Nap? We've been driving years."

"Not so many. I can't tell yet. If we had that dog of yours harnessed in front he'd take us straight."

"Rusto! I forgot him. Oh, Nap, do you suppose he got into the house? He'll be frozen."

"I'm not worrying about a dog tonight, my girl. I—gosh, I've struck it."

She could see his eyes grim with determination as he turned to her. "Now, we'll hurry!" He stepped on the accelerator. The car shot ahead.

"When I said 'Hurry!' I didn't mean to break our necks. Where are we? That looked like the entrance to La Mancha. Are you sure you are on the road?"

He bent forward without answering.

"Nap! Can't you hear? You've missed the road. I must get to Tony." A sudden sharp suspicion caught at her breath. "Where are you going?"

"To the border as fast as I can get there. You won't get to Tony. Anthony Hamilton has blocked me in every move I've made. Now I'll block him. I've got you. I'll keep you. Want to know my biggest ambition? To marry you."

"Nap! You are mad!"

"The madder the risk the more kick I get out of it. I've always been that way. I took those papers from the Tennants'."

"And you let people think that Daphne took them?"

"How can I help what people think? Fools! When at dinner at La Mancha Daphne echoed the word Texas I had a flash of intuition. She was frightened. I always felt there was something cagey about her engagement to Anthony Hamilton. I remembered that there was a girl named Tennant mixed up with a man who had served time for smuggling. I began to cultivate the family. The mother was only too willing to pour out her grievance. She promised to show me the evidence she had collected on the case."

"Why were you interested?"

"Because I had begun to suspect Sam Hardy of being the man."

Was he telling the truth, Rose wondered. Did he know that Daphne was married to Hardy? He was a shade too casual. She listened with only half of her mind. The other half was marshalling and rejecting plans for her escape. If she could keep him talking she might manage to stall the engine.

"I decided to have those papers and they were slipped to me on oiled wheels. Long's star! I went into the house to insist upon seeing them. I'd be politic if I could but I'd have them. The front door was ajar. Mrs. Tennant was in the living room—gone. I called. No one answered. I ran upstairs thinking that Daphne might be there. A handkerchief with S.H. on it confirmed me in my suspicion that Sam Hardy was the man who under a different name had been locked up. In my pocket was a vial I had bought for Santa Anna to use on the monkey. The beast was getting on our nerves. See how everything worked my way to throw suspicion on Hardy? I made one mistake. I shouldn't have touched that blue candle. I was back at the Club before five. I'm a fast worker."

He was boasting. Rose shivered uncontrollably. Nightmare? Was it all a horrid nightmare? Surreptitiously she touched the sleeve of the man beside her. He was real. Something beside the stolen papers was behind his running away. He was trying to take her with him. For the first time she remembered Tim's reference to the red-ink warning. She must keep her head. She tried to say lightly:

"Have you forgotten that we're both coming up for election tomorrow? Why not go back? Apparently you can explain about those papers."

"Back? I never turn back. That's one of the secrets of my success. I have a big deal on. I can't waste time here answering questions. Big interests, my girl, big interests. Years ago I made up my mind to marry you. I've slaved for you, schemed for you, now, I've got you. What a night! I've kept that plane in condition for months on the chance I'd need it. Now I can't use it."

The girl's throat died to the cracking point. How, how could she escape? Boards crackled and rattled under the wheels. The bridge! She crushed down the thought of Tony, hurt, calling for her. Somehow she would get to him. . . . Nap Long must not suspect that she was terrified. She tried twice before she could produce a voice. The words came unevenly but tinged with amusement as she reminded:

"You'll be stopped, Nap. I shall be missed. You've forgotten the radio."

"They'd have to supplement that with the telephone. Wires down."

A peremptory bark behind them. Rusto! Following! Rose sent up a little prayer of thanksgiving. She wasn't entirely at the mercy of Long. Her courage swept back in a vitalizing tide. Into her mind flashed the memory of her small self hugging decaptitated Annabel Lee, she heard her own little choked voice defying:

"I won't let him see me cry! I won't."

Long must have heard the dog. He stepped on the gas. The automobile shot forward. Skidded violently. He made a futile effort to swing it back. A splintering, ripping, grinding crash flung her forward on her knees. The car pitched downward. Stopped. What had happened? The front wheels seemed two feet below level. Long sat as though turned to stone. She peered through the icy windshield. She put her mittened hands to her mouth to shut back a cry of terror. Broken rails! The forward wheels of the car hung over the edge of the bridge. The headlights illumined the glittering gulch below. What held them from plunging down? Nap Long answered her unspoken question:

"Don't move! Don't even speak. If that rail holds we're safe until help comes. Believe in Long's star, my girl. Long's star."

A frantic bark. A prolonged howl behind them rent the air. The man turned livid.

"That dog again! My God, if he touches this car we're done for."

## Chapter XX

AS Anthony, Mark and Nicholas Cort entered the great hall at La Mancha Flora Hamilton sprang to her feet with a low cry of relief. The huge fire roaring up the chimney set flickering patterns dancing on gorgeous embroideries, sent ghostly shadows flitting up the winding staircases, turned lacy grills of iron to gold.

From one of the small balconies came the music of a symphony; church bells at a distance, the muted notes of violins. A steady glow from shaded electroliers stabilized the light in the corner where the woman stood. Two rouge spots high on her cheeks, her carmined lips, accentuated the whiteness of her face. She took an impetuous step forward:

"Thank heaven, you've come! I tried to 'phone again but the line was dead. I sat here and sat here," . . . her voice caught in an hysterical sob.

Anthony laid a gentle hand on her shoulders.

"Sit down, Mother. We made record time getting here, considering the night." He motioned to the coffee service on the low table beside the couch. "Suppose you give us something hot before you tell us what happened. You have enough there for a small army."

The steady voice restored her composure.

"That huge pot of coffee was ordered for effect. I told Santa Anna that I expected all the gentlemen from White Pillars, I really only expected Mark."

The slight effort of pouring coffee brought the color creeping back to her face. Mark piled cushions behind her back. Nicholas Cort lighted a cigarette as he sank into the luxurious depths of the couch. His face was white. There were tired lines about his mouth but in his eyes a deep content. Had Claire Grahame's tender solicitude brought it there, Anthony wondered. Perhaps that situation would clear up as would some others, he thought as he set his

cup on the tray. His mother's excitement had subsided.
She could tell her story calmly now. She must. Time was
flying.

"Now Mother, tell us what frightened you?" he encouraged.

Flora Hamilton leaned forward. The three men moved
nearer. The spangles on her green evening frock shimmered with every movement of her hands. Her voice was
low as she responded to her son's request.

"I dined alone. Santa Anna served with one of the men
as is usual when we have no guests. As he brought in the
salad I heard loud talking in the pantry. I spoke sharply
to him. Before he could reach the door it was flung open.
Carmencita, the parlor maid, burst in. She wore a cheap
fur coat, a red hat was crushed down to her eyebrows. In
her arms she clutched a monkey. I can see that creature's
beady eyes now, hear his shrill chatter."

She shivered. The three men waited. After an instant
she went on:

"I sprang to my feet furious at the intrusion, but the
girl took no notice of me. Her eyes glittered murderously
as she stormed:

" 'I tole you, Santa Anna, you take me away he find
me! You make me tell lie about that nice Sam Hardy—
w'ile all the time you know that Long man was the smug-
gler. He make t'ousands dollars. I not tell now if'—her
eyes literally blazed—'if you not try to harm my leetle
monkey. You try to keel him, put heem to sleep wif . . .'
Santa Anna who had seemed for a moment to be hypnotized by her tirade sprang for her. Her voice squeaked to
silence. He pushed her from the room. I started to follow.
The second man blocked the way. His smile was oily as he
cloaked command under suggestion:

" 'Señora, she stay where she is. She feenish her dinner.'

" 'I shall not finish my dinner,' I defied as though my
heart were not thumping in my throat. It was then I made
my grand gesture of ordering coffee for all the gentlemen
at White Pillars. The man obsequiously brought the tray
and backed out as servilely as he had entered. I waited. It
seemed hours. Then I telephoned Mark. More hours. Waiting. Waiting. Not knowing what might happen. If I hadn't
turned on the radio I should have gone mad."

"You have seen nothing of the men since? Have heard no sound?"

"No. Doubtless they are upstairs helping themselves to my jewels. If what Carmencita charged was the truth, I have employed a lot of smugglers, captained by Mr. Napoleon Bonaparte Long. There is one consolation, they can't get far with their loot on a night like this. Why don't you 'phone for the police, Mark?"

"With the wires down? I doubt if the servants are interested in your jewels. We've got Long surrounded at the Lodge. These people are only his tools. They can't get far in a storm like this."

"What a night! Oh, your New England. It's brutal. I leave this town tomorrow. Now what's happened," Flora Hamilton demanded querulously as the light went out. As though conscious that it alone was responsible for illumination the fire burst into high. Patterns shifted. Shadows on stairways, hangings and grills grew more grotesque. With weird effect the symphony rose to full-voiced sonorous heights of tone. Through the music boomed artillery. A crashing tree. The four persons in the great hall stood as though bewitched. Anthony was the first to break the spell:

"Ring for lights, Mark. No use waiting longer for Hardy and the others. We might as well know what we have to face. If Santa Anna comes . . ."

The butler stalked in bearing lighted tapers. The three men instinctively drew closer to Flora Hamilton. Anthony spoke with a composure he was far from feeling:

"Bring more candles, Santa Anna. Are the lights out all over the house?"

"Si Señor! We get more tapers. I come to tell the Señora to forget what Carmencita said. She no right here." He tapped his forehead significantly. "She think Sam Hardy heem fin'. He ver' bad—Nombre de Dios—ver' bad. Heem . . ." he swallowed the next word with a surprised gulp as a man appeared beneath the Moorish horseshoe fretted like a delicate fan which arched the entrance to the hall. Water rilled from his sleety hair, his clothes steamed in the heat. He jerked out his words between labored breaths:

"I'm a ver' bad man, am I, Santa Anna? I'll give you a

chance to repeat that before the sheriff. These men know, that Long is the man in whose place I served time for smuggling aliens. Long is the man who is back of that plane which has been dropping some of your countrymen on Headless Hill. Long is the man who stole those papers at the Tennants'. I found a drop of blue wax on his coat sleeve. Long is the man behind the destruction of those young trees." He stopped from sheer breathless inability to go on. His labored breathing, the jeweled notes of a harp, the accompanying rhythm of strings were the only sounds in the hall. Santa Anna manœuvered towards the Moorish arch.

"Stay where you are!" Anthony commanded sharply. The man wheeled and glared.

"You not my boss! You mak' all the trouble. You set that Hardy spying on me . . . me, Santa Anna. He try to tell you when we cut your trees, *Si! Si!* I smash his head. Mees Rose, I tie her up. She spy. Now he say, Get Long! You never get him. You stay here!"

He pulled a poniard from his belt. The full orchestra, horns, brasses, strings swelled into a jubilant climax. Flora Hamilton screamed. Nicholas Cort and Mark tried to step in front of Anthony. He pushed them aside and with incredible dexterity caught the man's wrists in a grip which brought a snarl of pain from the butler, loosened his fingers on the dagger. Anthony's face was white, his eyes blazed as he commanded:

"Pick that up, Mark. Search him for weapons. We won't take any chances with the cur. Some one shut off that radio!" he stormed, as horns and brasses crashed into finale. The succeeding quiet was like a sunny, silent countryside after a tempest. "Cort, bring me that scarf. Bind his wrists. No, you won't break away, *amigo*." He tightened his grip till the man with the red sash howled with pain. "Mark, tie his ankles. Tighter! All set?"

Santa Anna backed against the wall. His eyes were savage. There were flecks of white on his lips. He craned his neck eagerly at the sound of running steps. He grunted with furious disappointment as Peter Grahame appeared under the Moorish arch. His clothing was stiff with sleet. His eyes were frightened. His breath came in hard gasps. He clamped into the hall on ice-creepers.

"Where's Rose?" he demanded.

"Rose!" repeated Anthony sharply. "She is at White Pillars."

"No she isn't. Long's got her!"

The butler's laugh was demoniacal.

"So he get her! Not so bad, eh? I not haf to steal her for heem. Thees is one time w'en he do hees own beesness. *Bueno!* I get ver' drunk now."

"Mark, shut that man's mouth." Anthony's face was livid. "Now, Peter, how do you know that Rose is—is . . ."

"I don't know. I left the fires in the orchard and went to the house. Daphne seized me as I entered. She was hysterical. Said that Long had come there inquiring for Rose. She had told him that she was out. She watched him go down the steps. Saw Rose speak to him. Saw her jump into his car. Long's face had been terrible, she said. She—she was afraid that harm would come to Rose. She insisted upon my coming here. She said that Tony had been so good to her that if I couldn't get to La Mancha she would if she went on hands and knees. Then she fainted."

"Which way did Long go?"

"In the direction of La Mancha."

"Cort, you and Hardy stay here until the Sheriff comes. Come on, Peter, Mark, we'll follow Long."

The vision of the great room went with Anthony as he stepped into his brother's car. He saw it dim with rosy light, flickering with shadows. Santa Anna in his theatrical trapping cowering against a wall; a glittering shimmer of green where his mother huddled into a corner of the great couch. Nicholas Cort and Hardy in consultation.

"I'll drive, Mark. You did your share coming over."

"All right! Pile in, Peter. Where are you going, Tony?"

"Daphne said they started in the direction of La Mancha. There is only one road past this place. It crosses the bridge to Headless Hill."

In spite of the scourge of apprehension urging him Anthony drove cautiously. Sleet beat against the windows. Through the crack open for air sounded the crash of falling trees, the clash of frozen branches. The headlights shone dimly through the ice which covered them.

Mark laid a comforting hand on his brother's shoulder.

"Nothing will happen to Rose, Tony. I—I want you to know that until tonight I hadn't realized that you—loved her. Your engagement to Daphne was a smoke-screen. I didn't see beyond. Forgive me for butting in."

"It's all right, old scout."

Peter cleared his throat in nervous embarrassment.

"I won't say any more, Peter. How did you get wise to all this deviltry, Tony?"

"When the fruit disappeared we got busy. Nick put a secret service man at work. Slowly the snarl untangled. Long was tied to the other end of it. A visiting plane had dumped four or more smuggled humans per week on the top of Headless Hill. I believe now that Nap did it more for the kick he got out of the risk than for the money. His activities had absorbed the new arrivals and the towns-people were none the wiser. Think how he could have in-creased the traffic if I had taken some of them off his hands. Climb out Peter! Clean that windshield. Scraper's caught."

Peter forced open the sleety door. Above the throb of the engine shrilled the sirenic S O S of an automobile, the frantic bark of a dog.

"Rusto! The bridge! My God! Get in, Peter! Quick!" commanded Anthony Hamilton hoarsely. With every nerve in him, every pulse shouting "Faster! Faster!" he drove cautiously. He could take no chances. The storm was blinding. Rose in Long's car on the bridge? Rusto calling for help! Would he ever reach them?

Wooden planking crackled under the chains. He stopped the car but left the engine running. Within the radius of the headlights bulked the dark shape of an auto-mobile. Its red light flared like a demoniac eye. Its front wheels had plowed through the rails.

Was Rose in that? He wrenched open the door of the car. Peter and Mark tumbled out after him. Rusto sensed his presence, yelped a sharp note of greeting and resumed his hoarse bark for help. Anthony forced his mind to sub-mission, his hands to steadiness as he fastened straps around his ankles.

"Put on the creepers, boys. It's glare ice. Get the ropes. We'll fasten them to the rail posts this side. Carry them across and tie them to the rear wheels of Long's car. Thank God the bridge is narrow. We won't let him know we're here until we've made those ropes fast. He might lose his head and—and—bring those ropes."

Except for an occasional question the three men worked silently. The creepers cracked into the icy surface of the bridge. Rusto barked on but the tempo had changed. The siren call grew fitful. Hands stiff, eyes almost blinded by frozen lashes they made the ropes fast to the rear wheels of the imperiled car.

"Here's where one's yachting experience counts," Mark observed in an effort to break the suspense-racked silence. Rusto laid his nose on his master's shoulder as he knelt on the bridge.

"I know, old fellow, I know," Anthony encouraged through stiff lips. Ropes fast, the three stood for an instant contemplating the next move. Between spokes a broken fence rail held the right front wheel on the bridge. The left wheel hung half over the edge. A rail on that side had pierced the window—had shattered it until there was nothing left of the pane but a jagged edge. One would have to creep along the rail to reach the occupants on that side. Rose would be on the other.

Anthony called:

"Long! Long! Open the right door. We have the car roped!"

The siren ceased its wail with an almost human squeak. "Tony!"

Rose's voice. Thank God! He tapped gently on the window.

"Dear! You are safe. Safe. It's Tony! Tony! Open the door."

He heard the fumbling of the handle.

"It won't open."

He tried it. It was frozen shut. He shouted:

"Cover your head with a rug. Peter, give me that wrench we were using."

Carefully, with the fear of what any movement might precipitate crouching in his mind, he chipped the glass until not even a jagged edge remained. What was Long doing, he wondered furiously as he worked. Sneak! Blackguard!

"Mark! Grip me round the waist so that I can't slip! I'll pull Rose through that opening! Peter! Watch the ropes! Rose, dear, Rose! You are safe. Put your head and shoulders through the window. That's right! You can't fall, dear. Tony has you. Tony!"

"I'm not frightened, Tony. I'm cold—so—so cold."

Anthony Hamilton lived through centuries before safe in the middle of the bridge he held the girl's slender figure close in his arms. Mark was chafing her hands. Rusto collapsed, an exhausted ice-dog, beside them. Peter was patting her shoulder, choking:

"Rosy! Rosy!"

She was colorless. She smiled through tears into the tense face above her.

"Tony—I don't care for anything now that I know you are safe. Nap said that you were hurt." She shivered uncontrollably and turned her face against his iced coat.

"Hurt! I'm not hurt, dear. Can't you feel my arms close about you? I'll get her to your car, Mark. You and Peter pull Long out."

"Long!" Rose's scornful laugh was shaken by chattering teeth. "Nap crawled out along the rail on his side centuries ago. Said that he would take a chance on his star and try for help. I—I feel so—so—funny, To—ny!" With a long shuddering breath her eyes closed, her head fell back against Anthony's shoulder.

# Chapter XXI

ROSE forced up heavy lids. Had they been frozen down . . . she had been so cold. . . . Was she on the couch in the living room or was she still in the car hanging over the gulch . . . someone was bending over her. Mother. Someone gripped her hands. Tony. Safe! The warm room wasn't a dream. She tried to smile at Peter leaning over the back of the couch. Who was peering round the panel . . .

"Look! Look!" she heard her own voice warning: "Nap! The screen! He didn't see me cry he didn't . . ."

From under fathoms of water she heard her mother's voice:

"Even when she was a little girl she avoided that screen."

When next she opened her eyes the faces about her were clearer. She looked furtively in the direction of the Coromandel screen. Gone? Had they sent Nap with it? She counted the hours as the old clock boomed. Twelve! Midnight! What a long time . . .

"One! Two! Three! Four! Five! Six!"

The musical chimes of her jeweled clock? Rose gazed dreamily at the cloud of white encompassing her. Her own bed! Her mother's touch on her hair. She'd know that anywhere. Still clutching someone's hand—Tony's. Tony in the big chair. He smiled. Was there ever a smile like his? . . . She released her hold and cuddled one hand under her cheek.

"I'm all right, now, Tony. I'm warm. You and mother . . ." why wouldn't her eyes stay open?

Had the sun changed its course? Curious that it should come in that window in the morning, Rose thought hazily as she regarded the bar of light on the hooked rug. The objects in the room became clear. Assumed their right proportions. Was it possible? Afternoon. Four o'clock! She sat up and caught her knees in her embrace. Claire Grahame appeared at the door.

"Rose, dear."

With the exclamation her mother caught her close. The girl felt an overwhelming surge of love. Tears were near the surface of her dark eyes as she rubbed her satin black hair against her mother's sleeve.

"I am quite all right, Mummy. I have slept like a log. Confess, you gave me something to make me, didn't you?"

"Just a little. You seemed so—so . . ."

"You needn't say it. I know. I was some weak sister to go to pieces as I did last night. I'm perfectly all right now. I'll be down stairs in half an hour."

"But dear . . ."

"Don't coddle me, Mother. Good heavens, isn't this Town Meeting day? Have you voted? Are the roads impassible?"

"No, to the last two questions. Juno and Jupiter went to the village in the flivver. They reported the roads surprisingly clear. It has been a glorious day."

"Has Tony been to the polls?"

"No. He, Nicholas Cort and I have waited until we were sure that you were quite yourself."

"I am. This minute. Perfectly fit. Go, won't you? I need your votes. Where is Daphne?"

"Sam Hardy came for her early this morning. She is his wife."

"I knew it last night. No, no, I'm not hysterical. I just have to laugh when I remember the transformation wrought by coffee. Tim monologued steadily for five minutes. He told all that Sam Hardy had confided to him. Is —is Tony heart-broken?"

Claire Grahame's lips twisted whimsically.

"Not unbearably, I judge. I haven't had a chance to talk with him. You took stage-center last night. You are quite sure you want me to go?"

"I am quite sure that I need your vote. Toddle along, Mummy."

Rose resolutely kept her mind from dwelling on the terror of the night before. That was ancient history. How would the election go? Would Nap's desertion of her last

night count against him? Of course he would swear that
he had gone for help. Help! She shivered. How long had
she hung over that gulch? When he deserted anger had
burned up fright. He had warned her not to move. As the
minutes crept on—years they had seemed—the cold had
crept in and she had begun to lose hope. Reckless and
desperate she had tried the door. Better to go over than to
freeze to death. Rusto's bark had been a life preserver
flung to her courage. And then Tony's voice . . .

She must stop living over last night. She slipped into a
rose-colored frock as Juno puffed into the room. The woman caught the girl's hand in hers and mothered it against
her cheek:

"Yo' sure yo' all hunky-dory, mah Honey-Chile?"

"Sure, Mammy Juno. You and Jupiter have been to
Town Meeting. Were there many people out? Did you see
anyone I know?"

The black woman folded a filmy garment with lingering
care before she answered:

"Anyone yo' know! Chile, dat polls place was buzzin'
wid 'oomen lak workers in de hive w'en de queen bee's
tryin' outen her wings fer her weddin' flight. I walks into
de buildin' an' de fust pusson dat 'costed mah wus yuh
frien' Miss Polly Carter. She had a pencil an' paper an'
she says,

" 'Name please?'

"Jes's though she hadn't been to dis house agin an' agin
to wheedle mah into makin' rice waffles!"

"That was just form, Mammy Juno. She was checking
up the voters so that she could send for any of my constituents if they didn't appear."

"Checkin' up de voters! Fo' de Lawd, wus dat it? Well,
I says to her "Miss Polly Carter, yo' knows puffectly well
dat I's de candydate's Mammy, umph-umph, I is.' An'
wat do yo' tink dat sassy chile said to mah?

" 'W'ich candydate?' Jes's though dere was any of 'por-
tance 'cept yo'."

"Could you tell how the election was going?" Rose demanded eagerly.

"I ast de man walkin' roun' as though he owned de
place ef yo' wus gettin' all de votes an' he scowled at mah
lak I wus poison. Den dat Jup'ter he ketched mah ahm

an' dragged mah outen de votin' place. I tole him dat yo' would wan' to know but dat didn't mak no difference. Yo'd better put dis scarf ober yuh shoulders, ef yo' is goin' down stairs, Honey-Chile."

"Of course I'm going down stairs. Bring me some tea and toast in the living room, that's a dear. I'm so hungry I could bite."

"I guess yo's all right, Chile, an' comin' back to normalcy fas'."

The glittering ice-world was shading to pinkish dusk as Rose looked from the living room window. Outside the great oak which had been sanctuary in her childhood, lay prostrate. As far as she could see were topless trees. Cedars with decapitated heads on the frozen ground at their feet. Oaks shattered. Birches bent double. What a nightmare. Would she ever forget the sound of crashing trees?

"Jupiter told me that I would find you here, Rose-Pomona."

"Mark!" The girl turned quickly from the window. How good-looking he was, she thought as she extended a friendly hand. He had a genius—or his tailor had, for selecting his clothes. That gray homespun was most becoming. She had not treated him fairly. She had realized that when she had hung over the gulch. Had her life been years and years longer she could have reviewed them all.

"Sit down, Rose-Pomona. Do you—you feel equal to—talking?"

"*Et tu Brute?* Everyone persists in treating me as though I were on the verge of a decline. Except for an Ethel Barrymore husk in my voice I am perfectly fit."

"You had a tough experience."

"Agreed, but, as I have never had a sick day in my life barring the fifty-seven varities of childhood ills, why should one tough experience wreck my health."

"Now I know that you're normal. You are scolding me."

"Forgive me—I . . ."

"I understand, Rose-Pomona. I knew last night that you never could care for me."

"I'm sorry."

"It isn't your fault." He flung his cigarette into the fire. "Mother and I leave tomorrow."

"Tomorrow!"

"Yes. She had planned to stay until Tony would go with her, but the storm changed her mind—perhaps other factors influenced her decision. She doesn't care for your New England weather as per yesterday's demonstration. Besides, this morning the servants at La Mancha were removed in a body by the sheriff. He was held up on the road last night by wrecked trees."

"All? What happened?"

"All but Carmencita. She and the monkey are with Daphne and Hardy. It's a long story. Some day, ask Judge Cort to tell you the particulars."

"Has Nap appeared?"

"We think that he must have sneaked back to La Mancha. A car is missing from the garage. A great night for a get-away. Wires down. Lights out. No one on the road unless on a matter of life and death."

"Long's star! He had one chance in ten for safety when he crawled along that rail." She drew a long, shuddering breath. "I mustn't think of it. Are they voting on Long's name?"

"No. That was withdrawn. You have but one opponent."

"The men's candidate. If one of his constituents has assured me that while he admired me, etc., etc., he considered me too young and inexperienced for office, an hundred have. Never mind, thanks to you, Mark, I made a good try."

"That's the stuff! If at first—you know the rest." He held out his hand,

"Until we meet again, Rose-Pomona."

Her hand tightened over his.

"I shall miss you, terribly. I love you, really I do. Not the way you want but so much that—that I can't bear the thought that you may . . ."

He caught her by the shoulders.

"Look at me, Rose. I know what you mean. If ever the old habit tempts me, I'll think of Tony's set, ghastly face as he worked over those ropes last night. My God, what mastery of self! He knew that you were in that car. He knew that at any moment you might . . . Forgive me for bringing that memory back."

His tone lightened.

"You've made me vain, Rose-Pomona. I prefer the appearance of the clear-skinned man who looks back at me from the mirror to the face of the man who came here last spring."

With an unsteady laugh he removed his hands from her shoulders.

"Tony is looking at us."

Rose's eyes flashed to the man at the door. How white he was. Lines had been finely chiseled from his nose to his lips. They had not been there before last night. She put her hand to her throat. She tried to speak. Mark came to her rescue:

"You'll be up to see mother in the morning before she goes, Tony? I'll turn the keys of La Mancha over to the head man in Long's office. I must be off. Good-night, I won't say, 'Good-bye,' Rose-Pomona."

Rose controlled a childish desire to clutch his sleeve and hold him. She couldn't face Tony's eyes, alone. She walked to the window, the window from which she could see Headless Hill. The setting sun was turning the icy world into a glittering pink sapphire. She heard Tony cross the room. She knew that he was standing with one arm stretched along the mantel. She must speak. Her voice wouldn't come. She clenched her hands behind her.

"Have you heard from the Town Meeting?" the question was commonplace but there was a disconcerting timbre in Anthony's voice.

"No."

His low laugh was more disturbing than his voice.

"Get it behind you, dear. It has to be done."

"What has to be done?"

"You will have to turn away from that window sometime, won't you? You won't? Then I will come to you."

It seemed an aeon or two before she felt him gently part her clenched hands, felt a ring slipped on to her finger, felt his lips pressed to it as he laughingly reminded:

"You said that he was to have it waiting for you, dear."

Why, oh why, couldn't she move, say something, the girl thought turbulently. She was as tonguetied as the Chinese woman on the Coromandel screen. She—her heart shook her by its pounding as he laid his cheek against hers and asked, his voice unbearably tender:

"Dear, you are not afraid of me? It's only Tony, Tony, who wants you—for his wife."

With an inarticulate murmur Rose buried her face against his shoulder.

"Dear!"

The demanding huskiness of the appeal brought her head up. She lifted her face to his as instinctively as a flower turns to the sun.

"Rose! Rose!" shouted a voice.

She opened dazed eyes. She tried to slip away but Anthony held her tight in one arm as Peter accompanied by the three dogs came to a startled halt at the door. The boy was too excited to be observant—or too tactful.

"Rose, you're elected."

"Am I really, Peter?"

"A walk-over! I take off my hat to the women. They had every voter out! A lot of the men didn't care to take their cars out in the ice."

"Tony! Isn't it wonderful! Are you—sorry?" she pleaded with a quick change of tone. In exuberance of feeling she lifted her face to him.

"Sorry—about anything today?" he exulted. He kissed her possessively.

Heads tilted, mouths open as though in amused approval the three dogs regarded the man and girl unblinkingly.

"I'm still here," reminded Peter with an embarrassed cough, "and Mother has been here several minutes."

Rose colored adorably as she looked at her mother but Claire Grahame was not looking at her. Her eyes luminous through tears were fixed on Tony. Her face was white with emotion, her voice was shaken music as she rejoiced:

"Anthony! My son! My splendid son!"